IVY LETTERS

A Novel by Jesse Maas

Shellville Press

Printed by Shellville Press in the United States of America

Cover by Shelly Connor

ISBN: 978-1-7334487-6-5

Shellville Press
a division of Shellville Design LLC
www.shellvillepress.com

10 9 8 7 6 5 4 3 2

*For the love of my life, Josh
and our beautiful daughter, Mila*

Chapter One

Vienna awoke with a gasp and a shiver ran down her spine. She felt cool beads of sweat pooling on her forehead around her hairline. She brushed her curly, golden hair off her face and pushed it behind her ears. Although at first she was always taken aback, she was now used to these sudden interruptions in her night sleep. Unsurprisingly, they always seemed to occur on the first of the month.

She adjusted the pillow behind her and sat up against the wooden headboard. She mindlessly ran her fingers through the white, lace comforter as she focused to slow her breathing.

"Breathe in two, three, four, and out two, three, four. In two, three, four and out two, three, four." She exhaled, reminding herself it was just a dream.

Once her breathing had slowed, she opened her eyes once again and scanned the room. It was dark with the only light coming from a glowing streetlamp streaming in from a small crack between the curtains that spanned the large window on the opposite side of the room. The dark, mahogany bookshelf to her left was once a beautiful piece and though it still looked lovely, displaying various knickknacks, it had been neglected over time and its age was highlighted by various chips and cracks, and slightly drooping shelves.

Vienna stood up and her cream-colored, silk night-gown fell softly to her knees. She smoothly ran her hands down her side to straighten it out the best she could and began to walk quietly toward her bedroom door. She turned the knob without making a sound and began to tiptoe down the hall. It was hard to be quiet on the old, wooden floors of the 120-year-old home, but Vienna had made the walk down the hall to check on her brother countless times and knew every creak and loose floorboard to avoid. She passed the bathroom and linen closet without making a sound and stood in front of her brother's door. She grabbed the doorknob and silently turned it. She was slowly pushing the door open when it let out a loud creak.

"Oh no," Vienna thought to herself. She immediately stopped opening the door and peeked through the small crack.

Beckham was soundly sleeping, barely visible underneath his large pile of sprawling blankets. Although Beckham was Vienna's older brother (by only two minutes, of course, as she constantly had to remind him), Vienna had always felt the need to be protective of him.

Vienna breathed a sigh of relief at the sight of her brother peacefully sleeping but stiffened when she heard the sound of a chain light switch being pulled downstairs.

She walked as quickly as she could while still moving stealthily but her attempts were useless as she heard footsteps rapidly ascending the stairs before she was even halfway down the hall.

"Vienna Marie Tunston!" Her mother's cool words pierced through the air as she stepped up the last stair. "It's four in the morning," Margaret said, pulling her white, silk robe more tightly around her. Margaret's coffee colored hair fell to her shoulders and perfectly framed her thin face. Her ocean blue eyes complimented her light skin, which still appeared to be young and youthful. She was the kind of beautiful that was so natural, it was almost unnatural and even in the dim light of the early morning, with her pajamas and no makeup on, she could have been photographed for a magazine cover. Vienna had always spited her mother for her simple beauty. She felt her looks had always paled in comparison.

"Are you alright?" Margaret asked. "Did you have another nightmare?"

"Yes," Vienna quietly responded. She didn't care much for talking about her feelings and for this reason, she hated waking her mother up.

"I'm sorry, my darling." Margaret walked to Vienna's side and placed her arm around her. She led her back to her bedroom and to the bed. After Vienna climbed in, Margaret sat next to her and began to stroke her hair. "What was it about this time?"

"I don't want to talk about it, Mom," she replied.

"Was it the same as last time?" Margaret prodded.

Vienna gave a slight nod.

"I'm sorry." Margaret continued to sympathetically stroke her hair. "Someday you'll find that you wake up from that nightmare for the last time."

Vienna didn't believe her. It had now been three

years and still, without fail, on the first of the month she awoke from the same dreadful dream.

"You know next week marks three years, don't you?" Vienna asked.

Margaret was almost offended by the question (but only as offended as one can be by their youngest child's efforts to connect with them).

"Of course, I do." She leaned down and kissed Vienna's cheek. "Now get some rest," she instructed. "We have a big day ahead of us."

Vienna nodded as she turned to her side. She placed her hands on her pillow under her head and tried to fall back asleep.

Chapter Two

After closing the door to Vienna's room, Margaret walked quietly down the hall to check on Beckham. Once she was sure he was still sound asleep, she went downstairs and turned on the coffee pot in the kitchen. The dark, wooden floors contrasted the bright blue cabinets with glass doors. The cabinets were filled with plates and bowls and vases and all sorts of kitchen necessities. A lifetime ago, it seemed, they were organized in a picture-perfect sort of way, but now they were bursting at the seams and Margaret didn't have the same energy to fix them she'd once had.

It had been nearly three years since she'd lost the love of her life and since the dreadful December day, she'd barely had the strength to wake up each morning and care for her children. She most definitely did not have the strength to organize silly cabinets.

"And that's okay," she often reminded herself.

She glanced at the clock and was not phased when she saw it read 4:40 A.M. She used to have a perfect schedule. She'd wake up each morning at six o'clock sharp, make breakfast for Lewis and the kids, do the dishes and fold one load of laundry before heading out for work. She'd walk three blocks to catch the 7:35 A.M. train to downtown. The ride took precisely eight minutes and she got off on the fourth stop at Station One. Once off the train, she walked across the street to the immaculate marble mansion known as Carnot. After her nine-hour workday, she'd take the same route home, make dinner for her family and have it on the table at precisely 6:30 P.M. After dinner, her family would often play games or go hiking together until it was time for bed and then, she'd wake up the next day and do it all over again.

Now, however, it was not unusual for Margaret to wake up at four in the morning or go to bed at 1:00 A.M. Some nights she'd get ten hours of sleep and others, it seemed she'd get no sleep at all.

Margaret heard her coffee pot ding, signaling it was finished brewing and she poured herself a cup. She opened the refrigerator to get out the coffee creamer when the leftover sheet cake caught her eye. Hearing her growling stomach and realizing it had been at least twenty hours since she'd last eaten (she tended to forget to do that these days), she pulled out the cake and cut herself a piece. It was a vanilla sheet cake with white, whipped icing, colorful balloons and pink letters that originally read, "Congratulations on Fifteen Years!" All that was left now was "ons ears," and a couple of balloons.

She leaned on the kitchen island while she sipped her coffee and savored her cake. After a few bites, she felt a tear streaming down her cheek. She'd wept so much over the past three years that sometimes she didn't even realize when she was crying anymore. Her tear reached the corner of her lip and she tasted its saltiness. She grabbed a napkin and wiped her mouth and eyes.

"I guess that's to be expected," she thought to herself. The cake was from her fifteenth work anniversary as Assistant to the Secretary of State. Nearly twelve of those years, she'd served as assistant to her husband. When he died, she thought about quitting. In fact, she wanted nothing more than to quit but financially (and socially for that matter), it was not an option.

In Carnot, every member of society worked from the time they turned eighteen until they died. The only time one wasn't required to work was when a child was born. A mother was allowed to stay home with their baby for the first three years of their life, until the child could attend preschool. Carnot was a thriving city with almost limitless career options to choose from, though many individuals ended up working for the government.

Margaret used to love her job. She loved riding the train with Lewis every day when he wasn't working early or late. She loved sitting at the little desk outside of his large office, able to wander in and share her thoughts and dreams with him at any moment. She loved getting to help him and learning more about the government. And more than anything, she simply loved doing life with him.

Now that he was gone, some power-hungry young man had taken Lewis' place and Margaret did not have the energy (or desire) to get to know him. She could hardly remember his name. She went into work, did the bare minimum and left. She didn't care to talk to anyone. Although virtually every person in Carnot had faced great tragedy, Margaret had no interest in grieving with anyone. When Lewis died, she decided she was better off alone. She was not concerned with finding support or depending on someone around her. Plus, whether people would admit it or not, she knew her loss was different. She didn't believe anyone could truly relate to her.

She heard footsteps on the stairs and fanned her face rapidly, trying to hide the redness she could feel on her warm cheeks. She turned to see Vienna walking into the kitchen.

"I can't sleep." Vienna pulled her hair up into a messy bun on top of her head. "I really can't."

"It's okay," Margaret replied, understanding her daughter's struggles firsthand. "Would you like some cake?"

"I'd love some." Vienna sat down on a barstool opposite her mother standing at the kitchen island. Three years ago, an offer of cake for breakfast would have been a shock too big to imagine but now, Vienna didn't even give it a second thought.

"Can you believe you will be eighteen in just a couple of weeks?" Margaret asked in an attempt to change Vienna's mood.

"No." She shook her head. "Can you?"

"No." Margaret smiled softly. "I really can't. I was just thinking about it with this cake. I started at Carnot just before you and Beckham turned three. I can't believe I've been working there for fifteen years now. How have my babies gotten so big?"

"I don't know. I really don't know," Vienna whispered.

Chapter Three

Beckham rolled over in his bed to see the clock read 5:15 A.M. He rolled his eyes, knowing he wouldn't be able to fall back asleep because it was much earlier than he'd wanted to get up. He tried to sleep as late as possible on the first of the month, in hopes he could sleep away the entire day, but it never seemed to work. He rubbed his bright, blue eyes, brushed his hands through his shaggy, golden, blonde hair and sighed.

He got out of bed and threw on a crumpled t-shirt he picked up off the floor. He looked down at the shirt and was pleasantly surprised to see it was one of his favorites. It depicted four men on the front and read "Queen." Supposedly, the band had been rather successful more than one hundred years ago, but he had never heard their music. Not much from the old days had made it through the transformation, but of the few things Beckham's grandfather had handed down to him, this tee was one of his favorites. The shirt was slightly short and fit a little too snugly, even for his thin frame, but he wore it anyway. He opened a drawer to the dresser and pulled out a pair of black shorts. After putting them on, he walked out of his room through the hallway and down the stairs.

"Good morning," he greeted his mother and sister, both with empty plates sitting in front of them. He caught a glimpse of the white bakery box on the counter. "Oh no! Did I miss breakfast cake?" He dropped his jaw dramatically.

"Yep." Vienna teased, "Mom said only I get cake today because I'm her favorite twin."

"Oh, is that so?" Beckham took a step closer to Vienna and quickly moved his hands to her side. He started tickling her and when she moved to stop him, he tickled her armpits. "That's too bad," he laughed as he continued to tickle her.

"StOooOp." Vienna could hardly get the word out through her laughter.

"Say it," Beckham demanded.

"No," Vienna argued as she continued to try to escape his hands.

"Saaay it," he prodded.

"Okay, okay," Vienna finally gave up.

"Beckham is the bestest twin. Mom and Dad love him more. He wins," she sang.

"Ah, music to my ears." Beckham stopped tickling her. "Thank you."

"That is such a silly game you two play," Margaret commented. She knew there was no use in trying to stop them.

"No, it's not," Vienna and Beckham said in unison.

Margaret laughed. "Would you like a piece of cake?" she offered Beckham.

"Yes, please."

Beckham took a seat on the barstool next to Vienna as Margaret served the last piece of cake up for him.

"Yum," he said before he even took his first bite.

The three of them were quiet for a moment, one question lingering in all of their minds.

"How bad do you think it will be today?" Beckham finally asked. He had always been the type able to ask the hard questions.

"I don't know, darling," Margaret replied. "No one ever knows."

"Well, we know that's not true," Vienna retorted.

"Don't," snapped Margaret. "You know better than to speak poorly of the government, Vienna Marie."

Vienna looked down. She did know better.

"But you have to have a general idea, don't you, Mom?" Beckham continued. "You work there every day."

"I only work there five days a week," she corrected, "And no, I do not know." Leaving no room for response, she continued, "Speaking of work, I must go. I do not want to be late." She rushed out of the kitchen, through the living room, and into her bedroom.

"It's not even 5:30," Vienna laughed. "She doesn't need to be there for another two and a half hours."

Beckham shook his head. "You know Mom. She can't handle talking about it."

"I know," Vienna replied. "Don't you think she knows more than she lets on?"

"Of course, I do," Beckham said. "And someday soon, I will find out."

"Soon?" Vienna questioned. "Try, like, two weeks from tomorrow."

"Is that not soon to you?" Beckham questioned.

"No, it's, like, sooner than soon," Vienna laughed.

"What are you going to do?"

"I still don't know."

"Well, you have approximately two weeks until our eighteenth birthday, so you had better get that figured out," Beckham's tone was slightly more serious than Vienna had anticipated.

"I will." Vienna rolled her eyes. "Not all of us have known exactly what we've wanted to be when we grow up since we were five like you."

"I didn't know when I was five. I knew when I was three," he corrected.

Vienna threw her head back, annoyed.

"Are you thinking what I'm thinking?" Beckham asked.

"Count of three," Vienna replied, happy to change the subject. She knew she needed to decide her career path but truthfully, she'd never had any idea what she wanted to do, and she was content with continuing to put off the decision.

"One," counted Beckham.

"Two," said Vienna.

"Three. Hike day!" they exclaimed simultaneously. "Yes! Twin power!" They high-fived and jumped up from their seats.

"Be ready in ten," Beckham said as he started to run toward the stairs.

"Be ready in nine," Vienna challenged, quickly following him.

Chapter Four

Copeland slowly opened his eyes as light from the windows flooded into his bedroom.

"Good morning, Mr. Howth," Martin greeted as he opened the floor length curtains. Martin Pluto was a short man with tanned skin and wrinkles that covered his face. He was not as old as his face otherwise suggested but a fairly young man who'd lived a demanding life and the wrinkles on his forehead showed every ounce of it.

"Morning," Copeland groggily groaned as he rubbed his eyes. "What time is it?"

"It's 7:00 A.M., sir. Your father has asked to see you this morning."

"Why so early?" Copeland complained.

"He's planning to do the loop with you."

"The whole loop?"

"Yes, sir. He asked me to wake you at 7:00 A.M. precisely for the loop run," Martin clarified.

"Ugh," Copeland moaned as he rolled himself out of bed. Any normal kid needed to obey their parents but for Copeland, the standards were much higher. As heir to the Howth legacy and future leader of Carnot, he'd never had much control over his life. His every action, word, and emotion had been controlled since the day he was born, and he knew better than to hope it would ever change. He'd put off all possible responsibility for as long as he could, but he knew now, with his eighteenth birthday just one month away, he couldn't put it off any longer.

He dramatically sighed as he traipsed across the large room to the antique wooden dresser where Martin had perfectly laid out his workout clothes.

Copeland ran a hand through his thick, dark brown hair and leaned his head side to side as it cracked violently.

Martin cringed at the sound. "Are you alright, sir?"

"Yes, I'm up and I'll be down in five," he replied.

"Wonderful," Martin said as he walked to the door. He turned back and bowed slightly before leaving the room.

Copeland took off his shirt, unveiling his toned stomach and chiseled arms. He put on the lightweight, long sleeve shirt Martin had laid out and sloppily threw the t-shirt he'd slept in on the floor. He changed into the black running tights from the dresser and added a pair of loose shorts on top. Lastly, he put on a gray beanie. The weather was typically cold this time of year but if Martin didn't put gloves out, it must have been warmer than he'd expected. His light clothes and hat would be enough to keep him warm on the five-mile run that was ahead of him.

He started to walk toward the door when he caught a glimpse of the gold frame on his nightstand. The picture frame held two small photos. On the left, a picture of Copeland, as a young child, sitting on his mother's lap, and on the right, a formal portrait of the two of them taken on his fourteenth birthday. His mother had given him the frame only a few weeks before she passed away.

"Love you, Mom," Copeland whispered to himself as he blew her a kiss before walking out of the room.

He walked down the sprawling hallway lined with artwork that was supposedly very famous in the old world. When people visited the mansion, they'd comment on the vaious oil paintings, but Copeland didn't care much for art or learning about the way things used to be. The truth was that maybe a hundred years ago these paintings meant something to someone, and perhaps the art was once personal, once valuable, once inspiring, but in the world he lived in, the same art was nothing but a mirage of freedom hanging on the wall to remind him every day just how little of it was left.

He made his way to the formal entryway with servants stopping and offering him slight bows every so often. When he reached the foyer, he sat on a red, velvet bench and closed his eyes. He must have dozed off for a minute or two because he was slightly startled by the sound of his father's voice coming from the east hall. He stood up and moved to the center of the room to greet him.

"Good morning, son," Theodore said.

Copeland suppressed the urge to roll his eyes.

Son, he scoffed in his head. *You hardly act like a father.*

"Good morning," Copeland replied out loud. He'd never had a problem pretending to be civil. In fact, he doubted his father had any idea he was even pretending. Copeland felt only his mother had ever known the real him.

"I'm planning on the loop this morning," Theodore declared.

"That's what Martin told me," Copeland replied. "It's been a while since we've done that."

"It has been," agreed Theodore. "Shall we get started?"

Copeland nodded. Two guards opened the oversized double doors leading to the front lawn in perfect synchronization as they made their way out. They walked down the steps of Carnot and onto the sidewalk that led to the tall bronze fence that enclosed the property. The loop was a historic route that wound through the city. It was designed to efficiently pass the most important parts of the city and had originally been used for parades, funerals, celebrations, and more. Copeland's grandfather was the first to transform it into his own running route and it had become a Howth tradition ever since. He could remember the days when he was younger, and he'd join his father for half the loop. People would wave from their balconies or run beside them for a little while (of course, they could never get very close with the security detail surrounding them on every side).

He used to love when his father would invite him. He loved to get out of Carnot and see what was happening beyond the walls. He'd never been allowed to run the loop alone and there were not many occasions beyond running that he was able to get off the property, leaving him little exposure to the outside world. Although his dad was not his favorite person and he much preferred late nights to early mornings, he'd never really complain about an invitation to run the loop.

"Backwards or forwards this morning?" Theodore asked as they reached the entry gate the guard had just opened.

"Hmm, backwards," Copeland answered. He'd always liked to do things differently.

"You got it," Theodore replied as he turned right and began to jog.

His dad's upbeat tone promptly reminded Copeland that he sometimes did try to make an effort. Copeland often found himself stuck hating his father for a reason he could never pinpoint.

He really does have a lot on his plate, Copeland justified to himself.

He followed his dad's lead and ran on his left. They started down the middle of what Copeland assumed had once been a bustling street filled with honking cars and large buses. It was now filled with people walking purposefully in every direction. The only cars allowed in the city were those used for emergencies and official government business. Other than that, cars were only very rarely used to get to remote places where the train didn't travel.

They ran in silence for a few minutes, waving occasionally to the dozens of people who yelled and waved helplessly at them, enamored by their presence.

"Your eighteenth birthday is coming quickly," Theodore said, finally breaking the silence.

"Yes, it is." Copeland could see his breath as he replied.

"That makes me feel old. If you're almost eighteen, I

must be ancient," he laughed.

"True," Copeland laughed back.

Theodore jokingly gave him a shove.

There was a slight tension as they continued to run. They both knew what Theodore would say next.

"You know we have to talk about it sometime," he started.

"I know," Copeland sighed.

"We really should have started your preparation last year but given the circumstances, we agreed, as leaders, that it could be postponed, and here we are, a year later already..." he trailed off. "A very fast year later," he added, sounding less like a leader and more like a human, "and we have to discuss it." The latter part of his statement sounded more like his distant self.

"I know," Copeland said again.

"I have an idea. Well, more like a proposition for you," Theodore corrected.

"What's that?"

"If you agree to start training promptly after your birthday, and I mean promptly—the next day to be exact—" he clarified. "I will let you host your birthday party at the venue of your choice, anywhere in the city."

Copeland was caught off guard.

Anywhere in the city, he thought. *That would be amazing. Maybe he does pay attention to me. Does he really know how badly I want to get off the property?* Copeland suddenly realized he hadn't vocalized any of his thoughts. "That would be awesome. It's a deal!"

"Wonderful," Theodore beamed. "It's settled. I will have it arranged for Martin to take you around tomorrow to look at venues. We'll need to move quickly to give Mrs. Carter enough time to plan." It was as if you could see the wheels literally turning in his head when he came up with a new idea. "It will be magnificent! We'll ring in the new year with an extravagant eighteenth birthday party for the Heir of Carnot." He smiled.

"That sounds great!" Copeland agreed. For the first time in a long time, he was genuinely pleased with his father. *You don't even know how great this really is,* he thought to himself.

Chapter Five

Margaret sat silently on the train with her head leaning against the cold window; the glass fogging up slightly with each breath. Since Lewis had died, she'd made it a habit to do a better job of taking in her surroundings. She used to talk with him, or read the newspaper, or simply get lost in her own thoughts on the train, but now that he was gone, she didn't want to miss out on a single second of her life. She'd stare intently on her way to work, trying to take everything in. Whether it was a little girl skipping down the sidewalk or a grumpy old man walking to work, she enjoyed studying each face and making up their story in her head.

The ride felt particularly fast to Margaret this morning and as the train slowly came to a stop, she instinctively stood up.

"Station One," the automated voice announced over the loudspeaker. "Station One."

Margaret followed the bustling crowds through the underground station. The white and tan walls swirled by as people raced chaotically around her. She trekked up the steps toward the tunnel of light, and turned right when she reached the sidewalk. She was surprised by the large crowd gathered at the top of the steps.

What is going on? she thought to herself.

"Copeland!" she heard a high-pitched voice scream from behind her.

Margaret turned around to see a young girl frantically waving. She followed her gaze and suddenly the crowd made sense. Through the sea of people, Margaret could see a small group jogging in near perfect unison.

Ahh, Theodore and Copeland, Margaret answered her own question. "Excuse me, pardon me." Margaret began weaving through the throngs of people. "Excuse me, pardon me," she repeated over and over again until she had crossed the street and stood at the guard shack.

The small, red, brick building had been managed by the same security officer since Margaret had started. In fact, though Santi was much younger than her, they'd started on the same day.

"Good morning," Santi greeted her. His bright white smile contrasted his dark skin. He was tall and fit but not in a way that made anyone feel inferior. He was the kind of young man whose smile could make anyone forget all of the pain they'd ever felt.

"Good morning." Margaret smiled back. "How was your Saturday?"

"It was pretty good," Santi replied. "I had the chance to head out to the countryside to see my family. It was a nice little break."

"Oh, that sounds lovely," Margaret said as she fiddled through the brown leather purse hanging from her arm. "I'm so glad you had a little break."

"Me too. It's nice when I actually have a day off."

"Yes, it is. They work you to the bone." Margaret continued to rummage through her bag. "You'd think after all these years I would have figured out a better system for keeping track of my badge."

"I've come to the conclusion that you just use it as an excuse to talk with me longer." Santi winked.

"You caught me," Margaret teased as she finally found her white badge and flashed it at Santi.

Security was very tight at Carnot and though Santi knew every employee by name (he was very good at that kind of thing), it was still required that each person show their badge. If they forgot it, tough luck! They would have to go back home and retrieve it before they could enter the building (with the exception of the Howth family, of course).

Santi opened the gate and Margaret started toward it.

"Don't work too hard now," Santi called.

"You know I never do," Margaret laughed as she waved and continued to make her way up the sidewalk, toward the mansion.

It was the first of the month, so things were bustling more than normal. People were flying in every which direction, carrying white envelopes in their hands; these envelopes held the power to forever change lives. Margaret normally worked Monday through Friday but everyone in the government had to work on the first of the month, regardless of the day of the week.

"Good morning!"

Margaret was greeted with a smile as she set her purse down on her wooden desk.

Elton Smith stood broadly in the doorway to his office, nearly taking up the entire opening. His dirty blonde hair was neatly trimmed and always smoothed over to the right side. He wore virtually the same clothes every day: a neatly ironed button down, slacks with a belt and dress shoes. Although, despite its similarity, the color palettes were constantly changing, and Margaret was convinced he'd never worn the same shirt twice. Today's choice was a light purple shirt with almost invisible pinstripes, navy blue slacks, brown shoes and a brown belt. It was a combination most men couldn't pull off, but she had to give Elton credit, on his sleek, thirty-year-old body, his clothes looked good.

Poor kid... he still tries so hard, Margaret thought to herself. "Good morning," she replied, smiling convincingly.

"Did you have a nice Saturday?" he asked.

Margaret nodded. "I did. Short as always." After Lewis passed away, Elton took over his position. It had been nearly three years, but she still didn't care to get to know him. "And you?" she asked more out of obligation than curiosity.

"I did. Actually," he paused, scratching his head, deciding if he wanted to share the news, "I got engaged."

"You did?" Margaret was genuinely shocked. In the three years she'd worked for Elton, she'd only briefly talked to him about his love life.

"Yes, I did!"

She hadn't made eye contact before but now she could see that he was beaming from ear to ear.

"Congratulations!" Margaret smiled. "How very exciting!" She tried to rack her brain for his fiancés' name. *I guess that same brunette has been around for a while*, she thought. *What's her name? Brittany? No.*

Heidi? No.

"Jacqueline and I are so excited." Elton's genuine joy was radiating from every ounce of his being.

Jacqueline, Margaret answered in her head. "You should be! Have you set a date?" she asked aloud.

"We're thinking next November but we aren't certain."

"That would be lovely. I am so happy for you," Margaret replied. She was almost surprised by how convincing she sounded, but then, she realized she *was* actually happy for him. She'd spent three years dwelling only on losing the love of her life, and all the complexities entangled with it, and for the first time since Lewis' death, she was able to recognize and appreciate someone else's young love.

Chapter Six

"She should be home by now," Beckham paced the dimly lit kitchen.

Vienna stirred a pot of pasta sauce on the stove in the center of the island. "It's okay. It's the first of the month, I'm sure it was a busy day." Vienna hoped she sounded calmer than she felt.

"It's nearly seven o'clock." Beckham continued his panic, becoming increasingly more worried with each second that passed. He stared at the clock above the kitchen sink with its minute hand at fifty-five and the second hand nearly back to the top. "She has less than five minutes to get home."

"It's going to be okay, Beck." Vienna tried to encourage him as she suppressed her own increasing urge to join in his worry.

Silence fell in the room for a few seconds as both Vienna and Beckham stared at the three white envelopes placed perfectly spaced on the kitchen island.

"We're going to be fine," Vienna said finally breaking the silence, afraid if she sat in it any longer, she'd burst into tears. "It hasn't even been three years since Dad died, the odds of us—"

"The odds don't matter, and you know it, V," Beckham interrupted.

Unfazed, she continued, "The odds of us receiving a bad letter are still not high and—"

The front door flew open and Vienna was thankful she didn't need to continue her pep talk.

"Hi, kids," Margaret called, as she flicked the water off of an umbrella and placed it by the door. "I am sorry I am so late! What's the time?" She glanced up at the clock. "Good, two minutes to spare," She answered herself. "Dinner smells delicious, V."

Vienna was happy to see her mother in such good spirits, especially given the nature of the day. She'd come to accept the fact that her mother's mood was ever-changing and completely unpredictable.

"Alright, let's get it turned on," Margaret said. "Grab your envelope."

The letters were addressed in perfect calligraphy to their recipients:

Margaret Willow Tunston.

Vienna Marie Tunston.

Beckham Penn Tunston.

They each grabbed the envelope made out to them and made their way to the gray, fabric couch in the living room.

It was sad to Vienna, the way everything had slowly worn out over time. The couch was once vibrant, packed with colorful pillows, and now it was tattered and dull.

Beckham turned the only knob on the front of the small television screen until a picture appeared.

Theodore Howth sat superbly still in a large, brown

leather chair behind an enormous, oak desk. The walls behind him were lined with built-in shelves full of what Vienna imagined were empty, untouched books.

Beckham took a seat on the far side of the couch with his mother perched between him and his sister. The three of them watched the screen intently.

"Good evening," Theodore greeted.

Vienna glanced at the clock to double check but as always, he started at exactly seven o'clock.

"Today is the first of December and our 925th letter ceremony. Thank you for watching tonight's broadcast."

As if we have a choice, Vienna bitterly thought to herself.

Theodore licked his thumb and grabbed a piece of paper off of his desk. He adjusted it slightly in his hands, took a deep breath and began to read it assertively.

"It is with great privilege that I sit here tonight as the Paramount Chief of Carnot and read the Ivy Act our founders drafted many years ago. As we all know, ivy is a beautiful plant. It adds unique character to many buildings, streets and more, but at its root..."

"Its literal root," Vienna mouthed silently along with Theodore.

Theodore paused to smile at the same failed joke he made month after month. "We know that ivy can be detrimental if left unmaintained," he paused, "much like those who came before us realized the disorder that perpetual life can bring without regulation." Another pause. "Which is why, on the first of every month, we come together as a community to read our Ivy Letters. These letters help control our population and society. It is because of these letters that we have the spectacular opportunity to live our lives freely and appreciate a safe community."

Vienna stared intently at the television, fighting every fiber in her being to keep from rolling her eyes.

"You know I don't like to take up too much of your time," Theodore said. "So, without further ado, I ask that each of you peels the stamp off the back of your envelope."

Vienna hesitantly turned her envelope over and carefully peeled the green stamp shaped like an ivy leaf off of the paper. The sugary stamp began to curl slightly in her hand.

"Please repeat after me," Theodore instructed. "I, Theodore."

"I, Vienna," Vienna said aloud.

Everyone knew better than to jokingly repeat back Theodore's name in the pledge.

"take this ivy," Theodore continued.

"take this ivy," Vienna, Beckham and Margaret repeated together.

"as a vow to my nation," said Theodore.

"as a vow to my nation," they repeated.

"and to my neighbors"

"and to my neighbors"

"to continue the rich legacy"

"to continue the rich legacy"

"of Carnot"

"of Carnot"

"for the rest of my days."

"for the rest of my days."

"Be them many"

"Be them many"

"or be them few."
"or be them few."
"May the best ivy"
"May the best ivy"
"always continue to grow."
"always continue to grow."

Theodore took the ivy stamp from his own envelope and placed it on his tongue. Vienna, Beckham and Margaret did the same.

After letting the stamp melt in his mouth, Theodore continued. "Our current population count is 800,173, excluding those under fifteen years of age. After this month, it will be 790,835. As you know, the first of the year is next month and we will be adding all who turned fifteen this year into our official population count, thus the slightly higher demise rate for December," Theodore explained. "Thank you for your time tonight. I wish you all the best." He quickly moved on from the numbers. "It is my great pleasure to invite you to open your letters at this time. Good luck and goodnight." He smiled, and the television stream promptly shut off.

Silently, Vienna began opening her letter and she could see her mother and brother doing the same out of the corner of her eye.

She briefly read the decision line and quickly stuck her hand out, giving a thumbs up. She smiled to herself, remembering the first time she and Beckham understood the letters their parents were opening. Her father decided using a thumbs up to signal a good letter would be a fun way to ease some of their nerves and ever since, it stuck. Each month they signaled they were going to be okay with the simple gesture.

Beckham shot his thumbs up out next and Margaret quickly followed. With a sigh of relief, Vienna and Beckham leaned into their mother's sides and she put her arms around them.

"I told you there was nothing to worry about." Vienna winked at Beckham.

"You were right," Beckham admitted. "I guess now we'll just wait and see."

Chapter Seven

Copeland watched as the camera lights flicked off and staff members began whirling around him. Some picked up cords, others packed up cameras and some, Copeland noticed, simply pretended to be doing something.

"That's going to be you, you know?" Copeland was interrupted by a soft hand touching his upper back.

He turned to see the familiar face of Summer Nile. Her long, brown hair fell in large curls down to the center of her back. Her perfectly arched eyebrows highlighted her almond-shaped, green eyes and her naturally high cheekbones made her a textbook kind of beautiful.

"Oh, hi, Summer." Copeland was surprised to see her; her letter must have been okay or she wouldn't have been in such a good mood.

"Yeah, I guess it will be someday..." He didn't know how to feel. "What are you doing here?"

"My dad had to work," she gestured to a man in a black, tailored suit across the room who was sending people in many directions, "and he said I could come with him."

"Oh, yeah," Copeland replied, slightly embarrassed. Mr. Nile had been working for the Howth family as head of public relations for as long as he could remember. He should have known Summer would be tagging along.

"Word on the street is someone is about to host the birthday party of the century." Summer fluttered her eyes accusingly at him.

"Oh, is that so?" he questioned. "The century is probably a bit of an exaggeration."

"Doubt it." Summer flirtingly twirled her hair.

Mr. Nile had worked at Carnot for many years, but Copeland had only met Summer six months ago. Though many assumed he was, Copeland wasn't naive enough to think it was a coincidence. He knew with his turning eighteen that it wouldn't be long before he was expected to settle down with a nice girl and Summer checked all of the boxes. She was beautiful and captivating and well-liked by all. The few times Copeland and Summer had been photographed together, the newspapers raved over the young couple.

"I hope I get an invite." She winked and playfully touched his arm.

Copeland felt a knot form in his stomach. Of course, Summer would be invited, but he hadn't thought about asking a date and surely, that's what she was hinting at. Everyone assumed he had no idea what was going on, but it was so obvious the way Summer threw herself at him.

Summer is great, he'd think. *Summer is kind and smart and she would be a great wife by most standards,* he'd try to convince himself, but there was something off. He didn't know if he loved her and he didn't know if he ever would. But, like most things in his life, it appeared the plan was already in motion, so instead of dread it or consider changing it, he decided he would just let it happen.

"I'm sure you'll be invited." Copeland smiled. He knew he should ask her to be his date... and he probably would... but right now, he didn't feel compelled. "I'm sorry. I am pretty tired," he apologized. "I am going to head to my room for the night. The first of the month is always a bit much for me."

"I understand." Summer smiled through a deep breath and Copeland could see her disappointment. "Get some rest."

"Thanks." He began to make his way back to his room; down the hallways he'd walked thousands of times before. He stopped suddenly when a painting caught his eye. He'd seen it before but never in this hopeless of a mood.

The painting depicted a woman sitting alone at a table with a blue bottle next to her. She leaned on her left hand and her right hand looked tense. Her eyes looked sad and she looked like she was waiting for something that would never come.

Copeland stopped and stared up at the artwork.

Under the painting it read, "The Absinthe Drinker (1901)."

"You and me both," Copeland sympathetically laughed to himself. For one simple moment, he felt alone, yet understood. Copeland supposedly had everything one could dream of: money, power, authority. But he didn't care for any of it. He only wanted someone to share it with.

He continued to mindlessly walk to his room, thinking about the woman in the painting, when Martin's voice interrupted his thoughts.

"Good evening, sir."

Copeland looked up and was surprised to see him standing outside of his room.

"Hi," Copeland replied.

"I was hoping we could go over tomorrow's schedule if you have a moment."

At *this hour*, Copeland thought to himself, annoyed? He looked down at his watch and saw it was only 7:15 P.M. Feeling silly, Copeland agreed.

"Sure, Martin. That would be fine."

Martin opened the door and Copeland walked in. Per the customs of Carnot, members of the Howth family were required to lead the way into any room. Martin followed as Copeland led the way across the sprawling room to the sitting area with a brown leather, Victorian couch, two white, wingback chairs and a coffee table made of African Blackwood.

Copeland took a seat in one of the chairs. Martin bowed slightly and then took a seat in the other. He opened the black notebook he'd been carrying and quickly got to business.

"I have arranged for us to tour four venues tomorrow beginning at 9:30 A.M. We will start at the Zehr Opera House, followed by the Mattera Theatre, then we will break for lunch at Hulst Bistro. After lunch, we will go to Pillmonte Hall and finish with Wayne Ballroom. Ideally, you will select the venue by the end of the day tomorrow so we can give Mrs. Carter a full four weeks to plan," Martin explained.

"What about the piano factory?" Copeland asked.

"What about it?"

"I want to tour it."

"Sir, the Tellmen Piano Factory has been closed for quite some time now," Martin calmly replied.

"I know," said Copeland. "But I'd like to see it. I think it could have an elegant, vintage vibe."

"I highly doubt your father would be on board with an 'elegant, vintage vibe.'" Martin made air quotes as he nearly choked on the words and the thought of celebrating the future Paramount Chief of Carnot's eighteenth birthday in an abandoned factory.

"My father said I could host my party anywhere in the city," Copeland explained. "Tellmen Piano Factory counts as anywhere."

Knowing he had no choice but to fulfill Copeland's request, Martin replied, "We could go after Wayne—"

"I'd rather go first thing," Copeland interrupted. "Does 9:00 A.M. work?"

"No. I'm assuming you've scheduled every other venue for an hour. I would like Tellmen's to get the same," he countered.

"8:30, sir?" Martin asked.

"Perfect," Copeland smiled.

"Great," he replied, staying as formal and professional as possible. "I will get that arranged. We will leave promptly at 8:15 in the morning."

"Thank you. Goodnight, Martin," Copeland said giving him a slight wave.

"Goodnight, sir." Martin stood up, bowed and walked purposefully out of the room.

Copeland grinned to himself.

That one was for you, he laughed, thinking about the lonely woman in the oil painting. *You're too busy waiting on something that may never come but I'm taking a step toward it for the both of us.*

Chapter Eight

"Help!" a panicked voice called with a knock at the front door. Beckham quickly stood up from the couch, moving out of his mother's arms and hurried to answer it. Margaret and Vienna were quickly following behind him. He flung the door open and they met the watery eyes of Cassie Fredrickson, the young girl who lived next door. She was standing on the front porch; her hair was dripping wet from the rain and mascara streaked wildly down her cheeks.

"Cassie, what's wrong?" Beckham asked suspiciously.

Cassie's mother had died when she was only four, and she had no siblings. Her distress indicated something to do with her father.

"He's dead," she wailed. Cassie's uncontrollable sobs were halted only by her need to breathe.

"Dead?" Vienna asked.

Beckham immediately began running toward the neighbor's front door. The Fredricksons had lived in the adjoining townhouse the entirety of his life.

He ran up the cement steps leading to the front door and let himself in.

On the wooden floors of the living room, he saw the

pale, white face of Mr. Fredrickson. He was still gripping his Ivy Letter in his left hand.

Beckham hesitantly bent down to grab the letter. He had to pry Mr. Fredrickson's stiff fingers off the paper to loosen his grip. Beckham held the letter in his wet hands and began reading it to himself.

Mr. Tyler Lance Fredrickson,

The Committee of Demise has completed its monthly decision meeting. Each month the committee meets per Carnot's government policy to randomly select citizens whose time with us must come to an end. These decisions are based on numerical formulas and random number generators.

We regret to inform you that this will be the last letter you receive.

This month, you have been randomly selected to experience fatal cardiac arrest.

As you know, no substitutions or grievances are allowed.

Thank you for all you have done for our community! It is with great sorrow we say goodbye to a wonderful soul like yours.

All the best,

Theodore Steven Howth
Paramount Chief of Carnot

Margaret and Vienna walked in, supporting Cassie between them, while Beckham was reading the letter. When he was finished, he passed it to Vienna. She quickly scanned it before handing it to her mother.

The four of them stood silently in shock over Mr. Fredrickson's body. The only sounds were the rain pouring down on the roof and the occasional deep breath from Cassie. Faint ambulance sirens started to become louder against the sound of the heavy rain.

A few minutes later, two medical professionals in navy blue jumpsuits entered the room with a stretcher and a white sheet.

"Aren't you going to at least try to save him?" Beckham wanted to ask but he knew it was hopeless. The letter said "fatal" and fatal it would be.

The two men worked efficiently to place Mr. Fredrickson's body on the stretcher and cover him with the sheet.

"I've never heard of it happening so fast before," Vienna whispered to Beckham.

"Me either," Beckham agreed. "Normally, they at least give people a day to say goodbye."

Like clockwork, the moment they rolled Mr. Fredrickson out of the room, an assertive looking man in a black suit came walking in.

"Cassidy Beth Fredrickson." The man looked straight at her. "I'm going to need you to come with me."

Cassie almost choked on her tears as she hesitantly walked toward the man. Beckham knew there was nothing he could do or say to stop her from going. Children in Carnot were not allowed to live by themselves until they were eighteen, and Cassie was only thirteen.

Most likely, she would be taken to live in a group home until then. Although, occasionally, some orphans were lucky enough to be adopted.

"She can live with—" Vienna desperately tried to suggest before her mother gripped her arm so tightly she almost screamed.

"No, she can't," Margaret huffed through gritted teeth. "Have a nice night, sir." Margaret smiled politely as Cassie followed the man.

The young girl helplessly looked back one last time before she put her head down defeatedly and walked out the door.

Once they heard the car doors shut, Margaret reached out and slapped Vienna hard across the face.

"How dare you make a suggestion like that in front of a government official," she reprimanded. "You know far better than to do that."

"What is he going to do?" Vienna asked, pressing a hand to her stinging cheek, tears threatening to fall. "Kill me? They'll kill me if they want to anyway!"

"Vienna, stop!" Beckham pleaded. "Just stop. We're all a little on edge... and rightfully so," he added. "Let's just go home and call it a night. We all need some time to process."

Beckham took Margaret and Vienna's silence for an agreement and led the way out the front door. Vienna rubbed her sore cheek as she solemnly looked back at the empty townhome before shutting the door.

Chapter Nine

The alarm rang loudly, waking Vienna. She was pleasantly surprised she'd slept until her alarm, given the way the night before had gone. It wasn't the first time she'd seen a dead body and she knew, unfortunately, it wouldn't be the last.

She rolled over in bed, not wanting to get up.

What's today, she thought to herself? *Monday? Yes, Monday! That makes it so much easier to get up,* she continued the conversation in her head. *Okay.* She looked at the clock. *It's 7:30* A.M., *I have thirty minutes to get ready and out the door in order to stop for coffee on the way to school.*

For a few years now, Vienna had made it her routine to stop for coffee on her way to school every Monday morning. She had struggled to get back into a routine after her father passed away and she found that starting her week with coffee was good motivation.

She brushed her teeth and combed her hair before getting dressed. She put on a pair of jeans and an oversized, hunter green sweatshirt. After getting dressed, she sat down at her desk and began to fiddle through her makeup. Her mother always looked so naturally beautiful; she hardly ever wore makeup, so Vienna had to teach herself. She put on a touch of light, pink eyeshadow and added some mascara to her eyes. She brushed up her eyebrows and added some light blush to her cheeks.

I guess that will have to do. She smiled to herself in the mirror before she walked down the hall to see if Beckham was awake.

"Morning, V," he greeted her when she peeked in the doorway.

"Morning," she replied. "Any interest in joining me for coffee?"

"Not today. I'm not in the mood to walk to school. I'll take the train."

"Lazzyy," Vienna teased. "I'll see you there."

"Sounds good."

Vienna walked down the stairs and grabbed her winter coat off the coat rack hanging by the front door. She put on her coat, her black, suede Chelsea boots, flung her backpack over her shoulder, and headed out.

She loved to walk in the chilly, winter air. She breathed in the smell of the early morning and walked slowly down the street.

The Tunston family lived on the north side of the city. The walk to school was a mile east and took Vienna about twenty minutes. The first part of her walk was through a residential area of the city. Vienna's family lived in a government owned townhome and the matching government homes extended for five blocks. Since her father had worked high up for Carnot, they lived in the home free of rent. After he passed away, the government let them keep living in the house since her mother still worked there, even though she wasn't as highly ranked.

Once Vienna passed the last townhomes, she entered the restaurant district. Rich or Pour, her go-to coffee shop was about halfway through the restaurant stretch.

Vienna crossed the street before opening the glass door of the corner coffee shop. She was greeted by the shop owner, who was, ironically, named Joe.

The coffee shop had all glass windows that spanned the storefront. The inside was not big with a few small metal tables and chairs. The back wall was made of red, exposed brick and a little counter sat in front of it with a small menu hanging from the ceiling.

"Good morning, Vienna," Joe said.

She smiled. "Morning, Joe."

"Cinnamon latte?" he double checked, remembering her order.

"You know it."

"How was your weekend?" he asked. The coffee shop was pretty empty, but it almost always was at this point in the morning. It typically hit its peak around 7:00 A.M., when most people were on their way to work.

"It was alright," she replied. "My family got good letters, so I can't complain. How about you?" She handed Joe a ten-dollar bill.

"Same here. Luckily, the wife and I are in the clear," he said as he took the cash from her and rang in the total on the register.

"Glad to hear it."

Vienna had always liked Joe. He was kind. He spoke to her like a young woman and not like a child.

After handing her change back, Joe worked swiftly behind the counter, steaming the milk, pulling the espresso shots and adding the syrup to her paper cup.

"Any plans for the day?" he asked.

"Just school," Vienna answered.

"I always forget you are so young. You don't act your age."

"Sometimes, you have to grow up too fast," Vienna explained a little solemnly.

"I guess that is the sad truth," Joe said as he handed Vienna her latte with a reassuring smile. "Have a good one."

"Thanks, you too." She turned around and walked toward the door. "See you next week!" she called on her way out.

She started down the street again, sipping on her cup of coffee. The restaurant district ended a few blocks down the road, and she made her way into the factory district. She took in the mix of ever-changing buildings around her; some puffing smoke and some with windows boarded up. It seemed this area was constantly transforming and it was because of this that Vienna particularly enjoyed walking through it.

She admired a building to her right as she took a sip of coffee. The chimney at the top of the factory was letting out white smoke and Vienna watched as the smoke split into different shapes against the light blue morning sky.

Before she knew what happened, she felt the hot sting of coffee dripping down her arm.

She shrieked, half in pain, half in shock.

"I'm so sorry," an oddly familiar voice replied.

Vienna looked up to meet the honey-brown eyes of Copeland Howth.

"No, no, I'm the one who's sorry," Vienna frantically apologized. She hopelessly began trying to wipe the coffee she'd spilled off Copeland's linen shirt.

"It's alright," he said with a smile. "No worries."

Should I, like, bow or something, Vienna thought?

"You don't need to bow," Copeland answered.

"Did I say that out loud?" Vienna asked, mortified.

"No, I just assumed you were thinking it. Most girls who run into me and spill coffee all over my shirt typically ask." He smirked.

Is he always this snide, Vienna wondered? She forced a fake laugh, knowing better than to cause riffs with the Howth family. "Yeah, again, I apologize about that."

"It's alright."

Vienna was surprised by how genuine he sounded.

"What are you doing in this part of town anyway? I didn't think people like you were ever caught dead in the factory district?" Vienna asked. The ill-mannered comment came out before she could filter it.

"Oh," Copeland laughed. "You're a fiery thing, aren't you?"

Isn't he, like, the same age as me, Vienna thought to herself? *Why is he talking down to me? Ugh… the ego.* She refrained from rolling her eyes.

"If you must know, I am looking at venues to host my eighteenth birthday party," he explained.

"And you're looking here?" Vienna raised her eyebrows in disapproval, glancing at Tellmen's. "At an old piano factory?"

Copeland grinned. "Yes, I am. I like to do the

unexpected."

"Oh, is that so? Good luck with the unexpected," she said as she started to walk away. "I have to get to school."

"Have a good day," Copeland wished her well.

"You too," Vienna insincerely replied as she gave a single wave without turning around.

Chapter Ten

Copeland casually began unbuttoning his shirt as he walked across the street. There were three black town cars lined parallel to the road and he walked to the one in the middle.

"What on earth are you doing?" Martin exclaimed as he stepped out of the backseat.

"Shh," Copeland hushed. "Keep it down."

"Why did you insist we stay in the car? Manny is about to have a heart attack up there," Martin explained. Manny had served as Copeland's head security officer for many years.

"Don't worry about it." Copeland was unfazed by Martin's frustration. "Do you have my extra clothes?"

"Yes," Martin replied, still frazzled but regaining his composure. He walked to the trunk of the car and opened it, unveiling numerous spare pairs of pants, jackets and shirts. Copeland selected an ivory button-down shirt, nearly identical to the one he'd been wearing previously. He took off the coffee-stained shirt and surprisingly, his white undershirt was not wet.

"Shall we tour the factory now?" Martin suggested once Copeland had rebuttoned his new shirt.

"We shall." Copeland smiled. He'd always enjoyed making Martin squirm.

"All eyes on Fern," Martin whispered into the tiny microphone on the collar of his suit jacket. The Howth family all had botanical codenames for their security detail and Copeland's was Fern. "We are moving."

Like clockwork, the doors of the town cars opened and four men in all black suits and sunglasses moved toward Copeland. He was quickly surrounded by his security detail and Martin led the way to the front door.

Although the Howth family was constantly surrounded by security when they were out and about, it was only for show. Since the discovery of perpetual life, and the establishment of Carnot, there had been no reported crime in the city. If there was reason to suspect someone was thinking freely and could potentially commit a crime, they were taken into rehabilitation or, in some cases, subdued with medication.

The piano factory spanned the length of the block with worn, white brick lining the bottom third of the building and reddish-brown brick covering the remainder. The four glass entry doors were shaded by a red awning.

Before Martin reached the sidewalk in front of the building, the doors swung open and an older woman in a flattering blue dress came out.

"Good morning, Mr. Howth," she said greeting Copeland with a bow. "And Mr. Pluto." She turned her smile toward Martin. "We are so honored to have you touring our facility today."

"Thank you for making the time for us," Martin politely responded.

"Of course, of course," she replied. "I am Chelsea Tellmen. My father, Paul Tellmen, inherited this factory from his father and him from his father and so the story goes. We opened shop back in 1852 and as you can see," she gestured toward the empty entrance, "things have gone quite downhill over the last eight decades." She turned and opened the door. She held it as Copeland and Martin walked in, followed by the guards.

The sprawling lobby was completely empty except for a large, grand piano to their right in the center of the room. The wooden floorboards were worn but still in immaculate shape, considering the age of the building. The walls were made of the same white brick that covered the outside and windows lined the walls, perfectly spaced every three feet.

"I am happy to give you a tour of the entire building, but I figured if you're looking for a space to host a party, that this is the area you'd like to see most," Chelsea explained as she locked the door behind her. "Obviously, we do not make pianos anymore... though I truly wish we did," she added as if she was speaking only to herself. "But we do rent out this space for parties often. Usually, people set it up with banquet tables over here." She gestured toward the left side of the room. "And a dance floor over here." She pointed toward the side with the piano. "It's very cool, in my opinion, what many people do over here." She walked toward the grand piano. "I have seen people build a circular stage before, with the grand piano at the center and space for a few other band members, and then the dance floor surrounding it in a larger circle. It gives the room a very intimate feel."

"Ohh, I like that idea," Copeland commented.

"Yes." Chelsea agreed with a smile, failing to hide her enthusiasm that Copeland agreed with her. "These stairs make for a lovely entrance for the host." She motioned to the wooden staircase lined with a red pattern rug. "There is a service entrance at the back of the building so guests can come in the front door and you can make a grand entrance down the steps."

"What about catering?" Martin asked, clearly uninterested in anything but the logistics.

"Of course," Chelsea answered. "Follow me." She turned to her left and led the way to the only door on the back wall. She opened it and spoke as Copeland and Martin walked in. The security guards had spaced themselves out around the first floor and didn't follow. "We have a full catering kitchen here that you're more than welcome to use. I would offer you a list of our catering partners, but I am assuming you have staff you would like to bring in, which is more than acceptable."

"Yes, we do," Martin confirmed. "This is great." Even his sour attitude couldn't deny that the massive kitchen had everything they would need.

"Wonderful," Copeland commented. "Honestly, I think I've seen everything I need to see. I love it. We'll take—"

"We have four other venues we are looking at today," Martin interrupted. "We will get back to you by the end of the day tomorrow with our decision. Thank you for your time."

"That sounds great." Chelsea couldn't help but grin at the disapproval Martin clearly had toward Copeland's unfiltered comment. "You're very welcome. Thank you for coming!"

Chelsea led the way back through the lobby and opened the front doors. Copeland, followed by Martin and his security detail, walked back outside and to the cars.

Once inside the car, the reprimanding from Martin began.

"Your father would be so disappointed in the way you just acted in there. You can't promise people whose livelihood depends on every penny they bring in false business."

"I didn't promise anyone false business," Copeland replied. "I want to have my birthday party there."

"You know we cannot have your birthday party in the factory district," Martin sternly replied.

"I guess we'll just have to wait and see about that."

Martin took a deep breath in. He knew he shouldn't argue with Copeland, but he pushed so many of his buttons on purpose and even though he knew it, it still flustered him. "It's only 8:45 A.M.," Martin said. "It will only take us ten minutes to get to Zehr Opera House, which means we have about thirty-five minutes to spare. Did you get any breakfast this morning?"

"No, I didn't have enough time," Copeland answered. "I've always wanted to try that little coffee shop up the road. I think it's called... uhm—"

"Rich or Pour?" Martin guessed. He hadn't put two and two together yet, but suddenly, his wheels were turning.

"That's the one!" Copeland replied.

"Alrighty then. We'll get some coffee and be on our way." He grabbed his shirt collar and instructed, "Roll out to Rich or Pour. Fern is on the move."

They rode up the street and got out in front of the coffee shop. Without looking up from making the drink he'd been working on, Joe greeted them, "Good morning! Welcome to Rich or—" He finally looked up, clearly surprised. "Oh, Mr. Howth," Joe said as he bowed. "I do apologize. I had no idea—"

Copeland cut him off, "Don't sweat it."

"What can I get for you this morning?" Joe asked. "It's on the house."

"Let me ask you a question," Copeland replied. "Was there a girl in here earlier? She would have been about my age, relatively curly blonde hair, yay high." He estimated said-girl's height with his hand, holding it just below his shoulder.

"Yes, there was," Joe hesitantly answered.

"What did she get to drink?" he asked.

"She ordered a cinnamon latte," Joe replied slowly. He felt uneasy but knew better than to question those in power.

"I'll take the same," Copeland said.

"A cinnamon latte for Mr. Howth." Joe nodded as he wrote the order on the paper cup. "Coming right up."

Joe finished making Copeland's latte before he took the orders of his entourage. The coffee shop had been empty when they arrived, and Manny stood guarding the door to ensure it stayed that way. Word had evidently spread that Copeland was out in the city because a few photographers were now gathered outside the shop.

Copeland sat alone at the corner booth against the windows, ignoring the flashing cameras. He took the first sip of his cinnamon latte and closed his eyes, enjoying the flavor.

He moved slightly in the booth, adjusting his legs so he could reach into his right pocket. He angled himself away from the reporters and pulled out a tattered envelope, keeping it hidden in his lap, below the table. He admired the envelope with his name written in calligraphy, though it was not the same perfect calligraphy he was used to seeing on his Ivy Letters.

He rubbed the envelope. *We're making progress,* he thought to himself. *We're finally starting to get somewhere.*

Chapter Eleven

Beckham was walking across the schoolyard when he heard his sister call his name. He turned to see her flushed face and coat stained with coffee.

"What happened to you?" he asked.

"Uhm," Vienna hesitated, seeing how many students were within eavesdropping distance. "Can we go somewhere a little quieter?"

"Sure." Beckham raised his eyebrows, confused.

They walked around the right side of the school to an area outside of the cafeteria with four picnic tables. Only one table was occupied by a couple who shot them a disapproving look as they pulled away from each other; evidently, they'd interrupted something. The twins sat down at the wooden table furthest from them and Beckham asked again, "What happened to you?"

"I spilled my coffee this morning," Vienna answered obnoxiously, sensing she had her brother on the hook.

"I can see that." Beckham rolled his eyes. "How?"

"I ran into someone on my walk."

"Who?" he asked.

Vienna looked around again, ensuring no one was within earshot. The couple had gone back to making out, clearly not too bothered by their presence, and no one else was around.

"Copeland Howth," she whispered.

"Copeland H—"

Vienna covered his mouth before he could finish yelling his name.

"I didn't ask you to come back here where it was quiet so that you could scream it," she rebuked as she took her hand off his mouth.

"Sorry," Beckham apologized at a much quieter level. "I just... I was not expecting that... You ran into him? Like, he was just out and about without security?"

"Oh, uhm, I hadn't thought about that," Vienna replied. "But, yeah, I guess."

"Are you sure?" Beckham asked. "Or did he just look a lot like him?"

"No, it was him!" Vienna insisted. "He was out touring venues to host his birthday party."

"Where did you run into him?" Beckham asked.

"Outside of Tellmen's."

"You're telling me the future Paramount Chief of Carnot was looking in the factory district to host the biggest party of the year?" Beckham laughed and started to stand up from the table. "Good one, V."

"No, seriously, Beck, he was!" She stood up and placed her hands on his shoulders to push him down. "Have I ever lied to you?"

"You did tell me once I was adopted." Beckham sat back down.

"Be serious." Vienna was frustrated. If Beckham didn't believe her, who would? "I don't lie to you. It was him."

"Okay, okay. So, I believe you," Beckham replied. "What do you want me to do about it?"

Vienna pensively put her hand to her cheek and rubbed it softly. "I guess I don't know... I wanted to tell you so badly but now... I'm not sure why."

"Ohh... I know!" Beckham's eyes widened.

"Why?" Vienna sat up straighter, anxious for Beckham's interpretation.

Beckham sang, "Vienna and Copeland sitting in a tree, k-i-s-s–"

"Stop it." Vienna punched Beckham's arm, interrupting his song. "I do not have a crush on him. Plus, even if I did... which I don't," she firmly clarified again, "I'm sure I will never see him again in my life."

"Ahh, forbidden love," Beckham sighed. "How romantic." He turned away from Vienna, crossed his arms, and started rubbing his hands on his back, making lots of obnoxious kissing sounds.

"Ugh. This was a waste of time," Vienna sighed, shoving him. "I need girlfriends."

Beckham stopped his mimicking and turned back around toward Vienna. "But, like, totally," he started in a dramatic Valley-Girl voice. "Like, if you and Copeland ended up together it would be, like, so cool and, like, you would live, like, happily ever after."

To Vienna's relief, the bell sounded signaling first period.

"I'm going to class now." Vienna shook her head as she stood up and tossed her backpack over her shoulder. Despite her annoyance, she couldn't deny that her brother had always known how to make her laugh.

"Catch you later, Mrs. Copeland Howth," Beckham teased as she walked away. He could almost hear her eyes roll.

Chapter Twelve

"Good morning," Elton welcomed Margaret as she sat down at her desk. "Happy Tuesday."

"Happy Tuesday," Margaret replied.

"You have your work cut out for you today."

Margaret was surprised by Elton's rush. She hadn't even had a chance to get her cup of coffee this morning or put her lunch away. He was never this anxious to get to work.

"What's on the agenda?" she asked. The question felt strange coming out of her mouth as she was normally the one answering it.

"Well, you've just been assigned the task of planning Copeland Howth's eighteenth birthday party."

"What!?" Margaret was shocked. She was thankful she hadn't had the chance to get her morning coffee or she was convinced she would have spit it straight out of her mouth. "Why?"

"I have no idea," Elton answered with a shrug. "I was informed this morning that you would be temporarily serving as Madison Carter's assistant, effective immediately."

"What?" was all Margaret could get out. She couldn't

believe it.

"Madison works on the third floor. Do you need help bringing any of your stuff up there?" Elton offered.

"Uhm, no... I think I just need a box and I can get it all," she answered still surprised and a little confused.

Elton grabbed a box from inside his office door. "Here you go." He set it down next to her feet. He must have been prepared for her to pack.

"Thanks." She mindlessly began packing up her things, shocked by the start of the morning.

I was afraid this would happen, Margaret thought bitterly to herself. *He's replacing me... I should have been friendlier to him. He probably found some beautiful, more youthful woman to take my place and is having me sent to this lesser position.*

Packing didn't take her too long. She used to have a desk full of family pictures and decorations. Since Lewis died, however, she'd made it a point to be emotionally detached from her work, which meant she kept little on her desk so she could leave at a moment's notice. *Guess my plan is coming in handy,* she piercingly thought as she grabbed the box now filled with her things and walked toward the elevator bank.

"Have a nice day," Elton called from his desk as he caught a glimpse of her walking away. "See you soon!"

"Yeah, right," Margaret sighed to herself without responding to him. She stepped onto the elevator. *I've sat at that very desk for fifteen years and suddenly, I'm being exiled to the third floor. The third floor.* She shook her head, thinking. *The third floor is where they send people to squeeze the last bit of life out of them before they're selected to die.*

Margaret stepped out of the elevator and turned left. The level was filled with cubicles and the floor was bustling. It seemed everyone was either making a call, typing feverishly or hurrying to get somewhere. She walked between two rows of cubicles to the back wall lined with glass, separating those who were higher up. Madison's office was in the corner with a gorgeous view overlooking the city.

Madison saw Margaret coming and stood up from her desk. "Hello! Good morning!" she said as she cheerfully opened the door.

Oh no. Margaret's concern for what the day held grew substantially when she saw Madison. Madison was a tall and slender woman in her late twenties. She had blonde hair that fell in waves to her shoulders and her skin had a special glow. She was wearing a three-quarter sleeve black dress that hugged her tightly to her knees and perfectly accented Margaret's concern: a big, baby bump.

"Good morning." Margaret smiled. She'd briefly met Madison a few times before but hadn't spent much time with her. "You look stunning," she complimented and though she was concerned for herself, she truly meant it. "When are you due?"

"December twenty-second," Madison shyly smiled and bit her lip.

Margaret's mind began to whirl. *What in the world is going on here? I thought I came up here to start my slow death not to fill in for new life,* she thought.

"Would you come in and have a seat?" Madison asked. "We have a lot to talk about."

Margaret nodded. "It seems we do." She walked in

the door and Madison shut it behind her. She set her cardboard box on one of the black chairs across the desk from Madison and took a seat in the other.

"As you know," Madison started to talk as she sat down, "Copeland's eighteenth birthday is in less than a month."

Margaret nodded. She wasn't in an especially chatty mood.

"Yes." Madison nervously smiled. "And I am the executive event coordinator."

Margaret nodded again.

"And... I am eight months pregnant," Madison gestured to her stomach.

Again, Margaret only nodded.

Sensing her apprehension, Madison took a deep breath and cut to the chase. "Which means I will not be here to plan and execute Copeland's party," Madison continued. "And you've been selected to fill in."

"What?" Margaret finally spoke aloud. She thought Elton had been trying to get rid of her. She thought at most she'd help put stamps on invitations. But being tasked to plan the heir's most influential birthday party? No, this had to be a joke. The thought had never crossed her mind.

"Evidently, once it was reported I would not be able to entirely plan Copeland's birthday party, you were specifically requested," Madison explained.

"I'm sorry, what?"

"That's all I know. My last day of work is supposed to be the eleventh, which is a week from tomorrow. I am happy to help you as much as I can, but we have a lot to get done in seven days."

"That we do," Margaret agreed. She frustratingly rubbed her face and thought to herself, *I thought we'd moved on from the past... but I guess we have not.*

"We'll need to start with the guest list." Madison wanted to get right to work. "Four weeks' notice on a party they could have been planning for eighteen years," she sighed.

Margaret couldn't help but laugh at how ridiculously true that statement was.

Chapter Thirteen

Vienna and Beckham walked in the back door and tossed their backpacks onto the kitchen floor by the island like they did every day.

"Want a snack?" Vienna asked as she opened the refrigerator to scan what they had.

"Yes, I'm starving!" Beckham answered.

"You good with some cheese and crackers?"

"Yep," he agreed.

Vienna grabbed a block of cheese out of the fridge before opening a cupboard and taking out a box of crackers. She got out a cutting board and knife and then, cut a few slices off the Colby-Jack cheese. She could hardly keep up her cutting with the speed at which Beckham was eating it.

"Beckham, quit. I want some too." She slapped his hand away as he reached for more.

Vienna cut a few more slices and Beckham continued to eat, ignoring her pleas. She was about to protest again but a knock at the door stopped her.

"Who's that?" Beckham quickly asked.

"I have no idea," she replied. "I figured it was for you."

Their house used to be a lively space where friends

would gather on occasion but now, it was almost eerie how out of place the knock sounded.

They both stood still in the kitchen, waiting for the other to open the door.

"Aren't you going to get it?" Beckham asked.

"Are you kidding? It could be a serial killer," she jokingly suggested. There had not been a single murder in Carnot since before it was founded in 2043. "You're older and bigger."

"Only by two minutes," Beckham winked, "but alright." He got up and walked to the door. He looked through the peephole and turned around, his eyes suddenly wide open with surprise.

"It's Copeland Howth," he tried to mouth the words.

"What?" Vienna couldn't understand him from the kitchen.

"Co-pe-land Ho-w-th," Beckham tried to mouth it slower and he held his hands over his head trying to make a crown. Although Copeland wasn't technically a prince, he felt this would help the charade.

Vienna looked blankly at him, still utterly confused.

"Copeland Howth," he whispered.

"What?" Vienna whispered back.

"Copeland Howth," he finally said at an audible level.

"Yes," Copeland replied from outside the door. "It's Copeland."

Beckham put his hand to his forehead, embarrassed he'd been overheard. He turned back to the door and quickly opened it.

"Mr. Howth," Beckham bowed. "I'm—"

"Beckham Tunston," Copeland finished. "Twin of the lovely Vienna Tunston I have come to see."

Beckham raised his eyebrows; though he wasn't surprised by Copeland's arrogance, he was annoyed by it. He turned toward the kitchen, where Vienna stood with her mouth hanging open. "It's for you," Beckham kindly informed her, as if she hadn't heard the entire conversation.

Vienna was still wearing the wrinkled, knee-length black dress she'd worn to school. She tried to brush down the bottom of the dress in a failed attempt to make it look better and tucked her hair behind her ears before walking toward the door.

Beckham walked to the stairs and as she passed him, he made a kissing face at her. She rolled her eyes and continued on to Copeland.

"Uhm, hi." She shyly smiled.

"Hello," Copeland confidently replied. "Can I come in?"

Vienna hesitantly looked at the two large men standing behind him donning black suits, sunglasses, and death stares.

"Don't worry about them," Copeland replied, seeing her hesitation. "They don't have to come in."

"Uhm, okay," Vienna nervously agreed as she stepped aside and gestured for him to enter.

Copeland walked into the townhouse and took in every detail; the sagging shelves, creaking floorboards, and dusty decorations. He suddenly realized he'd never been in a commoner's house before, but he didn't want that to be apparent.

"Nice place," he commented.

"Yeah, right." Vienna didn't believe his compliment. "It's no royal mansion."

"I'm not royalty," Copeland retorted.

"Of course, you're not." Vienna winked. Since the fall of the old world and the founding of Carnot, leadership had decided it was best practice to not name a royal family. However, there was still one family controlling the country and leadership was handed down by bloodline, so in essence, Carnot was still ruled with a royal structure, just with different titles.

Copeland strolled into the living room and made himself comfortable on the gray couch.

"Would you like anything to drink?" Vienna offered.

"No, but I'll take some of those cheese and crackers." Copeland motioned toward the kitchen island where the food had been left out.

The nerve! Vienna thought frustratingly to herself. "Of course," she replied aloud with a smile, squinting her eyes slightly to show her dissatisfaction. She walked over to the kitchen and fixed him a plate before bringing it back to the living room. She set it on the coffee table and took a seat on the couch a couple feet away from Copeland.

"So," Vienna started, trying to sound casual. "What are you doing here?"

Copeland smiled at her and she hated that she almost liked it. *Ugh, he's so haughty,* she thought.

He took a bite of a cracker with cheese before answering.

"I have come to ask you a question."

Vienna creased her brows in confusion. "And what's that?"

Copeland reached into the inner pocket of the navy blazer he was wearing and pulled out a shiny, gold envelope.

"I wanted to invite you to my eighteenth birthday party," he said as he handed her the envelope containing, presumably, an invitation.

"That's not a question," Vienna contended as she reached to grab the envelope from his hand.

Copeland grinned. "You're correct." He moved the envelope slightly out of her reach. "My question is, will you be my date?"

A sudden burst of laughter erupted from the stairs. Beckham had been sitting on the steps, listening in on the conversation and couldn't control his amusement.

"Beckham! Go away!" Vienna shouted. Her face was suddenly flushed with color and though she wished Beckham hadn't been listening in, she was thankful his laughter gave her something to say. She'd never been asked on a date before and never in her wildest dreams had she anticipated Copeland Howth would be the first boy to ask her out. She didn't know what to say. "Sorry, about him," she apologized, waving toward the stairs and avoiding the question.

"It's alright. I'm used to having people listen to my every word," he admitted.

Vienna felt her stomach twinge. *Ew, was that sympathy*, she thought?

"So, what do you say?" Copeland asked again. "Will you be my date for my birthday party?"

"I guess..." Vienna started, "I guess I just don't understand why."

"What do you mean 'why'?" Copeland questioned.

"I mean why would you ask me? You don't even know me."

"I know you're a nice girl who drinks a delicious cinnamon latte," Copeland countered.

"How do you know I drink a cinnamon latte?" Vienna wrinkled her forehead, confused.

"You spilled it all over me," Copeland replied. "Remember?"

"Oh," Vienna sighed, embarrassed. "That's right."

She didn't know what else to say but she could tell from Copeland's face that he wasn't going to ask her again.

"Why aren't you going with your girlfriend?" she asked.

"Oh," Copeland's lips turned up slightly into a sly smile, "so, you do pay attention to me?"

Vienna didn't even attempt to hide her disgust. She rolled her eyes. "It's basically impossible to not know who you're hooking up with," she retorted.

"I'm *not* hooking up with her," Copeland quickly corrected a little defensively. "I actually don't even like her... but I probably shouldn't say that."

"Oh," was all Vienna managed to say.

"If you must know," he continued, "My entire life has pretty much been spelled out before me and I get very little say in any of it."

Vienna's stomach turned again. *Ew, more sympathy.*

"You know what, forget it." Copeland got up from the couch. "This was stupid. Yesterday, I ran into a beautiful girl on the street and I thought, maybe, it was more than a coincidence. I went out on a limb coming here today but I guess it was a mistake." He stormed toward the door.

Don't do it. Don't do it. Don't do it! Vienna fought in

her head to stay seated but to her dismay, she found herself instinctively getting up and chasing after Copeland. "Wait!" she called. "Wait, please. I'm sorry."

Copeland hesitantly stopped at the door.

"I was rude and I'm sorry. I don't know anything about you," Vienna admitted.

"It's okay." Copeland scratched his head. "I don't know anything about you either. I shouldn't have been so forw—"

"I'll go," Vienna interrupted. "I'll be your date."

"Really?" Copeland smiled.

Vienna nodded, unsure of what she'd just gotten herself into.

"Great," Copeland replied assertively. "I'll have Martin get in touch with you about your wardrobe and I'll think of something we can do for the announcement."

"The announcement?" Vienna questioned.

"Yeah." Copeland nodded. "We can't have the first time we're photographed together be the party. There's a lot of protocol surrounding the whole thing but not to worry, we'll be in touch."

Before Vienna could object, Copeland had opened the front door and was halfway to his car.

"Could I at least keep the invitation?" she called, realizing he'd never handed it to her.

Copeland turned around and continued slowly walking backward. "The invites aren't even printed yet. I just thought it would be a good icebreaker." He waved the empty, gold envelope in the air and turned back toward the car.

What did I just do, Vienna stood speechlessly wondering as the line of black town cars drove away?

Chapter Fourteen

Beckham sat at the top of the stairs and waited for the sound of the front door shutting.

"Oh my gosh!" he exclaimed, running down the steps. "What was that?!"

Vienna was leaning against the front door with her head tilted up toward the ceiling.

"I have no idea..." she sighed, stunned.

"Are you going to tell Mom?" Beckham asked.

Vienna's eyes widened. She hadn't even thought about having to tell her mom. "I... I..."

"Yikes," said Beckham. "Looks like you didn't think your way through this one."

"Do you really think that's helping?" Vienna sneered.

"I'm your older brother. My job is not to help," Beckham teased.

"By two minutes," Vienna reminded him. "And, yes, it is. Your job is to protect me from boys. It's in, like, every brother-sister handbook ever written."

"Oh, is that so?"

"Yeah. You're not supposed to sit on the stairs and bust out laughing when I get asked on my first date."

"Isn't there some kind of exception to the rule when

it's royalty?" Beckham asked.

"I'm not royalty," they imitated Copeland simultaneously and Vienna was thankful for the comic relief.

"Did he eat all of my cheese and crackers?" Beckham asked once he'd caught his breath from laughing.

"No," Vienna replied. "And I'm still hungry. Between you two idiots, I haven't even had one."

Beckham laughed as he went to get the plate off the coffee table. Vienna walked to the kitchen and started cutting some more cheese.

Beckham sat down and, lost in thought, they both silently snacked for a few minutes.

"What just happened?" Vienna finally broke the silence.

"I honestly have no idea. Yesterday, I thought you were lying about running into Copeland Howth and today, he's at our house asking you to be his date to the biggest event of the year."

"And for some unknown reason, I said 'yes' and now I have to explain to Mom that I am going on a date... or multiple dates... or I don't know... but I am doing something—"

"And very publicly, I might add," Beckham interjected.

"Thanks for that." Vienna rolled her eyes. "With a member of the Howth family... who Mom absolutely despises."

Beckham pursed his lips and nodded. "Yep, I think that about sums it up."

"Ugh, what am I going to do?" Vienna put her face in her hands.

"You have to tell her."

"Do I though?" she asked.

"How would you possibly keep it from her? It's going to be front page news."

"Maybe, not right away," Vienna countered. "It sounds like he really wants me to go with him," she talked through her thoughts out loud. "So, maybe, I could ask him to hold off on the announcement for a bit... even a week could buy me a little time. I just need time to think. I need time to play out all the scenarios and decide the best way to explain it to Mom."

Beckham breathed in. "Ahh, the sweet scent of forbidden love."

"It's not love. I don't even want to go with him," Vienna argued.

"Oh... Really? You don't want to go to the event of the year with the world's most eligible bachelor?" he questioned.

Vienna's face turned bright red. "No!"

"V, I'm your brother. More than that... I'm your twin. I can tell you're into him," he said.

"I'm not! He's so arrogant and smug and his smile is too," she racked her brain for words, "too perfect... and the way he dresses and strolls all around like he owns the place—"

"Well, he kind of does," Beckham interjected.

"It's sick," Vienna finished.

"If you say so," Beckham laughed.

"Whatever." Vienna rolled her eyes. "I just need a week," she declared. "Just give me a week." She confidently walked out of the kitchen and up the stairs.

She is in real trouble, Beckham thought to himself.

Chapter Fifteen

"How did it go?" Martin asked as he opened the car door for Copeland.

"Splendidly," Copeland replied. "I have a date for my birthday party."

"You what?" Martin questioned, surprised.

"I have a date for my birthday party," Copeland repeated, nonchalantly.

"Sir, forgive me, but are you not supposed to be taking Miss Summer Nile? I thought you were just apologizing to Vienna for spilling coffee on her shirt and offering to buy her a new one... not asking her to your party."

"I don't want to take Summer. I want to take Vienna, which is why I asked her, and she agreed. So, there you have it, I have my date for the party all set. Would you please have Zelda start designing some ideas?" Copeland said changing the subject.

"Yes, sir," Martin replied. It was clear he wasn't going to change Copeland's mind. It wasn't Copeland he was worried about answering to though. He was worried about answering to Theodore.

"We need to plan a date or two before the party,"

Copeland thought aloud.

"Yes, sir. The protocol is two dates with a potential girlfriend before a formal event," Martin explained.

"Perfect," Copeland replied. "I think we should do a hike and a dinner date."

"That sounds like a fine plan," Martin agreed. "Hike first, I presume?"

"Yes," Copeland answered. "Hike sometime this week and please arrange for it to be highly photographed. Then, we'll do dinner at Salan's next week. After that, we can officially announce that Vienna will be accompanying me to my party."

"We'll have to run it by Mr. Nile, of course," Martin reminded him.

Copeland knew this would be an issue. There was no one he wanted to know less about his intentions with Vienna than his semi-ex-girlfriend's dad. Well, he'd probably rather tell Mr. Nile than his own father... but even then, he wasn't sure.

"Do we have to?" Copeland asked.

"Yes," Martin replied. "Everything we display publicly needs to run through him."

"I know," Copeland sighed. "Okay, just give me a day or two to think it over. I need to figure out how to best go about this."

It took everything in Martin to refrain from saying, *Best going about it would have been simply asking Summer. You're making things more difficult than you know, dearest Copeland.* But he instead said, "Of course, sir."

They pulled into the gates of Carnot and Copeland was dropped off under the porte-cochère on the backside of the mansion.

He walked through the vast halls replaying his conversation with Vienna.

I think she bought it... She seemed to think I was sincere. The thing with the coffee was almost a mistake but I covered it well. At least, I hope so, he thought. She's going to be my date for the party and that's what's most important. I have bought myself more time with her; time is what I'm after.

His mind continued to wander and soon enough, he was back in his room. He walked in and grabbed the gold frame from the nightstand before sitting down. He stared longingly at the pictures of him with his mother. She had been beautiful. She had short brown hair that sat curled on the top of her head and her smile radiated all sorts of happiness. Copeland missed her dearly. He felt like she held the answers to all of his questions.

If only you were still here, he thought to himself. He flipped the frame over and took off the back cover of one of the photos, unveiling the same tattered envelope he'd held at the coffee shop the day before. He knew his room was searched often, so he had to go to great lengths to keep things hidden.

He opened the envelope and took out the letter, which to the general eye, looked identical to an Ivy Letter. It was spaced almost exactly the same with its words, lines and paragraphs, but the information it held had changed Copeland's life forever.

Mr. Copeland Beau Howth,

The Committee of Demise has completed its monthly decision meeting. This month, the committee met per Carnot's government policy and decided my time with us must come to an end. This decision was not based on numerical factors, and it rarely ever is. I am in dire need of your help.

We are pleased to inform you that you will receive another letter next month.

This month, I will die from a cause I do not yet know. You must find Vienna Marie Tunston.

Her father will die on the same day from the same cause.

We need you both for the betterment of our community! Please refer to the note in the back of the golden frame for further instructions.

I love you,

Camilla Audrey Howth

Camilla Audrey Howth
Paramount First Lady of Carnot

Copeland reread the letter as he'd done hundreds of times.

I'm getting there, Mom. He closed his eyes. *I am sorry it's taking me so long, but you know how things are, I can only get so much information at a time without causing suspicion.*

He opened the other side of the frame and pulled out a handwritten note.

November 25, 2117

My Dearest Copeland,

What once started as a beautiful discovery, the ability to no longer suffer from diseases, death, and sickness, has tragically transformed over the years. Carnot, in its simplest form, was a grand idea. It was a way to keep the earth moving, despite the introduction of perpetual life. It allowed for chance to determine those next to die, rather than incurable and uncontrollable causes. However, over the years, the government system has become corrupt, with leaders slowly taking control and making decisions based, not on chance, but instead, on their own personal vendettas.

A dear friend and colleague of mine, Lewis Matthew Tunston, and I have been working tirelessly to learn more about the system at its core and to find its weaknesses, so that we can restore Carnot to its glory.

Unfortunately, we now believe our efforts have been discovered and we suspect that we will be selected to die soon.

I am asking you, on behalf of Lewis and the people of Carnot, to find his daughter, Vienna, and continue our quest for restoration. I wish it wasn't so, but you will not be able to request the help of your father in this matter. As for

Vienna's mother, I cannot say for certain where she stands.

What we know is this—

Copeland heard footsteps down the hall and frantically tossed the letters and frame in the top drawer of his nightstand.

He untucked the covers and quickly climbed under them. He placed his head on his pillow, closed his eyes and pretended to be asleep.

He heard the sound of the doorknob twisting and stayed as still as possible.

"Sir," he heard Martin start and suddenly stop, seeing he was disturbing Copeland's rest. Martin quietly backed out of the room and shut the door.

Phew. That was close, Copeland thought to himself.

Chapter Sixteen

The cool, brisk air blew against Margaret's face as she walked home from the train station, the events of the day swirling in her head. The sky was growing dimmer with her every step and just as she got to her front door, the streetlights flicked on for the night.

"Helllooo," she called as she walked in.

"Hi." Vienna and Beckham greeted her from the kitchen where they stood snacking on cheese and crackers.

"How was your day?" she asked as she took off her coat.

"Good. Nothing special," Vienna lied.

Beckham shot her a look while Margaret was turned around, hanging up her jacket on the coat tree.

"Mine was good," Beckham added.

"How was yours?" Vienna quickly moved on.

"It," she paused, deciding how best to describe it, "it was interesting." She began making her way to the kitchen.

"Interesting?" Vienna asked. She had not heard her mom use any word but "fine" to describe her day at work since her father died. "How so?"

"Well," Margaret began as she sat down on the stool next to Beckham, "I was asked to help plan Copeland's eighteenth birthday party."

Vienna started choking on the cracker she'd just taken a bite of and coughed violently.

"Are you okay?" Margaret was suddenly concerned.

Vienna nodded as she tried to slow her coughing. "I'm good," she finally got out.

"Why did they ask you?" Beckham questioned, dubious.

"Don't act so appalled," Margaret laughed. "Your mother does have the capability to plan a nice event... but the truth is, I have absolutely no idea." She rested her elbow on the table and put her chin to her hand. "Well, I mean, I know in part, Madison Carter is the woman who normally plans official events and she is eight months pregnant. What I don't know is why they want *me* to fill in for her. I have been trying to make sense of it all day... I don't know if it has anything to do with your father, but it's been nearly three years, so I don't think it would—"

"Maybe, it's just because they think you'll do a fantastic job," Vienna kindly suggested.

"Maybe," Margaret chuckled. "But you know who would do an even better job than me?"

"Who?" Vienna asked.

"You."

"Me?" Vienna was thankful she wasn't eating, or she might have choked again.

"Yes." Margaret smiled. "I was thinking about all of the help I am going to need and the fact that you aren't exactly sure what career path you'd like to take. I figured this could be a good opportunity for you to try out event planning," she explained. "Plus, you'd have an exclusive invite to the party of the year."

Beckham tried to refrain from laughing but couldn't keep it in. He tried to cover his amusement with a coughing fit.

"Geez, those crackers are dangerous," Margaret commented, seemingly not noticing Beckham's laughter.

"So, what do you say?" Margaret continued, her eyes beaming with light Vienna had not seen in years.

Vienna's eyes grew wide and she bit her lip. How could she say "no" to her mother now? She'd never asked for her help with anything. "Sure," she finally said. "I'm not sure how helpful I'll be but it sounds like a great opportunity."

"Wonderful!" Margaret smiled. "Madison's last day is next week, and you'll be done with school, so I will try to get things in order this week with her and then, I can use your help when you're free."

"Great." Vienna forced a smile.

"How fun." Margaret excitedly clapped. "I guess we will both try to make the most of this odd and unexpected opportunity."

Chapter Seventeen

Vienna stared at the ceiling with her head on her pillow, watching the narrow stream of light from outside move slightly each time the fan blades passed it.

What happened today, she wondered? How have the last five hours changed everything so much? Is this how life happens? You go along, one day after another, until suddenly, without warning, one day changes the course of them all—

The sound of the door quietly creaking open interrupted her thoughts and she was thankful. She sometimes got stuck going down rabbit holes in her head for what seemed like forever, wondering if she'd ever climb her way back out.

"V," Beckham whispered, "are you awake?"

"Yeah," she whispered back and sat up in her bed.

"Sorry it took me so long," he apologized. "I had to make sure Mom was asleep." The twins had had an unwritten rule for as long as Vienna could remember; if one of them had a big day (a fight with their parents, a date, or really anything exciting or out of the ordinary), the other snuck into their room and gossiped with them after their parents were asleep.

"That's alright. You know me... just thinking through every scenario over and over again," she laughed.

"I figured." Beckham sat down next to her on the bed.

"Can we just agree that the oddities of today truly have surpassed all other days we've ever lived?"

Beckham chuckled, "I think we can agree on that."

"Like, Copeland Howth, King slash not King of Carnot, came to our house this afternoon to ask me to be his date for his eighteenth birthday party." Vienna scratched her head.

"And your plan was to hide the whole thing from Mom... even though it will be front page news very soon," Beckham added.

"But then, to everyone's surprise, Mom came home and asked me to help plan Copeland's birthday party," Vienna continued.

"And bribed you with an invitation you already had," Beckham finished.

"Ugh," Vienna sighed, throwing her head back, "I'm lost."

"Hmm," Beckham hummed. "Do you think it's weird at all that both of these events randomly happened? Like... don't you think it's an odd coincidence." It wasn't a question.

"Would I even be your sister if I hadn't already thought through all of that?" Vienna joked. "I thought it could be contrived at first, but I can't figure out why or what the purpose would be. If they had something against Mom, I don't think they would drag me into it and if they had something against our family, I don't know why they wouldn't just write us letters. Plus, I don't understand why Copeland would play any part in it."

"Touché," Beckham replied. "I figured you'd already played out all the scenarios. I can't figure it out either... I think I've decided today is simultaneously the luckiest and unluckiest day of your life," he laughed.

"Yeah, right." Vienna rolled her eyes. "You think it's going to be that easy to bait me into saying I like Copeland? It's like you don't even know me," she laughed. "I don't even want to go with him." Her mind flashed to the moment she'd first touched him, trying to wipe up the coffee she'd spilled all over his shirt. *At least, I don't think I do*, she thought to herself.

"Uh huh," Beckham replied. "Sure, you don't."

Vienna grabbed one of the throw pillows next to her and swung it hard at Beckham's stomach. Beckham grabbed the pillow out of her hands mid-swing and hit her with it in the arm.

"You're going to have to be faster than that," Beckham teased.

"I'll get you someday," Vienna replied determinedly.

"So, what's your next play here?" Beckham asked. "Do you just wait for Prince Charming to pick you up in a horse and carriage for your first date or...?"

Vienna rolled her eyes as far back into her head as she could. "Beckham, here's the line," she raised her right hand in the air to show him, "and here's where you are." She took her left hand and placed it just below her right. "If you keep pushing, I will completely cut you out," she threatened.

"Okay, okay," Beckham relented. "I will back off a bit."

Vienna knew her threat would work. Beckham loved nothing more than being "in" on something and this was definitely something worth being "in" on.

"Good." Vienna smiled.

Chapter Eighteen

argaret stepped onto the elevator and almost instinctively pressed the button for the second floor.

Nope, we don't work there anymore, she reminded herself as she pressed the button labeled "3." The elevator doors opened, and she was surprised to see a nearly empty floor. She looked down at her wristwatch and saw it was 7:58 A.M.

I guess I'm early, she thought, confused. She walked toward Madison's office and took a seat at the cubicle across from it. It was a dull space with light gray walls and a black desk. She'd placed one picture frame with a photo of Vienna and Beckham on it next to her computer, but other than that, the space looked rather lifeless. She sat twiddling her thumbs for a few minutes, periodically looking up to see if others were arriving. If she'd arrived at 7:58 on the second floor, the place would have been roaring. Most people were already on their second or third cup of coffee by eight o'clock.

It wasn't until 8:15 that she saw Madison getting off the elevator with a few others.

"Good morning," Madison greeted her with a smile.

"You're early this morning."

"Am I?" she asked.

"We normally don't start work until nine."

"Really? The second floor is normally up and at 'em by 7:30."

"Well, we'll give you a break to sleep in," Madison laughed. "They're a bunch of overachievers down there anyway." She unlocked the door to her office and made it look very difficult to set down everything she'd been carrying. "I'm sorry, I tried to get here early so I could prepare some stuff for you to work on, but it seems I didn't achieve that goal."

"No worries," Margaret quickly replied. "I could use a cup of coffee anyway. Would you like one?"

"No, thanks," she answered. "I think the stuff in the break room tastes terrible."

"Well, I'd hate to watch over your shoulder as you get things ready. I could go pick us up something better," she offered.

"Oh, I could really go for a cinnamon roll and decaf vanilla latte from Eckle's." Madison's eyes lit up. "Mama's got to eat," she laughed, lightly tapping her bulging baby bump.

"I love Eckle's," Margaret agreed. "Their dirty chai tea latte is delicious."

"Yes, it is!"

"Perfect," said Margaret. "I will go get us some coffee and you can take your time and get some stuff in order here."

"Sounds like a plan."

Margaret started to walk out of the room when Madison called, "Oh, wait! Let me get you some money."

"You don't have to," Margaret replied.

"I'll expense it." She smiled warmly. "Don't worry."

Margaret couldn't argue with that.

Madison grabbed some money out of her purse and handed it to her. "Just get a receipt, please."

"No problem. Be back soon," Margaret said as she walked out the door. She decided to take the long way out of the building. She weaved her way through hallways until she reached the grand stairs. The immaculate stairs were the centerpiece of the formal entryway. On the ground floor, two pristine staircases led to the second-floor balcony, where the steps then split again to lead to the third floor. The ivory steps were perfectly accented with a black, intricately designed iron railing.

When looking at the grand stairs, the left side was the west wing of Carnot, designated to official government work, while the right side was the east wing where the Howth family resided.

Margaret made her way down the steps and out onto the sidewalk of the front lawn. She followed the sidewalk to the front gates where Santi clicked open the gate for her.

"Where you headed?" he asked.

"Eckle's," she answered. "In need of a little extra caffeine this morning."

"I understand." Santi raised his own cup of coffee. "I hear you've been promoted."

"Oh, is that what they're calling it?" Margaret laughed. "I am not so sure planning Copeland's birthday party is a promotion."

Santi sympathetically chuckled. "I'm sure you'll do great, though," he encouraged.

"Thank you." Margaret sighed, not totally accepting his compliment. "I'll be back soon."

"Have fun." Santi waved.

Margaret unzipped her coat as she walked down the road; it was unseasonably warm for early December. She walked a few blocks and saw the coffee shop up on her right. She was pleasantly surprised by the short line. Oftentimes, the line was out the door during the morning work rush.

"Good morning," the clerk greeted her. His bushy brown hair was piled on top of his head and sporadically flopping over his red visor. "What can I get for you today?"

"Morning! I will take two cinnamon rolls, a decaf vanilla latte and a dirty chai tea latte," Margaret replied. "Please," she added, realizing she hadn't been polite.

"You got it. I have two cinnamon rolls, a decaf vanilla latte and a dirty chai tea latte," he repeated back to her to double check.

She nodded.

"What's the name on that?" he asked.

"Margaret."

"Perfect. Your total will be $14.35 today," he replied.

Margaret pulled the money Madison had given her out of her pocket and handed it to him. "Keep the change," she said.

He smiled. "Thank you. We'll have that right out for you."

A few minutes later, a young and bubbly barista called out, "Margaret!" She walked up to the counter and grabbed the drink carrier and white, paper bag stuffed with cinnamon rolls. Each cinnamon roll was much too large to be considered an individual serving, but Margaret was sure she could handle finishing it herself. She walked down the middle of the street, sipped on her chai, and focused on keeping her feet perfectly on the faded, double yellow lines. Since Lewis had died, Margaret had surprised herself every once in a while, with her enjoyment of simple things. Her attempt to stay on the lines was one of those times and she smiled to herself. She missed Lewis deeply, but she felt a sense of relief each time she could smile at his memory and keep living her life.

In what felt like no time, she was back at Carnot. She walked toward the guard shack and reached into her pocket.

Oh no, she thought. She shifted the coffee and paper bag and tried her other pocket. "Ahh." She threw her head back in frustration.

"What's wrong?" Santi asked, seeing her hesitation on the sidewalk.

"I left my badge inside." She sighed.

"Oh, no," Santi replied, sympathetically. "I'm sorry."

"Is there anything you can do?" Margaret pleaded. "Just this one time."

"I am truly sorry, Margaret, but you know I can't. I'd certainty lose my job." He paused. "And... well, you know what else is on the line."

Margaret frustratingly rubbed her forehead. "That I do," she replied. "I figured it was worth an ask." She sighed again. "So, what's the protocol here?"

"Well, we have two options," Santi explained. "The first is easiest, if you know where exactly your badge is."

Margaret could picture right where she'd left it. "Yes,

it's sitting out on my desk."

"Good. Then, option one is definitely our best bet. I will page Joey to swing by your desk and he can grab your badge and bring it out."

"Oh, perfect! That won't be too bad… except for our coffee getting cold," Margaret half-heartedly laughed.

"Go for Joey," Santi spoke into his walkie talkie.

"This is Joey," the muffled voice came back through the speaker.

"Could you do me a favor and stop by Margaret Tunston's desk on the second floor—"

"I'm on the third floor now," Margaret interrupted.

"Pardon me, third floor," he corrected, "and grab her ID badge? It should be sitting on her desk."

"You got it, boss. I'm just down the hall. Shouldn't be too long," Joey replied a few seconds later.

"Perfect. Thank you." Santi set the walkie talkie back down on his desk. "Easy peasy."

"You're awesome," Margaret complimented.

"Just doing my job. How's your new gig?"

"New," Margaret laughed. "Today is really my first day and you see how that's going."

Santi chuckled.

"I'm sure it will be fine," she continued. "Actually, I think Vienna is going to help me a bit."

"Is that so?" Santi asked. "That would be fun."

"Yeah," Margaret agreed. "I think it will be good for her to start trying to figure out what she wants to do. She's nearly eighteen and I have no idea what field she's—"

The static sound of Santi's walkie talkie cut her off.

"Go for Santi," Joey called.

"This is Santi," he replied.

"Boss, I am not seeing an ID badge on her desk," he explained.

"Are you sure you're at the right desk?"

"Yeah. I asked Cara and she told me it was Margaret's new desk."

"Hmm," Santi hummed. "Any ideas?" He looked at Margaret.

"Gaahh." She let out a loud sigh, ignoring his question. "Why is this protocol so strict?! I've worked here fifteen years and—"

"If you'd like to file an official complaint, I'm happy to point you in the direction of our human resources office," a familiar voice interrupted Margaret.

The hair on the back of Margaret's neck stood up. She slowly turned around to see Theodore Howth standing with a posse of bodyguards behind him.

"That won't be necessary," she calmly replied. "I sincerely apologize for my complaints. I made a mistake by leaving my badge inside when I went to run an errand."

"You still there, boss?" Joey called from the walkie talkie. Santi quickly grabbed it and turned the volume down completely.

"I see." Theodore pursed his lips.

The way he spoke made Margaret sick to her stomach. The last time she'd been this close to him was the week before Lewis passed away. Since then, she'd seen him but only from a distance. She'd forgotten how uninviting he could be; his greenish-brown eyes served as inescapable daggers and his solid frame was just big enough to be intimidating. Plus, there was the added fact that he held all of the power and could (quite literally) decide to kill you anytime... well, almost anytime.

"I guess it's your lucky day." He smirked. "Santi, open the gates," he instructed. "I will vouch for Mrs. Tunston today."

Margaret felt a pit deep in her stomach and it took everything in her to keep from hurling. *Ugh. He makes me sick. I don't need his help.*

"Thank you," Margaret forced herself to say aloud as the gates started to open.

"Of course." Theodore smiled a sadistic smile.

Chapter Nineteen

Copeland awoke to light streaming into his bedroom from the large windows.

"Good morning, sir," Martin greeted as he opened the last set of curtains.

"Morning." Copeland rubbed his eyes.

"You have a day filled with meetings," Martin explained. "It's 8:30 and your first meeting starts at 9:00 in the Jupiter Suite. Zelda would like to discuss your vision for the party."

Copeland groggily nodded.

"Mrs. Smith will be here in a few minutes with your breakfast and coffee, and after that, we will go from there."

"Thank you, Martin," Copeland replied as he got out of bed.

"Of course, sir." Martin bowed and left the room.

Copeland let out a big yawn and stretched his arms high above his head. He opened his eyes, and the nightstand caught his eye. His picture frame was perfectly intact, displayed exactly where it always was. He quickly grabbed it, sat back down on the bed and opened it.

"Phew," he sighed with relief and closed the frame

after seeing that both letters from his mother were hidden in the back. *Did I do that, he wondered? When did I fall asleep?* He retraced his steps. *I got back from Vienna's and I pulled out the letters. Then, I heard Martin come in and I pretended to be asleep... What happened after that? Did I actually fall asleep? How did these get put back here?* Copeland's heart was racing. *How could I have made a mistake like this? If my father finds out, I'm dead. Maybe, I woke up and just don't remember. Ahhh!* Copeland rubbed his temples. *Think.* He hit his hand on his forehead. *Think!*

There was a light knock at the door before it opened.

"Good morning, Mr. Howth," Mrs. Smith greeted him, pushing a silver cart with a coffee pot and an array of goodies.

There is no such thing as privacy in this place, Copeland sighed to himself.

"I have hot coffee, fresh fruit, bagels, muffins, and croissants for you to choose from this morning," she offered.

"Thank you. I'll take coffee, fruit, and a blueberry muffin."

"Of course, sir," Mrs. Smith replied. "You know... blueberry muffins were her favorite." She smiled, seeing Copeland was holding the pictures of him and his mother.

"Mine too."

Mrs. Smith, like most of the staff at Carnot, had been working there for many years. She was a short and stout old woman with light gray hair and a heart of gold. Mrs. Smith had cared deeply for Camilla and when she passed, she made it a priority to take care of

Copeland. She'd made special late-night trips to bring him his favorites snacks and desserts and though he could always request whatever he wanted anyway, there had been something special about the way she'd gone above and beyond to care for him.

Mrs. Smith poured a cup of steaming hot coffee and stirred in a bit of cream and sugar. She took a small plate and piled on some kiwifruit, pineapples, and oranges. She added a blueberry muffin, cut it in half and slathered butter on it. She placed the items on a silver tray and carried it to the foot of Copeland's bed.

"There you are, sir," she said.

"Thank you." He tried to be intentional about being kind to Mrs. Smith, but his mind was racing, still trying to figure out what had happened with the frame.

"Have a wonderful day," she said as she curtsied and pushed her cart out of the room.

"You too," Copeland stood up and grabbed a piece of pineapple as he walked over to his dresser to find the clothes Martin had laid out for him. He got changed, brushed his teeth, and finished his breakfast before heading out of his room to his first meeting; his mind spinning with every action.

He walked down the halls of Carnot trying to comfort himself. *Surely, I put it back in there and just don't remember. I was tired... It was a big day... I used to sleepwalk when I was a kid, so I'm sure I could handle putting the frame back in its place.* He tried to rack his brain but before he knew it, he found himself sitting in his first meeting.

"Goooood morning," Zelda greeted with excessive elation and a curtsy. Zelda Hydrangea was a tall and slender dark-skinned woman with long, black hair that always seemed to be changing. Today, it was extravagantly placed on top of her head in seemingly endless braids and knots, with silver beads scattered throughout it. She was now in her late thirties but in her early years (or as she liked to say her "former life"), she had been a runway sensation. Her unique features made her undeniably intriguing to look at. After she retired from the runway, she started working behind the scenes and quickly worked her way up to being the top designer in Carnot, hence the reason she now dressed the ruling family.

"Morning," Copeland replied. He walked to one of the oversized, orange accent chairs in the middle of the room. There were black curtains hanging at the back of the room and a small, T-shaped runway jutted out from them. Martin took a seat in the other orange chair and Zelda clapped her hands. The moment she did, the overhead lights clicked off and spotlights lit the runway.

The curtains opened and models began walking out. The first was in a shimmering black gown with thin straps over the shoulders. The dress was snug at the top and then flared dramatically out from the waist. The second model donned a sparkling, silver gown with a strap over one shoulder. The dress fit tightly down the model with extra material flowing off the back. The last model wore an ombre blue, glittering gown. The strapless top was full of frills and started as a dark, navy purple color. It hugged her chest and flared out at her hips, softly changing to a lighter sky-blue color by the time it reached the floor. The women walked the runway and disappeared back behind the curtain. Then, three men walked the same runway path and Copeland truly couldn't tell the difference between the three tuxedos. All the while, Zelda was rambling on about each piece.

After the men finished their walks, the six models filed back out on the stage and stood at the end in a perfect line.

"What do you think?" Zelda asked. "Or better yet, what speaks to you?" She gestured dramatically with her hands.

"Hmm." Copeland tilted his head. "I think I like the blue one. It's very different."

"Splendid!" Zelda celebrated. "I personally love that piece and think it will look absolutely stunning on Summer."

"Oh," Copeland replied hesitantly, "I'm not taking Summer."

Zelda tried to keep from displaying her shock, but her eyes said it all. "Who are you taking?"

"I'm not ready to share that," Copeland said. "But it's not Summer." He was so tired of people asking him about her.

"Sir," Martin interjected, seeing the concern on Zelda's face, "we don't have to publicly announce anything yet, but as you know, Zelda's pieces can take quite some time to be tailored and it's important we give her enough time to measure and fit your date."

Copeland huffed. "Can I have until tomorrow?"

Martin looked to Zelda for approval.

"Yes, sir. That would be fine," she agreed.

"Thank you."

"Which tuxedo would you like?" Zelda asked, trying

to move past the tension.

"I truly don't care." Copeland tried to sound polite. "I don't even know what's different about them so please, pick what you think will look best with V—" he caught himself, "with the blue dress and that will work for me."

"Wonderful. I can do that," she agreed.

"Are we done here?" Martin asked.

"Yes, I think we should be all set," Zelda confirmed.

"Perfect." He stood up and Copeland followed suit. "Thank you, Zelda."

"Yes, thank you," Copeland added.

"Of course." She smiled and curtsied again, unnecessarily.

Copeland led the way out of the room with Martin in tow.

Once in the hallway, Martin led the way down the hall, giving him the rundown for the day as he walked.

Copeland wasn't paying attention to Martin's instructions; his mind was still occupied with the picture frame.

"And then, an early lunch with your father—" He heard Martin say, snapping him out of his daze.

"Lunch with my father?" he repeated back.

"Yes," Martin replied. "He'd like to speak with you about the party."

"You told him, didn't you?" Copeland asked accusingly.

"Sir, I did not tell your father about your date," Martin sternly replied. "He simply wants to discuss party plans with you before we meet with the planning team later this afternoon. Although, I would encourage you to tell your father about your plans to bring Vienna. I'm sure he'd prefer to hear it from you first."

Copeland sighed aloud. *I never hear anything from him first*, he thought to himself.

They continued to walk in silence for a few moments.

"Do I have anything after lunch?" Copeland asked.

"The meeting with the event planning team is at 3:30 and that's the only other item on today's agenda."

"Perfect. Could we make a trip to the Carnot High after lunch? I'd like to ask Vienna on our first official date myself."

"Sir, won't she be in class this afternoon?" Martin questioned.

"Probably," Copeland replied, not exactly sure how public high schools worked. "But I am sure with your help and my influence, we can find a way for me to get a few secret minutes with her." He smirked.

"I'm guessing we can," Martin hesitantly agreed.

Chapter Twenty

Beckham sat tapping his pencil in study hall. He'd never been a huge fan of school—with the exception of Governmental Law and Leadership—and considering he was almost done, he disliked it more than ever. He should have been preparing for his test next period but instead, he stared out the window and mindlessly watched the trees blow in the wind. He was zoned out, watching a squirrel running around, when he saw slight movement out of the corner of his left eye. He turned his head slightly to get a better view of what was happening.

He saw two black cars pull up and a short, tan-skinned man step out of the first car. The man walked on the sidewalk toward the entrance of the school. The cars were not parked in front of the building but rather on a side street, a short walk away. He didn't recognize the man, but he knew it must be official business if he was riding in a car within the city limits.

Beckham ripped a small edge off a piece of paper from his notebook and crumpled it into a ball. Vienna was sitting in the row to the right of him a couple of desks back, working on homework. He tossed the paper ball at her, hitting her cheek.

She looked up, threw her hands up at him and went back to writing.

Beckham ripped another piece of paper, crumbled it, and threw it at her again. This time, it hit her in the neck.

Vienna looked up again, visibly more annoyed than the last time and mouthed, "What?"

Not wanting to cause more attention from his classmates than he already had, Beckham silently shaped his hand into a "C" and then pointed out the window with his thumb.

"What?" Vienna mouthed again.

Beckham tried to spell it out with his hands. He successfully made a "C," "O," and "P," before a knock at the door interrupted him.

Their study hall teacher, Mr. Beene, stood up from his desk and walked to the door. He whispered quietly with the secretary before he turned around and called, "Vienna." He waved his hand for her to come to the door.

Vienna looked at Beckham with unsure eyes and slowly stood up. She made her way to the door and Beckham couldn't make out any of their whispers. Vienna followed the secretary out and Mr. Beene returned to his desk, like nothing had happened at all.

Beckham anxiously tapped his pencil as he stared at the clock. Five minutes of study hall remained before lunch.

His classmate in front of him turned around, "What was that about?" he asked.

"No idea," Beckham shrugged.

Evidently, that answer had been enough to satisfy him because he turned back around with no further questions.

Beckham continued to stare at the clock, watching it tick by second by second. When the bell finally rang, he quickly stood up, grabbed his backpack, and hurried out of the classroom. He walked down the hall, opposite the crowd moving toward the cafeteria until he reached a hallway with windows that gave him a better angle to look at the cars.

Sure enough, he saw Vienna out in the distance talking to someone. He could hardly see the other person, but he didn't have to; he knew it was Copeland.

He watched as Vienna continued to talk. The hallways were growing quieter each second with students disappearing into classrooms and to lunch. After what felt like an eternity, Vienna turned around and started walking back to the school. Beckham made his way to the front entrance. He was standing inside, casually leaning on a wall, with one leg bent and propped against it when she walked in.

"Oh, fancy meeting you here," he teased.

Vienna rolled her eyes, acting unamused, but her rosy cheeks gave her away.

"What was that about?" Beckham asked as they started to walk to the cafeteria together.

"Nothing," Vienna replied.

"I don't know why you act like you're not going to tell me things when you always end up telling me," Beckham chuckled.

Vienna couldn't argue with that. "He wanted to officially ask me on a date."

"Oh, did he now?"

"Yep. It's protocol for a minimum of two dates—err, let's call them outings," Vienna corrected herself, "two outings before he can take me to a formal event. He asked me to go hiking."

"It's a date," Beckham corrected. "And you like it. When and where?"

"No, it's not and no, I don't," Vienna replied. "Tomorrow after school."

"Where?" Beckham repeated.

"Uhm." Vienna scratched her head.

"Not Mickinley." Beckham shook his head. "Is it Mickinley? Is he taking you to our go-to spot?"

"Beck, it's the best trail around here," Vienna countered.

"Ugh, true," he said. "What are you going to do? Watch the sunset and make it all gross and romantic?"

"I don't know," Vienna lied, knowing full well that was the plan. "I told you. I don't even like him."

"Uh huh, so you've said," Beckham doubted. "I guess we'll see how you feel after he kisses you."

"No way he kisses me on the first date," Vienna replied.

"So, it is a date!" Beckham exclaimed as they walked into the eerily quiet cafeteria.

A few heads turned and they both stopped in their tracks. To the right, a large circle of students was gathered, standing over a student. Teachers were unsuccessfully trying to get them to calm down and go back to their tables.

"Nothing to see here."

"He will be fine," one teacher lied. "Get back to

your lunches."

"What happened?" Beckham asked the table of students just inside the door.

"It's Zachary Morris. He was walking to his table after getting his food and we think he had a seizure. Word on the street is he got a bad Ivy Letter this month, so it's probably fatal," one of the guys answered.

"That sucks," Beckham commented. And though it really did, there wasn't anything he could do. It wasn't terribly common for high school students to get fatal Ivy Letters, but they'd seen enough deaths in school by now to know it was better if they just moved on.

"Ugh, that's too bad," Vienna commented. She didn't care to talk more, so she started to walk to the back of the cafeteria and Beckham followed. They always sat at the same table in the back corner of the room. The table was big enough to seat eight people. Two other kids sat there as well but they never talked to them. They used to have many friends in school, but since their dad's passing, they'd pulled away from everyone, and today was a perfect reminder of why. They didn't want to risk getting close to anyone else and losing them too.

As soon as they sat down, Beckham continued his interrogating. "Why did he come to the school?"

Vienna shrugged. "I don't know. Because he can do whatever he wants."

"I guess." Beckham set his backpack on the ground and pulled out his lunch.

Vienna followed suit and they started to eat in silence for a few minutes.

"So, you have until tomorrow to tell Mom?" Beckham finally broke the silence with his mouth full of a peanut butter and jelly sandwich.

"I guess so," Vienna sighed.

"How are you going to break the news to her?"

"I am still not sure. Maybe, I won't tell her and instead, I'll say I have plans with a friend tomorrow night."

"Yeah, that won't be suspicious, considering all of the friends we have." Beckham gestured to the basically empty table.

"I knoOow," Vienna huffed. "I will figure it out. It's only one in the afternoon. I have over four hours until Mom will be home. I can think of something."

"Good luck with that," Beckham doubtfully replied.

"You could help, you know?" Vienna retorted.

"I know." Beckham took an oversized bite of his sandwich. "But what are older brothers for?" he obnoxiously teased through his mouth full of food.

"Two minutes." Vienna rolled her eyes. "You're only older by two minutes."

Chapter Twenty-One

"Are you ready?" Madison asked.

"Yes." Margaret turned her head to see Madison was standing at the edge of her cubicle.

"Perfect. The meeting is in the Aphrodite Suite, so it's not too far of a walk for us."

"Great." Margaret stood up and followed Madison's lead down the hall.

"The purpose of this meeting is to get a general sense of the direction Copeland is hoping to go with his birthday party." Madison spoke as they walked. "When we plan an event, we typically touch base once to get the overarching idea, then a second time to home in on it and a third time to solidify everything is on schedule and aligned with their vision. Sometimes the host attends all of the meetings, some of them, or none at all; it just depends on their desired level of involvement. Truth be told, this is the first party Copeland has had the option of contributing to so I am not sure if he will be there or not." They continued to wind through the expansive halls until they arrived at the suite.

Inside the room was a large, oak table with fourteen

white, leather chairs surrounding it. They were the first to arrive. They chose two seats next to each other on the far side of the table. Madison pulled out a pen and a notebook filled with pages and pages of hand-written notes.

"I must stress the importance of the meeting and the utmost respect and honor we must carry ourselves with today. It is a privilege to get time with the Howth family and we must treat it like the pleasure it is. You must smile, agree, and actively listen to everything they say. I am sure this is your first interaction with them but please, do not show any ounce of awe toward them. We must simply do our job."

Margaret was surprised at the authority Madison suddenly spoke with. *That's quite an assumption,* she disapprovingly thought.

Madison looked at her watch. "It's 3:28," she said. "We should stand for their arrival."

Margaret hadn't been nervous for the meeting until she stood up. She suddenly felt a knot in her stomach and the collar of her shirt felt much too tight around her neck.

The two of them moved closer to the door. Margaret straightened out the black skirt she was wearing, and Madison brushed her hair with her hands before tucking it behind her ears.

A moment later, the doors opened, and Copeland walked in first, followed by Martin.

"Good afternoon, sir," Madison addressed him with a curtsy. Margaret followed suit with the curtsy but didn't speak.

"Hello," Copeland cheerfully greeted.

"Hi, Martin," Madison added.

"Hello, Madison," he smiled back.

"This is my colleague, Margaret," Madison gestured. "Martin, Margaret and Margaret, Martin."

"Yes, I know Margaret," Martin replied. "Hello."

"Hello." The knot in Margaret's stomach felt slightly looser after seeing his familiar face.

"Oh, I didn't realize that," Madison said, surprised.

Copeland, who had already lost interest in the awkward introductions, took a seat at the table. The others followed his lead.

Once seated, Madison started, "We are so excited and honored to be throwing your eighteenth birthday party. We have a few ideas of our own we'd like to go over with you today but for starters, we'd love to hear your thoughts."

What was I worried about, Margaret thought to herself? *This is easy. Just a casual conversation.*

"I am picturing something formal but with an air of creativity and fun," started Copeland. "I'd like for it to be a black-tie event, of course, with a strong and respectful coming of age spirit but not overly stuffy. I don't want it to be like the party—"

Copeland was interrupted by the doors behind him opening.

"Sorry, I am late," Theodore apologized as he fixed his cufflink. "My two o'clock meeting went," he paused, looking up and seeing Margaret for the first time, "very late." He almost lost track of his sentence.

Madison quickly stood up and seeing Margaret was still sitting, she pinched her arm.

"Ow," Margaret groaned but then realized she hadn't

moved. She stood as well and they both greeted him with a curtsy.

"Hello, sir," Madison said. "This is my colleague, Margaret."

"Yes," Theodore replied. "I know Margaret."

"You do?" Madison was dumbfounded.

The knot in Margaret's stomach grew tighter than it had been before.

"Why, yes, just this morning she was locked outside the gates of Carnot and I let her in," Theodore explained.

"Yes." Margaret played along with his charade. "Silly me."

"Plus, at one point in time, I worked rather closely with her husband," he added.

Margaret felt sick again. She hadn't anticipated Theodore's presence and she didn't like it one bit.

"Of course," Margaret courteously replied.

"Such a shame we lost him so young," Theodore feigned, with a sigh. "Dear Lewis."

Before Margaret could even fully process Theodore's fake compassion, Copeland perked up, "Lewis? Lewis, who?" He curiously asked.

Martin shot Copeland a disapproving look.

"Lewis Tunston," Theodore answered. "Why the sudden interest, son?"

"Oh, I thought it might have been someone else," Copeland quickly played it off. *Tunston? Is she Vienna's mother? Ugh, what was her name again? I should have been paying more attention...*

Feeling the undeniably strange shift in the room's energy, Madison tried to get everyone back on topic.

"So," she said, "we were in the middle of hearing

from Copeland about his vision for the party. Please continue."

Everyone took their seats as Copeland started again, "Well, I really don't have much else to add." He could hardly think about anything but Vienna's mother. *Does she know? Could she help me? Was there tension between her and my father? Maybe, she really does know? Does he know?* His mind raced.

"As for me," Theodore cut in, "I think the grand entrance is the most important aspect of the night. The food, decorations, and guest list mean nothing if we do not successfully portray the immense authority Copeland has over Carnot. It must be made abundantly clear that he is the future ruler, and respect at all levels must be given to him."

"Of course, sir," Madison agreed. "Tellmen's has beautiful stairs—"

"Tellmen's?" Theodore questioned.

"Yes, the venue, sir," Madison explained.

"As in Tellmen's Piano Factory?" he clarified.

Madison hesitantly swallowed. "Uhm, yes, sir."

"What does she mean by Tellmen's?" Theodore looked accusingly at Martin and Copeland.

"That's where I'm having my party," Copeland nonchalantly replied.

Martin was thankful he didn't have to speak first.

"Martin," Theodore snapped. "Why did you take him to Tellmen's?"

"Sir, I had to follow his orders," Martin explained.

Theodore's face turned red with anger. "Why on earth would we have his birthday party at Tellmen's in the filthy factory district?!" he yelled.

"I thought it would make me seem more relatable," Copeland paused. "I think it's important the people of Carnot see me as approachable." He tapped his chest.

Margaret couldn't help but smile at Copeland's fortitude.

"They don't need to see you as approachable. They need to see you as noble and commanding." Theodore spit a little through his gritted teeth.

"Sir," Martin bravely cut in, "the venue really wasn't too bad. I think with Madison's expertise, we could transform it into a lovely space. Plus, Copeland might be right about creating a slightly more, err," he searched for the least offensive word he could find, "congenial atmosphere."

"Yes, Dad," Copeland added. "Tellmen's had a grand staircase that would make for a very noble entrance. Plus, you said I could have my party anywhere I wanted."

The room was silent for a few moments and Theodore took slow and heavy breaths.

"Okay," he finally sighed. "I am not approving it yet, but I will try to warm up to the idea. Let's at least move on and focus on the entrance itself... wherever it may be."

"Wonderful!" Madison took the opportunity to shift gears quickly. "I assume you'll be taking Miss Summer Nile as your date," she started again.

"Uhm," Copeland hummed.

Martin glared scornfully at Copeland and shook his head ever so slightly.

"Uhm, what?" Theodore asked contemptuously.

"Uhm, about Summer," said Copeland. "I'm... I'm not taking her. I'm taking someone else."

"You're what?" Theodore stood up and slammed his hands on the table. "Are you trying to kill me?" he yelled.

"I don't like her, Dad." Copeland's palms suddenly felt sweaty.

"Oh, you don't like her?" Theodore pretended to be sympathetic. "Well, boohoo!" he screamed. He moved around Martin, who had been seated in between them and grabbed Copeland's shirt by his shoulder. His face was red, and he spoke sternly, spitting a little through his tightened jaw. "In our family, with the position and power we hold over Carnot, we do not always have the pleasure of doing what we want or what we like." He aggressively let go of Copeland's shirt. He sighed and regained his composure. "I thought you were ready for this next step but I'm not so sure anymore." His tone was eerily calm now. "I want you to think about your actions, son. I want you to reflect on your choices, come back to me tomorrow and let me know if you're really ready to take this next step. Do you understand?"

"Yes, sir," Copeland respectfully replied. He knew better than to push his father further. *But I wasn't the one who said I was ready in the first place,* he bitterly thought.

"Good," Theodore said and with that, he left the room.

"Thank you for your time." Martin tried to bring the meeting back to a professional level. "I will be in touch regarding future plans if needed." He tapped Copeland on the back. "Let's go, sir."

"Thank you," Copeland managed to get out even though he was still a little shook from the last few minutes.

"You're welcome," Margaret and Madison simultaneously replied.

When the door shut behind Martin and Copeland, Madison let out a gigantic sigh. "Oh my, that has never happened before!"

"That was... uhm... a lot," Margaret agreed.

"Well, maybe you won't have to plan a birthday party after all." Madison closed her notebook.

"Maybe not," Margaret chuckled.

Chapter Twenty-Two

Vienna and Beckham walked in the back door and dropped their backpacks on the kitchen floor.

"Hello," Margaret called from her bedroom.

"Mom?" Vienna called back. "What are you doing home so early?"

Margaret walked out. "No, really, don't act so excited to see me," she teased.

"Sorry," Vienna apologized. "I was just surprised."

"It's okay." Margaret kissed her forehead.

"How was your day?" Beckham asked.

"Let me tell you, I had the most interesting day," she explained. "You would not believe the drama!"

"Drama?" Beckham questioned.

"I don't think I've ever heard you describe your job as dramatic," Vienna added.

"That's because it never has been. I probably shouldn't tell you but honestly, I think if I don't tell anyone I won't believe it really happened.

"Do tell," Beckham encouraged. He leaned on the kitchen counter and looked intently at his mother. She sat down on a stool and Vienna did the same.

"Well, this afternoon I had a meeting scheduled with,"

she paused, "Wait, scratch that, geez, I forgot how filled my day was. This morning I went to get coffee for Madison and myself and I forgot my ID badge."

"Oh no," they commented.

"'Oh no' is right," Margaret replied. "I got back to the gates and of course, Santi couldn't let me in—even though he knows me—and I started complaining about it, only to be overheard by Theodore Howth."

"No!" Beckham didn't believe her.

"Yes!" Margaret exclaimed. "And he smugly made an exception for me and opened the gates. I was flustered all morning about it, but then, my day made a turn for the better in my afternoon meeting."

"What happened?" he asked.

"Theodore and Copeland got in a raging argument. Well, I should clarify... Theodore was exploding at Copeland and Copeland was kind of asking for it," Margaret explained.

"What about?" Vienna asked, trying to act the right amount of interested though her stomach was turning rapidly.

"Well, it started with Copeland's request to have his party at Tellmen's Piano Factory," she began.

"In the factory district?" Vienna asked as if she didn't already know, slightly relieved it was only about the venue.

"Yes," Margaret confirmed. "He said he felt like it would make him seem more approachable or something... it wasn't a bad idea."

"Why was he so mad then?" Beckham asked.

"See, that's where it gets interesting," Margaret replied.

Oh no, Vienna thought. She nervously rubbed her hands together under the kitchen island.

"After Theodore calmed down a little about Tellmen's, he suggested we talk about Copeland's grand entrance and Madison mentioned Summer Nile and Copeland said he wasn't going to take her and Theodore about lost it." Margaret grinned. "I can't lie… It was kind of fun to see him squirm."

"Did he say who he was taking instead?" Beckham asked, knowing Vienna wouldn't have the guts to say anything.

"No," Margaret shook her head. "But poor girl… it will surely be a mess for her. Evidently, he's going to end up with Summer whether he likes it or not."

Vienna's stomach dropped. *How can I possibly tell her he asked me to be his date to the party?* She dreaded the thought.

"So, how did things end?" asked Beckham.

"Theodore threatened to cancel the party altogether if Copeland didn't take time to really think about what he wanted. He has until tomorrow to let his father know his plans and I guess we'll go from there." Margaret laughed. "Ha! What a day."

"What a day indeed," Beckham agreed.

"Yeah," was all Vienna could get out.

"But anyhow, that's enough about me," said Margaret. "How were your days?"

"Good." Beckham shrugged. "Nothing special."

"Same," Vienna agreed.

"Only a little bit left until you're done with high school," Margaret commented. "How are my babies so old?"

"Stop asking us that, Mom," Beckham whined.

"Hey, Beck," Vienna said, ignoring the current conversation. "Want to go hiking?"

"Right now?" he asked confused.

"Yeah," she replied.

"It's going to be dark in, like, two hours," he complained.

"Okay, well that still gives us an hour to hike."

"Uhh, I don't know if I really feel like—"

"Beck," Vienna sternly interrupted. "Please hike with me." Her threatening stare left him no room for disagreement.

"Okaaay," he sighed.

"Geez," Margaret commented. "I come home early for the first time in fifteen years and you two are leaving me?"

"Yeah," Vienna replied. "Sorry, Mom. Let's go." She stood up from the stool and waved Beckham along.

"I guess we're going." He shrugged.

"Be careful," was all Margaret had time to say before they'd disappeared out the back door. *What strange moods they are in*, she thought to herself.

When they were a few steps away from the house, Vienna started rambling.

"This is such a mess. Oh my, what a mess. Why did I think I could actually go with him? Mom is going to be furious. His dad *is* already furious. Summer will be angry. Everyone will be talking." She picked up the pace with each sentence. "Oh my! Oh my." She panicked, unable to fully catch her breath.

Beckham grabbed Vienna's shoulders and pulled her to a halt. "V, calm down! It's going to be okay."

Vienna was now shaking with tears streaming down her face. She had never been one to cause trouble.

"I know how we can fix it." Beckham squeezed her shoulders and looked at her with certainty.

"You do?" Vienna questioned.

He nodded.

"How?"

"At this point, Mom doesn't know, and from the sounds of it, Mr. Howth doesn't know exactly who you are either. If you could speak to Copeland before he tells anyone your name, then there would be no harm done. He can go with Summer and you can move on like nothing happened. No harm, no foul," Beckham explained.

Vienna wanted to agree. She wanted to say, "Yes." She wanted to explode with gratitude and exclaim, "That's a perfect plan! You're a genius, Beck!" She wanted to agree... she knew she should agree... but her heart ached at the thought.

She stared blankly back at him.

"Oh," Beckham sighed, seeing the look on her face. "You *do* really like him."

"No," Vienna started her usual defense. She deeply exhaled. "Well... maybe," she finally admitted. "I don't know."

"I knew it," Beckham teased.

"Beck, please, not now," Vienna pleaded, her face still wet with tears. "I really don't know what to do." Realizing they'd captured the attention of a couple of bystanders, Vienna started walking again and Beckham followed her lead.

To get to Mickinley Park, they had to take the train two stops out of the city and walk half a mile.

"If you still want to go with him, I would really advise telling Mom sooner rather than later," Beckham said. "We both know things are going to be a lot better if she hears it from you and not someone else."

"True," Vienna nodded.

They walked into the train station, which only had two tracks. The trains ran on constant loops exactly opposite each other; only crossing paths at the half-way point, station five, which was the closest station to their house.

They sat down on a wooden bench, waiting for the next train. The high-speed trains ran from station one to station ten in a total of twenty minutes including stops, so it was never a long wait for the next one.

Vienna rested her elbows on her knees and put her face in her hands. "Ugh. I can't go with him, can I?" she finally asked.

Beckham looked at her with sad eyes. "I don't know if you can, V. It's dangerous territory you're playing in right now and you have the chance to back out before anything serious happens. For the sake of our family, I think it would be best to call it off..."

Vienna hesitantly nodded. "I know you're right," she admitted. "I try to be tough, Beck. You know I have to be tough for Mom and I have to always keep my guard up... but I guess there was still this small part of me that held on to every little girl's dream of marrying a prince," she confessed.

"Well, good thing he's not a prince." Beckham winked.

"Ha-ha! True," Vienna laughed.

Chapter Twenty-Three

opeland paced around his room, replaying the afternoon meeting in his mind.

I should have been more careful, he rebuked himself. *I demanded too much. I've never asked for anything and then, suddenly, I demanded the venue and the girl... I should have known that would never work.* He pinched the bridge of his nose and closed his eyes in frustration. *How can I fix this?*

He continued to pace, brainstorming all of his options.

I don't care about the venue... I would happily move it anywhere but I'm afraid that is no longer the negotiable part of this dilemma. I need to speak to Vienna and get some alone time with her... but I can't go on a date with her if I am supposed to be going to the party with Summer. If I go with Summer as a formality and simply invite Vienna as a guest, I will not be able to speak to her alone. Plus, if I invite Summer, an engagement announcement will be expected and I really don't want that... and what about Mrs. Tunston? If that was really her mom, does Vienna already know about the fight today? Has she even asked her mom if she can go with me to the par—

A knock on the door interrupted his wandering thoughts.

"Good evening, sir," Martin greeted him as he walked in the room and bowed.

"Hello, Martin," Copeland reluctantly replied. He wasn't in the mood for another lecture today.

"Have you come to any conclusions about today's meeting?" he asked, shutting the door behind him.

"Uh, no. Not yet," Copeland replied. The door shut very loudly. *Does he normally shut the door*, Copeland wondered, feeling like something was off?

"Good," Martin began speaking quieter. "I was hoping you wouldn't make any decisions without my help."

"What?" Copeland questioned. He was offended Martin thought he couldn't make decisions for himself.

Martin moved to Copeland's dresser and opened the top drawer. He tore through the folded clothes until he reached the bottom. He pulled out a pile of clothes and held them neatly in his hands.

"I am going to place this pile of clothes in the employee bathroom on the third floor. It's a single person restroom and I will leave the door locked so that no one else goes in." He handed Copeland a small key. "This is the key for it. You will need to change into these clothes and follow other employees out of the building. It's nearly five o'clock and they tend to leave in big groups; keep your head down and walk quickly. Once you're outside the gates, take a right on the sidewalk and then a left into the first alleyway and I will meet you there."

"What?" Copeland was beyond confused.

"I will explain more there," Martin said. "Just count

to sixty and head to the bathroom."

Before Copeland could reply, Martin was out of the room.

What is happening, Copeland wondered to himself? He nevertheless decided to listen to Martin's orders. "One, two, three," he started to count.

He paced the room and continued counting.

"Fifty-nine, sixty," he finished and left the room. He hadn't spent much time in the west wing, but he didn't have to venture far to find the restroom. He approached the white door and as promised, it was locked. He took the small, silver key out of his pocket and unlocked it. On the counter, he found a pair of black chino pants, a half zip dark green sweater, a hooded black winter coat, a gray scarf and a black beanie. He took off his pants and with reproach, put on the black chinos. He followed suit with the other items until he was fully dressed. He looked in the mirror and took in a dim view of his reflection.

These clothes are not tailored to my size, he thought. *And how do you even wear this thing?* He tried to tie the scarf around his neck a few different ways before landing on looping it once and letting the sides hang down. He put on the beanie, flipped up the hood of his coat and turned to walk out before noticing all of the clothes he'd thrown on the floor. *I can't leave these—* Before he could finish his thought, he saw a brown messenger bag hanging on the back of the door. "Martin really does think of everything," he commented to himself. He tossed the clothes into the bag, threw it over his shoulder and walked out of the restroom. He figured the stairs were a better option than the elevator, so he walked quickly toward the steps. Sure enough, there were many people making their way out of Carnot for the day. Copeland tried to keep his head down and walk quickly but not too quickly to draw any attention. He was soon out of the gates and turning down the alleyway.

Martin was standing at the back of the dark alley behind a dumpster. He had changed out of his uniform and into an inconspicuous pair of black pants and a dark gray winter coat.

"What is going on?" Copeland asked.

"Thank you for coming, sir," Martin kindly replied but did not bow. "I am sorry to rush you out like that, but we don't have much time. I felt it was important to share information with you as soon as possible after today's meeting."

"Martin, what are you talking about?" Copeland asked, annoyed by his beating around the bush.

Martin glanced around the alley and up at the windows looking down on it, ensuring no one was around. "I'm talking about your mother," he paused, "and the work she left for you to do."

Copeland's mind raced. *What is he talking about? Did he find the letter she wrote me? How does he know? Or better yet, what does he know?* He took a deep breath, trying to portray an illusion of indifference. "What in Carnot are you talking about, Martin?"

"You know precisely what I am talking about," Martin snapped back. "And you're certainly lucky I already knew, considering you've been getting rather sloppy lately."

Copeland thought back to the picture frame with his

mother's letters. "Did you put it away?" he asked.

"Of course, I put it away."

"What do you know?" Copeland tentatively inquired. He wanted to trust Martin and he knew he should, but he'd never truly trusted anyone but his mother.

"Let's walk," Martin instructed. He led the way out of the alley and walked quickly down the street, keeping his head down. Copeland followed his lead. They walked a few blocks in silence until they reached a residential area of the city. By now, most people were home from their days at work and the streets were rather quiet with only a few people still out and about.

"Your mother was right," Martin finally said. "She had always been a curious mind and God bless her; she had the brains to go with her beauty." They continued to walk down the street, though their pace was slowing.

"Right about what?" Copeland asked.

Martin stopped and stared intently at Copeland.

"The corruption," he answered.

He started walking quickly again but Copeland stood still, trying to process Martin's actions. A few moments later, he ran to catch up with him.

"What are you talking about, Martin? I am lost."

"Come along," Martin instructed. "I'm going to tell you, but first, we must get someplace we can talk privately."

They walked for what felt like an eternity to Copeland, his mind racing, until they arrived at an abandoned brown brick building. The front doors had boards sporadically covering them with a small opening that Martin climbed through. The inside was rundown and smelled of rotting wood. The paint was chipping off of every wall in a pattern that was almost pleasing to the eye. The floor was covered in old pieces of wood, velvet chairs, trash, and countless, unrecognizable items.

"What is this place?" Copeland asked.

"An old theater," Martin answered. "Supposedly, before the fall, people used to come here to watch other people perform musicals and plays; a form of entertainment I've been told."

"Interesting," Copeland commented.

"Indeed," Martin agreed. He took a seat on one of the red, velvet chairs. Although, the red was now a much darker color, having been stained with who knows what over who knows how many years.

Copeland hesitated, analyzing the filth of the chair next to Martin and sat down.

"How did you find this place?" Copeland asked.

"I didn't. My sister did. She used to take me here all of the time when she wanted to talk privately. She always had a more adventurous soul than me," Martin confessed. "If I saw a door boarded up with wood, I would never dare to enter, but my sister always saw the openings, never the wood."

"I never knew you had a sister," Copeland replied.

Martin took a deep breath in and nodded slowly. "I did and she was absolutely wonderful."

"What was her name?"

"Camilla."

Copeland furrowed his brow and stared at Martin. He'd never looked closely at his features before but suddenly, he couldn't unsee it. His wide-set blueish green eyes. His coarse brown hair. His naturally tanned skin. And of course, his narrow, slightly crooked nose.

"My… My…" Copeland could hardly get out the words. "My mother was your sister?" he finally asked.

"Yes," Martin nodded. "Yes, she was."

"How can that be? I thought she came from a wealthy family in the Crosley District not…" He gestured toward Martin, indicating his lower class but not wanting to speak the words.

"We did," Martin confirmed.

"Then, how—"

"Let me just start at the beginning," Martin cut in. "I can explain everything."

"Okay." Copeland hadn't exactly known what he'd expected but this news was far from it.

"For generations, my family, the Beckett family, has been on opposing sides of the government of Carnot. Since the fall, most opposing families have been disposed of but, because of my grandfather's wit, our family has lived on. He knew from the beginning that open opposition would not end well. He knew that the government would eventually need to be conquered from the inside out, which is why he devised a plan that has been slowly in action for over eighty years now."

"What?" Copeland couldn't hide his disbelief.

"In 2043, when it was discovered that disease, death, sickness, and brokenness could forever leave the world, Carnot was formed. Actually, let me correct myself… in 2035, those things were discovered and they started injecting every person and child with the medication. Within a year, everyone was immune to death. Now, as you know, when babies are born, they are injected with the medicine to continue to ensure the world's immunity. However, it didn't take long for people to realize the true distress eternal life brought to the world. Most specifically, the concern for overpopulation; which led men with power to work together to form Carnot. These powerful men designed the rules and regulations we now live out and officially formed Carnot in 2043. They are the ones who drafted the plan for Ivy Letters and designed the perfect community. However, there were men that didn't believe in this alteration to the world."

"You mean of regulating the population?" Copeland questioned.

"No," Martin replied, "of perpetual life."

"Oh," Copeland tried to follow.

"My grandfather," Martin paused and added, "and your great grandfather, Edwin, dedicated his life to designing a long-term plan that could eventually change our society. Edwin strived to create a plan that would negate the modern discovery and restore the world back to its natural order. When I was fifteen years old and eligible to receive my first letter, it said I would die from leukemia within six months. At the time, my father was a member of the Committee of Demise. He knew he could report the death, and no one would question him on it. He instructed me to not ingest the ivy stamp. I dyed my hair dark brown—it used to be a platinum blonde—and hid out for a few years. During that time, my sister was climbing the social ladder and working her way up to Theodore. It wasn't too difficult, thanks to my father's status in the government and your mother's remarkable looks. Before long, Theodore proposed to Camilla, which meant I could come out of hiding. With the way the government works, no one suspects anyone can avoid certain death, so I really never got a second glance. Camilla hired me immediately after she married Theodore as her assistant and obviously, you know I was later transferred to watch over you."

Copeland tried to absorb all of the new information. Martin paused, seeing he needed a second.

"But why didn't you tell me sooner?" he finally asked.

"It was not my position. Who am I to rush a plan that's eighty years in the making?" After a few silent seconds, he admitted, "Plus, I actually did end up rushing the plan slightly."

"How so?"

"I found the letters from your mother the other night, and you're really lucky it was me who found them," he again reprimanded. "I was not supposed to talk to you until your eighteenth birthday but after the eruption at the meeting this afternoon, I felt it was necessary to speak with you early."

"Because of Vienna?" Copeland asked, trying to put all of the pieces together in his mind.

"Yes," Martin replied. "She is part of the reason... but also, because I am worried about some rumblings I've been hearing lately. I am worried they will find you out."

"How?" Copeland asked. "How would they possibly find me out?"

"Well, for starters, you're not exactly the best under-cover agent." Martin winked.

Copeland uncomfortably chuckled. He didn't think he'd ever heard Martin tell a joke and he assumed that's what that was supposed to be.

"But really, it seems there has been a lot of suspicion

lately and the government leaders seem to be on edge. After your mother's death, everyone and everything began to be observed more closely but in the last six months, security and monitoring have become increasingly stricter. I am not sure the exact reasoning behind this change, but I assume they are starting to feel that a revolution is coming."

"A revolution?" Copeland asked.

"Yes," Martin replied. "A revolution that we will lead."

Chapter Twenty-Four

Margaret sat on the couch in the living room reading *The Great Gatsby*. The book was her prized possession and her only remaining one from before the fall. It had belonged to her father and his father before him, and his father before him. The blue cover pictured sad blue eyes, red lips and a shining cityscape. Its tattered edges and torn pages displayed years of well-worn and well-loved pages. Though Margaret couldn't picture a far-off America or anything like New York City, she treasured the pages and the ability to try to imagine such a magical and unorderly world. She was lost in the book when a knock at the door startled her. She jumped slightly and looked quickly to the blinds to ensure no one had seen her reading the forbidden work of fiction. Thankfully, the blinds were closed. She stood up, lifted a couch cushion, and threw the book underneath it. As she walked to the door, she adjusted her robe slightly and pushed her hair behind her ears before opening it.

Her jaw dropped slightly, surprised by the sight.

"Archie? What are you doing here?" she asked.

"Archie?" Copeland, who had been hidden behind

Martin, stepped out. "Who's Archie?"

Seeing Margaret's shock and concern, Martin suggested, "How about we step inside and discuss?"

"Of course," Margaret curtsied to Copeland and opened the door wider. She gestured for them to come in.

As soon as the door was shut, Martin put Margaret's mind at ease. "He knows," he said.

Margaret let out a sigh of relief. "Phew."

"Who's Archie?" Copeland asked again.

"I am," said Martin. "Sorry, I forgot to tell you my name when I was a child. It was Henry Archibald Beckett, but I went by Archie."

"Oh." Copeland raised his eyebrows. "But I thought you said no one recognized you after you 'died.'" he made air quotes with his hands.

"Well, they didn't exactly," Martin explained, "but those who were waiting on me knew who I once was."

Copeland hesitantly nodded. The last hour of his life had been a lot to take in and his mind scrambled to process it all.

"I was wondering when you'd be stopping by," Margaret commented. By now, the three of them were sitting comfortably in the living room.

"After this afternoon's meeting, I felt it was important to move up the timeline," Martin acknowledged.

"Yes," Margaret agreed. "I am glad you did. Since Lewis died, I have not been able to speak with anyone about what I know. I am thankful the time has finally come."

"Me too," Martin concurred.

They sat in silence for a few minutes before Copeland

finally admitted, "I guess I am still a little confused about what's going on. Two hours ago, all I knew was that I needed to find Vienna, which I had done, but now everything has changed. I have a long-lost uncle and we're leading a revolution and somehow, you're involved, and I don't know. This is all suddenly seeming like too much." He stood up and began to pace. His hands were shaking slightly. "I just think I need more information. Can you two please stop speaking in code and shoot straight with me? I want to know what's going on. No," he placed his hands on his hips and stared intently at them, "as Heir to Carnot, I demand to know what's going on."

Martin and Margaret exchanged glances and exploded with laughter.

"That was so cute," Margaret said through her chuckling. "Did you see the way he stood with his hands on his hips demanding information?" She imitated Copeland.

"I did," laughed Martin. "He was so proud for a moment there." He looked at Copeland. "That was good practice in being assertive," he complimented. "You'll need that confidence later on."

Martin and Margaret continued to go back and forth, sharing comments and laughing at Copeland. Defeated, he crossed his arms and frustratingly sat back down. He didn't know how much time had passed when his thoughts were interrupted by the opening of the back door.

Vienna and Beckham had been energetically chatting when Beckham took sight of the living room and stopped suddenly in his tracks. He reached out his arm to stop Vienna. Her heart skipped a beat when she saw the group of people sitting in the living room.

"What's going on here?" Beckham asked. Vienna was once again thankful for Beckham's willingness to address every situation head on.

"Have a seat," Margaret replied.

She knows. Vienna's mind whirled. *She knows and she's mad and this was such a mistake. Why did I even say 'yes' in the first place?* Without thinking about her steps, she found herself seated in the living room. She was thankful to be sitting because the room seemed to start spinning suddenly.

"Do you want to start?" Margaret asked Martin.

"You go right ahead," he replied.

She nodded and began, "There are many things you three do not know about this world; things you cannot begin to imagine. To be frank, it is a sick and twisted place... but it wasn't always this way."

"I thought it was the opposite?" Beckham interrupted.

"Let her talk," Vienna chided him.

"Thank you," Margaret acknowledged Vienna. "You know what," she paused, "I think you know more of the history, Martin. Why don't you take over?"

"Okay," Martin agreed.

Copeland was becoming visibly frustrated with their continued beating around the bush.

Martin started, "My family has been on opposing sides of the government of Carnot for generations now. This opposition is due to the regulation of perpetual life. Many, in the beginning, believed the opportunity of eternal life brought great distress, but they, along with their opinions, were quickly weeded out. However, my grandfather, Edwin Beckett, worked diligently and quietly to outline a plan that could eventually overturn the shifted society. You see, he knew the government would need to be conquered from the inside out."

"What?" Beckham breathed. He couldn't help voicing his confusion.

"My grandfather was a wise man. He didn't agree with the alteration Carnot made to regulating the world's population, and most of all, he didn't believe in exploiting endless life," Martin explained.

"You mean, he wanted things to go back to the way they were before? Like, before they cured death and disease?" Vienna tried to clarify.

"Yes," Martin calmly replied. "They may have found the fix for death and diseases with the injection, and for crimes like theft and murder in the design of the city, but the fix didn't cure all. Deep envy, deep darkness, and deep corruption still exist in the world today." He paused. "The question is this: Is it better to live a safe and predictable life with little independence or to live a life of free will with transgressions looming around every corner?"

"In other words," Margaret chimed in, sensing Martin's poetic approach might be losing the audience, "is it better to live like we are now, relatively safe but with no ability to control our lives, or to live like those before us used to, with fear of crime and car accidents and unpredictability and all that goes with it, but also with free will?"

Copeland, Vienna, and Beckham sat still with their thoughts, pondering the question.

"I guess I'd rather live with choices," Beckham finally shared. "But, don't we have choices?"

"I don't get to decide anything about my life," Copeland commented. "I'd rather fear death but have independence."

"I guess I am confused," Vienna replied. "Don't we fear death now? How does our current reality save us from fear of death any more than the old reality did?"

"Exactly the question," Martin commended her. "While we may not fear death every second of the day, I agree with you, we still fear it. We fear it on the first of the month and the days leading up to it. We fear it when we open our letters and when our loved ones open theirs. We fear it far more often than we even realize, so what is the difference?"

"Is there one?" Vienna asked.

Martin and Margaret exchanged glances, communicating with their eyes about who should answer.

Martin nodded slightly and Margaret replied, "No, darling, there is no difference in the fear of death. Carnot's system has reintroduced the fear of death in exchange for regulating overpopulation. The government has taken too much control, and therefore, lost many of the benefits perpetual life was designed to bring."

"We live now with fear of death and no independence when we could instead be living with the same fear of death but," Martin paused dramatically, "but with freedom."

Beckham's mind raced with all the new information. *Death and fear and independence and what did they say, freedom? What are they talking about? Would Dad approve of this nonsense? This is the government I want to work for... or think I want to work for. A few days ago, I thought Vienna was crazy for saying she ran into Copeland on the street and now, he's sitting in our living room.* He looked over at Copeland comfortably seated in an accent chair. His eyes were fixed on Martin's every movement. *I think I'm gonna be sick,* Beckham thought as he put his hands over his mouth.

"Are you alright, Beckham?" his mother asked.

He could barely shake his head to say "no."

Margaret quickly got up and grabbed the trash can from the kitchen. She set it next to him and slowly stroked his back.

"He tends to get sick when he's stressed," Margaret explained.

"That's unfortunate," Copeland commented.

"Yeah," Vienna agreed, "when we were ten, he got a B on a test and threw up for hours. Poor guy."

"Vienna, be kind," her mother reprimanded.

Despite Beckham's nausea, he managed to shoot her a dirty look.

Copeland laughed at Vienna's story and she was glad he acknowledged her. Since she'd walked in, it was the first time he'd made eye contact.

"I'm just saying, if he wants to work in the government and be a leader someday, he might need to toughen up," she continued.

"Vienna, quit. Mockery is not your best color." Margaret glared.

"Okay," Beckham said. "I think I am going to be okay." He sat up a little straighter and some color rushed back into his cheeks.

"Are you sure?" Margaret continued to rub his back.

He nodded.

"Okay," she said. "I will leave the trash can here just in case."

Beckham nodded again.

Margaret returned to her seat on the couch and addressed Martin. "I think we are good on explaining the issues." She gestured to Beckham.

"Yeah," Vienna cut in, "how about you explain how you two know each other?"

"Please," Copeland seconded.

"Uh huh," Beckham quickly added.

"Of course," Martin replied. "Your mother and I go way back." He stopped. "Actually, I think it would be best if we worked our way backward." He reached into his pocket and pulled out a worn letter.

"Hey!" Copeland shouted. "That's mine!"

"It's ours now," Martin replied. "This letter is crucial for the revolution."

"The revo-what now?" Beckham distressingly asked.

"Uh oh," Vienna quickly grabbed the trashcan from in front of Beckham and hurled into it.

"Who needs to toughen up now?" Beckham sneered under his breath.

"I don't care if it's for the revolution." Copeland jumped up. "That letter is the last piece I have of my mother!" He flung himself at Martin and tried to grab the envelope out of his hands. Martin stood up, grabbed the collar of Copeland's sweater, and held it tightly.

"You listen here. Outside these walls, you may be Heir to Carnot and I'm only your assistant, but right here, right now, I am your uncle and your elder. You sit down and you listen to what I have to say. The fate of our world depends on it," Martin firmly instructed. His face was red with determination and the veins in his neck were visible.

Copeland didn't have anything to say. He sheepishly nodded and Martin let go of his shirt. He sat back down and saw Vienna by the trash can across the room. He'd hardly noticed her getting sick in his fury with Martin stealing his letter. He suddenly realized he'd never really looked at her. Up until now, she had simply been a girl he needed to find. A girl he needed to use. A girl he needed to help his mother. But now, in a room full of people ready to help him, he could see her more clearly. Even with a bit of color drained from her face, he saw the way her golden hair fell softly on her cheeks, the way her forehead wrinkled when she smiled and the way her hazel eyes glistened against the light from the window.

He brushed down his sweater, evening it out once again and smiled at Vienna. For the first time, he really smiled at her. And, despite her extreme embarrassment, she smiled back.

Moving on from the chaos, Martin continued, "This letter was given to Copeland by his mother, the late Camilla Howth. She secretly delivered it to him in a frame she gave him as a gift only a few weeks before she died. It holds valuable information for us and will help in explaining our connection. Is it alright if I read it out loud?" he asked.

They all nodded in agreement.

He read:

My Dearest Copeland,

What once started as a beautiful discovery, the ability to no longer suffer from diseases, death and sickness, has tragically transformed over the years. Carnot, in its simplest form, was a grand idea. It was a way to keep the earth moving, despite the introduction of perpetual life. It allowed for chance to determine those next to die, rather than incurable and uncontrollable causes. However, over the years, the government system has become corrupt, with leaders slowly taking control and making decisions based not on chance, but instead on their own personal vendettas.

A dear friend and colleague of mine, Lewis Matthew Tunston, and I have been working tirelessly to learn more about the system at its core and to find its weaknesses, so that we can restore Carnot to its glory.

Unfortunately, we now believe our efforts have been discovered and we suspect that we will be selected to die soon.

I am asking you, on behalf of Lewis and the people of Carnot, to find his daughter, Vienna and continue our quest for restoration. I wish it wasn't so, but you will not be able to request the help of your father in this matter. As for Vienna's mother, I can't say for certain where she stands.

He paused. "Camilla did not know but I did," he added with a quick glance at Margaret before continuing:

What we know is this, the very foundation of Carnot is cracking. We are starting to see faults in the structure and our time is coming. Wait patiently my darling. When you turn eighteen it will all be clear. Trust those around you and submit to their instructions. With Vienna's help, you will be able to overcome the opposition.

I love you,

Camilla Audrey Howth

"Is that why you asked me to be your date?" Vienna asked. She was surprised at the words flying out of her mouth. That shouldn't have been her first question.

"Your date?" Margaret questioned. "To what?" Her eyes widened as the day's events became clearer. "His birthday party? You're the girl he's planning to bring?! Why didn't you tell me?" Her tone shifted from confusion to genuine disappointment.

"I'm sorry, Mom," Vienna replied. "Obviously, this is all news to me. I didn't know you had some sort of alliance with the Howth family... actually, I thought you hated them. I didn't want to tell you I was going on a date with Copeland."

Margaret couldn't argue her daughter's reasoning. "I understand," she replied. "Wait," she looked at Martin, "why did you let Copeland ask her? Shouldn't you have waited until his birthday to talk to him? I thought you were supposed to follow your grandfather's instructions to a T?"

"I am," Martin sighed. "I do have to admit we're a little bit off course. A while back, Copeland asked me to do some digging on Vienna's habits. Obviously, I knew his intentions, but at the time, I could not admit to that. I did some tracking and reported back information to him."

"You've been stalking me?" Vienna accused Copeland.

"Technically, he's been the one doing the stalking," Copeland shifted the blame.

Vienna disapprovingly raised her eyebrows.

"Anyway," Martin continued. "When we were looking at venues for his birthday party, he asked to add Tellmen's Piano Factory and I did not realize he was facilitating a run-in with Vienna... which was my mistake," he admitted.

He planned that, Vienna thought to herself?

"The next day, he asked to stop by the house, and I figured it was fine... little did I know he was planning to ask her to the event of the century. I thought he'd start to form a relationship and truly, I figured all would be fine. Then, the small sparks turned into a wildfire. The party was going to be in the factory district and a commoner would be Copeland's date and Theodore was angry and I really lost control," Martin explained. He was rambling a bit now. "I don't have anyone to talk to anymore now that my mother and father and sister have passed. My grandfather's plans rest solely in my hands." He began to hyperventilate. "So, I went a little rogue and decided to tell Copeland early and now, I don't know what to do and I really need your help." He spoke with desperation.

"Don't worry," Copeland calmly replied. "Your grandfather's plans now rest in *our* hands." He gestured around the room. "You're not alone anymore."

"Thank you," Martin looked up at Copeland with sincerity. He looked around the room and the others met him with kind eyes, nodding in agreement. He caught sight of a clock on the wall. "Oh my!" He stood up suddenly. "Is that the time? Come on." He gestured for Copeland to follow him. "We've got to get you back before anyone starts looking for you."

Copeland got up and they moved quickly to the door. They put on their coats and shoes as the others followed them to the entryway.

"We will be in touch very soon," Martin said, but before anyone could respond, they were out the door.

Chapter Twenty-Five

"Wow," Vienna sighed a few seconds after the door was shut. "That was a lot."

"Uhm, yeah," Beckham agreed.

"I knew they would be coming to us soon but that was... that was a lot more than I anticipated." Margaret began to walk back to the living room with Vienna and Beckham close behind. They all sat down in the same seats they'd been sitting in.

"So, what do you know, Mom? What did Dad know?" Beckham asked. "I still have so many questions."

"Of course," Margaret calmly replied. "I am happy to help answer any of the questions I can. Unfortunately, I do not know everything, and Archie knows a lot more than I do, but I will try."

"Who's Archie?" Vienna interrupted.

"Oh, that's right, you missed that part. Martin is Archie. Gosh... this is a big part of the story I would have forgotten about. When Archie was fifteen, the first Ivy Letter he received said he would die from leukemia. At the time, Archie's father was a member of the Committee of Demise and he faked Archie's death. They kept Archie in hiding for a few years and died his blonde hair the dark brown it is today."

"How is that even possible? Didn't people recognize him? How could he fake his death?" Beckham questioned.

"Well, your exact disbelief is part of it," Margaret replied. "With the way the government controls everyone, no one suspects anyone can avoid death, so no one thought anything of him. And with his father on the board, he was able to report the death and alter records without much hassle. After Archie had been in hiding for a few years, his father was able to alter the records again and added Martin Pluto, at age eighteen, to Carnot society."

"That's insane!" Beckham commented.

"It is indeed," Margaret replied. "Edwin Beckett was a genius. He dedicated his life to outlining a plan that would someday save us all. Every minute detail must be executed accordingly, or it will all crumble. At this point, eighty plus years of work could fail in an instant."

Vienna and Beckham sat silently for a second, thinking about that.

"Keep going," Vienna directed, then realized she sounded rude. "Please," she added.

"Your father's relationship with the Becketts goes back a long time. He grew up next door to their family and his parents were very close with their parents. If I am not mistaken, your father's grandfather was also friends with their grandfather, but I am not positive how far back the partnership dates. Lewis' parents even helped Archie during the years he was hiding. A critical part of Edwin's plan was getting his family connected with the Howth family. He knew it would be necessary to have people on the inside to truly be able to conquer the government someday."

"So… we're really talking about a revolution?" Beckham asked.

"I'm afraid so," Margaret sighed.

"How could Edwin have known Camilla would end up with Theodore?" Vienna asked.

"He didn't," Margaret plainly replied. "His plan, from what I understand, is more of an outline. There are steps that must be made for other ones to follow. In other words, the plan was not 'Camilla marry Theodore,' but rather 'get an insider as close to the ruling family as possible and establish trust.'" She paused. "Truthfully, we got very lucky with Camilla marrying Theodore and from what I understand, he fell head over heels for her." She added to herself, *Or so she believed.*

"What else do you know?" Beckham questioned. "Did you know Camilla well?"

"Oh, heavens no," Margaret waved her hand. "The Howth's have very little contact with the outside world."

"But you work for the government," Vienna countered.

"It doesn't matter," Margaret replied. "I was, and still am, no one of status. Your father on the other hand worked very closely with Camilla. She's the reason he got the job in the first place."

"I never knew that," Beckham replied. "He always said he worked very hard to gain his position in the government."

"He did work very hard," Margaret quickly defended. "He did very well in school and studied endlessly to understand the ins and outs of the government. Camilla most definitely helped get him in the door, but he had to prove himself to get the job."

"I guess I just don't understand what the next step is," Vienna admitted.

"To be honest, darling, I don't exactly know either," Margaret admitted. "At this point, it's really up to Martin to lead us all…" She paused, "and between you and me, I am a little worried about that."

Chapter Twenty-Six

Copeland walked with his head down and tried to keep pace with Martin on the way home. They didn't say much. After all, there had already been a lot said for one night.

As they walked, Copeland tried to recall every detail from the evening. He couldn't believe everything he had learned. *Martin is my uncle... or better yet, Archie is my uncle, and my great grandfather has been slowly working to overthrow the government for over eighty years. And Vienna is going to help us lead a revolution... maybe? Or that's just us? Why do I need her if I have Martin?*

Before he knew it, they were back in the alleyway where they'd met earlier.

"Do you have any questions?" Martin asked plainly.

"Do I have any questions?" Copeland lowered his eyebrows into a quizzical frown. "Do I have any questions?" he repeated for emphasis. "How about one million questions? I have one million questions," he rhetorically answered himself.

"I know, I know," Martin calmly replied. He reached out and placed his hand on Copeland's chest. "It's going to be okay. Just breathe."

Copeland breathed in slowly. Martin's hand oddly soothed him; it felt so familiar. It took him a second to realize that Martin's touch reminded him of his mother. He hadn't felt any sort of physical love since she'd passed away and for once, amidst all of his anxieties, someone was there for him.

"Forget the questions," Martin said. "Let's take it one day at a time. Right now, we need to decide what you're going to tell your father about your birthday party. I know I messed up by telling you all of this before your birthday, but I also messed up by not telling you some of it sooner." He paused. "We need to figure out the best course of action."

"What do you think it should be?"

"I am not sure," Martin replied. "We obviously know you'll have to give a little, so you definitely can't take Vienna *and* host your party at Tellmen's. I don't know at this point that you can say no to both though either. You already stood up to him, so giving in altogether might be a step in the wrong direction. I guess that leaves us with picking between Tellmen's and Vienna. I think you need to go back to him with one or the other and stand firm."

"Okay, which one?" Copeland didn't really care to hear all of Martin's reasoning. He just wanted him to tell him what to do.

"That, I don't know." He hesitated. "Well, I do kind of know. I know the answer should be easy and it should be to fight for Tellmen's and forget about Vienna. In that case, your father would never need to know her name, which is good, because it would most likely raise an air of suspicion if he did—"

"Good, it's settled then," Copeland cut him off. "I will forget about Vienna."

"Buuut," Martin started again, "without taking Vienna, it will be very difficult for you to get any time with her. If you don't take her, you won't be able to go on any dates and if you don't go on dates, then you won't be able to leave the premises and it will be extremely difficult to communicate with the Tunstons about anything—"

"Then, I will take Vienna," Copeland replied.

"It's not that simple." Martin once again began to hyperventilate. "It's not that simple and I don't know what to do. I've never been good at making decisions." He started to rock back and forth, breathing more heavily with each movement. "I don't think I can do it... I can't decide... I can't orchestrate this plan."

He sat down on the cobblestone ground and put his head in his hands. He continued to rock back and forth. Copeland couldn't tell for sure, but he thought he might be crying.

"Sure, you can," Copeland encouraged him. He squatted down next to him and placed his hand on his shoulder. "You were destined for this. Your grandfather created a plan and knew you would be able to handle it—"

"No, he didn't," Martin wailed.

"He didn't what?" Copeland asked.

"He didn't plan on me handling it!" Martin's hands shook uncontrollably. "This was never how it was supposed to go. Your mother wasn't supposed to die. She was supposed to be the one leading us," Martin explained. "I have no idea what I am doing."

The words hit Copeland like a dagger in his chest. "She's supposed to be leading this?" His hand fell off Martin's shoulder. He slumped onto the ground and his body slouched. "That's kind of a bummer," Copeland admitted. He honestly didn't know if he meant it light-heartedly or not, but Martin chuckled a little.

"Bummer is quite the understatement."

Copeland couldn't help but laugh too. After all, his mother had always told him a cheerful heart was good medicine.

After a few moments of silence, Copeland sat up straighter. "Enough of this," he declared as he stood to his feet. "I believe in you. Margaret believes in you. We all believe in you, and we *need* you." He reached out his hand to help Martin up. "You can do this! You can help lead this revolution and I know you will make the right decisions along the way. You hold all the power and without you, nothing will change. It's up to you to bring your grandfather's plan to fruition and it doesn't matter if it was originally intended for you because you know who else is counting on you?"

Martin looked up at Copeland who was still reaching out his hand. "Who?" he asked, though he already knew the answer.

"Your sister," Copeland sincerely replied, "and my mother. She wouldn't want her death to be in vain. It's up to you to make it worth something."

Martin took a deep breath and finally grabbed Copeland's hand with both of his. He stood to his feet and stared intensely into Copeland's eyes.

"It's up to *us*," he declared.

Chapter Twenty-Seven

Margaret sat silently eating lunch in her cubicle. Her peanut butter and jelly sandwich, cup of fruit, and cheese stick were nothing exciting, but she packed the same lunch every day and she liked consistency (especially since nothing else in her life seemed steady at the moment).

Just as she took a bite into her sandwich, she felt the tap of a man's hand on her shoulder. Startled, she turned to see a bodyguard she recognized as being one of Theodore's standing broadly behind her; nearly taking up the entire cubicle.

"Come with me," he instructed.

Knowing better than to disregard Theodore's orders, Margaret quickly stood up, left her unfinished lunch on her desk, and followed the bodyguard. As they walked through the halls of Carnot, each passerby moved swiftly out of the way, making an easy path for them to follow. Margaret walked closely behind the guard and tried to avoid making eye contact with anyone. When they reached the grand stairs, the bodyguard led the way down them. Margaret desperately wished they would get off on the second floor but when he continued down the next flight, Margaret's heart began to beat faster. When they reached the bottom of the steps, Margaret once again falsely hoped they would turn right but instead, he took a sharp left and Margaret knew for certain where they were going. She continued to follow the man and focused on slowing her breath.

It will be okay, she encouraged herself. *It's going to be okay.*

In what felt like no time at all, they had weaved through the downstairs hallways, and she found herself standing outside of Theodore Howth's executive office.

"Wait here," the bodyguard instructed, signaling toward a brown leather chair next to the double doors.

Margaret hadn't felt so little in years. Despite being a grown woman with two, teenange children, she suddenly felt like a child waiting outside the principal's office.

She sat outside of the office for what felt like an eternity.

"He's ready for you," the bodyguard finally came out and informed her.

Although Margaret was terrified for what the meeting would hold, she was momentarily thankful her spiraling thoughts were interrupted. She stood up and followed the guard as he held the door to the office open for her.

Theodore sat stiffly with his hands clasped together and arms resting on the large, cherry desk. He stared blankly at Margaret as she hesitantly entered the room.

"Have a seat." The guard motioned toward one of the tufted, leather chairs that sat opposite Theodore.

"Thank you, Amos," Theodore replied. His gracious

tone didn't match his harsh body language and Margaret feared its clashing was due to her presence.

Amos bowed and left the room, leaving Margaret and Theodore alone.

"Good afternoon," Theodore greeted.

"Hello, Theodore," Margaret replied. "To what do I owe the pleasure?"

"I think you know precisely why I've called you here today," he paused, "but if you insist on me spelling it out for you, I will. It is because, for some unknown reason, my son has taken an interest in your daughter."

"Is that so?" Margaret innocently asked.

"Indeed," Theodore replied. He unclasped his hands and reached for his glass of whiskey on ice. He took a sip, waiting for Margaret to bite, but she did not respond. "Do you have any idea how something like this could have happened?" He licked his lips.

"Well, my Vienna is beautiful." She grinned. "Perhaps Copeland simply has good taste." She didn't anticipate having such confidence in Theodore's presence, but she also didn't anticipate holding the power.

"I think we both know that is not the case," Theodore replied. "Why are you being this way? Why so defensive?"

Margaret bit her lip and sighed deeply.

Theodore pushed his chair back and stood up. He began slowly walking around his desk and Margaret's heart beat faster with each step he took. He walked until he stood behind Margaret. He placed his hand on her shoulder and ran it down her arm.

"You used to be so kind," he whispered in her ear and then gently kissed her neck.

She pulled away. "That was before you killed my husband," she breathed.

"We both know I didn't kill him," Theodore replied as he continued to kiss down her neck.

"You had him killed," Margaret pulled away. "It's the same thing."

"I did it for you..." Theodore defended, "for us. I wanted you to be free of that dreadful man."

"You did it because you knew they were after you," Margaret countered. "You didn't do it for me."

"Well, of course, that played into my decision." Theodore paced behind Margaret. "But it was also for you. Without Lewis and Camilla, I thought we could finally be together."

"You knew that wouldn't be the case," Margaret contended. "It was all a mistake anyway."

"Really?" Theodore slammed his hand on the desk. "A mistake, Margaret? You make a mistake once, maybe twice, not for years. You know what we had was more than a mistake."

"Theodore," Margaret sighed heavily. Her chest felt like a weight was crushing it. "Things have changed. I've changed." She wanted the words to be true. "It's been years and you haven't missed me."

"You know that isn't true and you know you haven't changed." Theodore smiled a derisive smile. "You're the same old Maggie I know." He moved closer to her once again and ran his hand down her cheekbone. "And dare I say it," he softly bit her ear, "Love."

Margaret's stomach felt like a million butterflies had taken flight. The logical part of her brain wanted to say 'no.' She wanted to throw her hands up and angrily storm out of the room, appalled by Theodore's actions. She wanted to tell him off. She wanted to do so many things... but instead, she threw her arms around him and placed her lips on his.

Chapter Twenty-Eight

"Are you excited for tonight?" Beckham asked as they sat down at their usual lunch table.

"I guess," Vienna nonchalantly replied. "If it's even happening still."

"What do you mean?" Beckham was confused. "Yesterday, you wanted nothing more than to go on a date with the prince."

"Not a prince," Vienna corrected.

Ignoring her, Beckham continued, "And now you're not excited at all? And what do you mean 'if it's still happening?' Of course, it's happening."

"You don't know that," Vienna countered. "Copeland needs to decide if he's fighting for the venue or for me. He can't have both. And based on what he said last night, he doesn't even want me... He just wanted to use me."

"Ohh, I see what this is about," Beckham sighed. "You're upset because it wasn't all happenstance."

"Not upset," Vienna corrected. "Just," she searched for the right word, "bummed, I guess."

"Same thing. It's okay though, V. Even if it wasn't happenstance, that doesn't change the way he was looking at you last night."

"What on earth are you talking about?" Vienna asked, trying not to appear too interested.

"His body language, his tone, his frequent glances in your direction? What else would I be talking about?" Beckham stated as though it was as obvious as the sky being blue.

"When did you become so observant?" "If someone is interested in my little sister, I have to be on my best guard." "You're older by two minutes." Vienna rolled her eyes. "Nevertheless, it doesn't matter anymore. There's too much on the line and I don't like him anyway."

"What? Since when?!" Beckham nearly shouted.

"Let's just say it's not exactly attractive when someone stalks you and then pretends to be romantically interested but really needs you instead to help lead a…" she paused and got quieter, "a revolution." She shook her head slightly, feeling like the word was too intense. "That's not exactly what every little girl dreams of. It's strictly business from here on out."

"Touché." Beckham couldn't argue with her logic.

"Plus, I can't even think about trying to navigate a relationship in the midst of everything else," she added, trying to further convince herself and less to convince her brother.

"You make a good point," Beckham agreed. "So, are you still going to go to the birthday party with him?"

"That's completely up to him at this point," Vienna said. "Whatever he decides is fine with me. I'm assuming I will know more tonight."

"Hopefully, so," Beckham replied. "I just hope I still get an invite to the party."

"Really?" Vienna glared. "With everything else going on right now, you're still holding out hope for an invitation to his birthday party?"

"What can I say?" Beckham shrugged. "It's the event of the century. And you might be a pawn, but if you're the ticket in, I'm embracing it." He winked conspiratorially.

Chapter Twenty-Nine

Copeland followed Martin's lead as he wound through the halls to his father's office. He was nervous about how the conversation would go (considering how poorly the last conversation with his father had gone) but he still walked confidently. The last twenty-four hours had changed his entire life and he knew this discussion was simply one of the first steps he needed to take to start practicing his dominance.

Martin stopped abruptly outside the office and Copeland, who had been looking down, ran into him.

"What the heck?" Copeland rubbed his head after smashing it against Martin's back.

"Sorry, sir. I thought I saw something... err... someone at the end of the hall," Martin explained.

"Who was it?"

"No one," he lied. "I think my mind was playing tricks on me." He changed the subject, "Are you ready?" Martin brushed the shoulders of Copeland's jacket down.

"Yes," Copeland assertively replied.

"Good," said Martin. "You're going to do great."

"Thank you."

Martin opened the door to Theodore's office and

Copeland walked in. The second the door was shut, Martin took off down the hall as quickly as possible without drawing attention to himself.

"Hello," Theodore greeted Copeland.

"Good afternoon." Copeland respectfully bowed his head.

"I'd like to start off by apologizing for my actions yesterday, son. I shouldn't have gotten so angry at you for wanting to share your opinions and for that, I am sorry," Theodore sincerely apologized.

Copeland's stomach knotted. All of the confidence he'd built up on his walk over escaped him. *An apology? In all my life, he's never once apologized and now, when I am ready to stand up for myself for the first time ever, he decides to do this?* Copeland's mind raced. "Uhm, thank you," was all he could get out.

"I'm so proud of you, son, and the man you are becoming. You're going to be a great leader of Carnot and I want your birthday party to symbolize your coming of age. How can it do that if I don't allow you to make any of your own decisions?"

Copeland was speechless. This conversation was not at all what he'd expected. He was not prepared. "I guess you're right," Copeland said, finding an ounce of courage. "However, I did have time to think about what you said, and I am happy to compromise. I am willing to host the party wherever you think is best, but I would like to take someone other than Summer Nile as my date."

"I think I can agree to those arrangements," Theodore calmly replied. "I am assuming you'd like to take a Miss Vienna Tunston as your date?"

Copeland wanted to scream. He should have known

his father would have eyes and ears everywhere. He would rather his father yell at him than play these silly mind games.

"Yes." Copeland refused to acknowledge his father's cunning tone. "I would like to take Vienna as my date."

"Why such a sudden interest in the lower class?" Theodore taunted.

Copeland's emotions were all over the place. He knew his father could be twisted and conniving, but he'd never experienced this kind of behavior firsthand.

"I ran into her... quite literally," he explained, "the other day when we went to look at venues for the party. We really hit it off. She is kind and beautiful and she has a good sense of humor. I'm so young... I feel it's only right I experience a bit of dating before settling down for the rest of my life."

"I didn't date anyone but your mother before I married her and we were very happy," Theodore stated. "But, if you insist, you may take Vienna."

"Thank you."

"However, you must be the one to break the news to Summer."

"Why?" Copeland complained. "I didn't even ask her."

"It has always been assumed you'd be going with her, so she deserves the right to hear it from you and not the newspapers," Theodore explained. "Do we have a deal?"

"Yes, sir," Copeland agreed.

"Wonderful! And you know what, son?"

Ugh, quit calling me son, Copeland groaned internally. "What?" he asked aloud.

"You can host your party at Tellmen's."

"What? Why?" Copeland couldn't hide his surprise.

"I'm feeling generous this afternoon," Theodore smiled.

"Really?" Copeland still didn't believe him.

Theodore nodded.

"Thank you. I will let Martin know and get things rolling right away."

"Sounds good," Theodore agreed.

Copeland turned to leave, wanting desperately to get out of the presence of his father. As he reached the door, Theodore called, "Hey, son."

Copeland turned around. "Yes?"

"Be careful," he warned.

Careful, Copeland thought? *Does he know? Is he on to us already?*

Before Copeland's mind could race further, Theodore added, "It's never easy watching a heart break."

Copeland moved his lips to respond but nothing came out. He nodded and left the room.

Martin was walking quickly up the hall when the door closed behind Copeland.

"Where have you been?" Copeland asked. Martin never left his post.

"Doesn't matter," Martin replied. "How did it go?"

They started walking down the hall.

"It... It..." Copeland tried to find words to describe the meeting. "It was interesting," he finally said.

"Interesting in what way? Are you taking Vienna? Where are you hosting it?"

"Yes, and Tellmen's," Copeland replied without giving out any more details.

"You got both?" Martin questioned, clearly surprised.

"How did that happen?"

"I don't know. Something was off. He was in a very strange mood... I think he might be on to us."

Martin rubbed his hair frustratingly. "I'm afraid you might be right, but we cannot talk about it here."

"Then, where?" Copeland asked.

"We will talk about it tonight. I will insist you be left alone on your hike, with the exception of me, of course, and we can talk about it with Vienna," Martin suggested.

"Sounds good," Copeland concurred. "What time is the hike?"

"Four o'clock, sir."

"And what time is it now?"

"Quarter after one."

"Perfect," said Copeland. "Then, we have time to go to Summer's house."

"Why do we need to go there?" Martin asked.

"My father is allowing me to take Vienna under the stipulation that I break the news to Summer myself about not taking her," Copeland explained, filled with dread.

"I see," Martin replied. "I will arrange for the car."

Chapter Thirty

Vienna added a touch of lip gloss and evaluated her reflection in the mirror. She ran her fingers through her hair and nervously tucked a few strands behind her ears, then pulled it back into a pony-tail, then down around her face and over again. Finally, she left it down, hanging naturally around her face.

I guess that will have to do, she thought to herself.

She had on dark blue jeans, a white sweater and brown hiking boots.

"Is that what you're wearing?" Beckham leaned in the bathroom and asked.

"No, really, what a kind thing to say when I'm about to go on the most photographed date of my life." Vienna was instantly defensive.

"Woah," Beckham raised his hands in defense. "I meant you'd be cold, not that you looked bad."

"Oh," Vienna sighed, realizing she'd snapped at him too quickly. "Sorry, I'm a little on edge."

"That's understandable," Beckham replied. "What time will he be here?"

"I think around 4:00."

"Nice. I'm just glad you're not into him so I don't have

to give him the talk." He flexed, trying to act tough.

Vienna shook her head and laughed. She was thankful Beckham knew how to make her smile even when she was nervous.

The doorbell rang and Vienna's stomach dropped.

"You grab a hat," Beckham instructed. "I'll get the door."

Vienna nodded and he left the bathroom. She went to her closet and grabbed a white and blue beanie her dad had bought for her when she was in middle school. She'd pointed it out to him one day when they were shopping and said she liked it because of the little, fuzzy ball on the top. The next day, Vienna got home from school and it was on her bed. Wearing it had always made her smile. She put on the beanie, grabbed a pair of white gloves and walked down the stairs. She didn't know exactly what to expect but she was thankful photographers weren't outside her door... at least, not yet.

Copeland was casually talking to Beckham when Vienna walked up. She took her black winter coat off the rack and put it on.

"Hi, Vienna," Copeland greeted.

"Hello." She smiled back.

"Are you ready for our hike?"

Vienna couldn't help but giggle at the way Copeland stood awkwardly in the door. It was clear he'd never gone on anything like a real date before and although, Vienna no longer cared about it being a date, she still thought it was cute.

"Yes," she replied. "It's a good day for it. The sky is relatively clear, so we should be able to see the city."

"Nothing like awkward weather talk to start off the

night," Beckham teased.

Vienna rolled her eyes.

"Should we get going?" Copeland suggested.

"Yeah," Vienna agreed.

"You two crazy kids have fun," Beckham called as they walked down the sidewalk to the line of black cars.

Vienna had never ridden in a car before and she'd never taken roads to Mickinley Park. She sat in a window seat and left the middle seat open between her and Copeland. She stared out and watched as the city blocks slowly became less congested, fading to suburbs and then to woods. Vienna was amazed at how quickly the city ended. When she rode the train, it was underground for the first two-thirds of the ride, and when it was above ground, it wound through the woods. She'd never thought about what the edge of the city looked like.

"I have to warn you," Copeland, who had been nervously fidgeting with his hands, finally spoke. "When we get to the park, I expect a large number of photographers to be there."

"I assumed." Vienna shrugged. "I'm sure it will be fine."

"I want to again emphasize that there will probably be *a lot* of photographers."

"Got it." Vienna was slightly annoyed by Copeland's tone. She didn't like when anyone doubted her comprehension.

"Okay," Copeland replied, sensing her irritation and changing the subject. "Martin will join us on the majority of the hike. We have a lot to cover for..." he paused, realizing he shouldn't talk about anything with the driver in the car, "the birthday party," he saved himself. "There are a lot of details and plans to be made."

"Oh, right." She was surprised, and almost impressed with herself, that she'd caught onto his cover. She barely knew him, yet she could already tell what he was thinking.

They rode in silence the rest of the way. As they pulled into the parking lot of Mickinley Park, Vienna's blood ran cold. It was filled to the brim with press and photographers. She felt silly now for brushing off Copeland's warnings.

They slowly pulled into the lot as security officers moved in front of the car, paving a path for them by moving the press out of the way.

How will we even get out, Vienna thought seeing how closely the people were standing to the car doors?

"Oh, that reminds me," Copeland replied.

"Did I say that out loud?" Vienna asked a little panicked.

"No." Copeland raised his eyebrows, wondering what she'd been thinking. "I was just going to say that it's protocol for me to get out first and grab your hand to help you out. We'll want to keep holding hands as we walk onto the trails. Once we're out of sight of the photographers, Martin will let us know and we can stop holding hands. Unless, of course, you don't want to stop." He winked.

Is he flirting with me, Vienna wondered?

Her thoughts were quickly interrupted by the shouts of photographers.

"Vienna, over here!"

"Vienna, look to your left!"

"Copeland, look at me!"

"Copeland, where's Summer?"

"Are you ready?" Copeland asked.

"I guess," Vienna shyly replied. She rubbed her hands together, trying to dry them of the nervous sweat she could feel gathering on her palms.

Copeland gave the driver a nod, signaling they were ready to exit. The driver got out of the car and walked to the back to open the door. Copeland graciously stepped out of the car, gave a slight wave to the roar of press and then turned back and reached his hand out for Vienna. She took hold of his hand and moved out of the car to stand next to him. The flashes from the cameras were blinding and the shouts of the crowd were a constant, undecipherable hum.

Copeland started toward the trail as security officers surrounded the two of them on all sides. Vienna walked a step behind Copeland, tightly gripping his hand; it felt warm and comfortable in hers. She squeezed, and he squeezed it back reassuringly.

Vienna's mind whirled as they moved through the crowd. They made it to the trail entrance, where Martin was waiting for them. He bowed slightly to greet them.

"Follow me," he instructed.

The three of them walked closely on the narrow, dirt path as it began to wind through the tall trees. Vienna had walked the trail countless times before, but it felt different without her brother. Her heart was still racing from the crowd and her legs felt unsteady. She'd never had a problem navigating the uneven path, but today, her legs felt unstable and every fallen tree branch seemed more like a boulder she needed to climb over.

"Alright, I think we're in the clear," Martin announced.

Copeland stopped walking and looked at Vienna, still holding her hand. "Are you alright?" he asked.

"Yeah." Vienna breathed a heavy sigh. "I'm alright."

"I tried to warn you," Copeland teased.

Vienna rolled her eyes. She hated being wrong, but she didn't mind Copeland's playful chaffing.

"Have you filled her in?" Martin looked seriously at Copeland. He didn't want to waste a second of their limited time together.

"On what?" Vienna asked.

"Uhm," Copeland hummed.

Sensing Martin's seriousness, Vienna let go of Copeland's hand. "On what?" she demanded.

"I... well, with my decision to take you as my date to my birthday party," Copeland started.

Guess that answers my question of whether or not he decided, Vienna thought to herself.

Copeland continued, "I had to tell Summer I wasn't taking her."

"Had you already asked her?" Vienna didn't mean to say the words out loud.

"No," Copeland answered. "But my father felt it was assumed I would take her and that she needed to hear it from me directly."

"Oh," Vienna replied. "I guess that makes sense."

"Yeah." Copeland shrugged. "So, this afternoon, Martin went with me to her house and..."

"And what?" Vienna sensed his hesitation.

"And it didn't go well," Martin cut in. "Summer was appalled and very angry. She threatened to go to the newspapers."

"With what?" Vienna was oddly annoyed at Summer's vexation.

Copeland and Martin exchanged glances.

"With what?" Vienna asked again a little impatiently.

"We're not exactly sure..." Copeland replied. "Her dad is the head of our public relations team, so she could know anything.

"Or she could know nothing," Martin added, trying to sound reassuring. "But we have to proceed with caution."

"This doesn't exactly seem like caution," Vienna gestured back toward the photographers whose shouts could still faintly be heard behind the trees.

"True," agreed Copeland. "But we had to calculate the risks. We could either move forward with the plan and be able to openly communicate with you and see you on a regular basis..."

"Or revert to taking Summer and attempt to sneak around and communicate with you without anyone knowing," Martin finished.

"We went with the former," Copeland said. "We're crossing our fingers Summer doesn't know anything damaging and that it was just an empty threat. We need you in the picture."

Vienna's heart fluttered. *Stop,* she scolded herself. *This is not a date. He needs you for a revolution, not a relationship.*

"Plus, I'm afraid my father is onto us," Copeland added. "It's more important we work together as quickly and efficiently as possible, rather than trying to keep things a secret, when in reality, he might already know."

Vienna furrowed her brow. "That seems really concerning if he already knows."

"Yes," Martin agreed. "But, luckily, even if he does, he can't do anything about it until next month. It's only the fifth, so we have twenty-six days before he could make a detrimental move."

"I guess you make a good point." Vienna couldn't argue with his logic, though her stomach turned at the thought of receiving her last Ivy Letter. "So, where do we go from here?"

"That's precisely what we need to figure out," answered Martin.

Chapter Thirty-One

Beckham was sitting upstairs in his room when he heard a rumbling coming from outside. He got up and walked to the window where he was shocked to see photographers gathering on the street below.

"Mom!" he called. He hurriedly left his room and went downstairs. "Mom!"

"Yes?" she shouted back from her bedroom.

Beckham followed the sound of her voice. "Are you seeing this?"

"Seeing what?"

"Outside! There are dozens of reporters lining up in front of our house.

"Oh my! Really?" Margaret walked past Beckham and he followed her to the front door. She pulled back the edge of the curtain that covered the window next to the door and peeked out. "Wow!"

"Right?!" Beckham agreed. "I knew the date would cause a stir, but this is insane."

"Yeah," Margaret concurred. "It's getting pretty dark. I am sure they'll be back any minute."

"Do you think Copeland will come in?" Beckham asked.

"Ha!" Margaret let out a big laugh, then realized Beckham had been serious. "Oh, no, honey," she answered sincerely. "It's going to be a big enough deal already that Copeland went out with a commoner. There's no chance he comes inside our home. We will have to get all of our new information from Vienna."

"Oh." Beckham shrugged. "I guess that makes sense."

"Yeah," Margaret replied. "So, let's hope Vienna can relay everything we need to know."

Beckham nodded.

"Want to play Elygra while we're waiting?" Margaret suggested. "It might help us keep our minds from wandering."

"Sure," Beckham agreed. "I'll grab the board."

He went to the coat closet where they kept the few games they had. Elygra was a board game played with marbles on a wooden board. It was a classic game that Margaret's mother had taught her, and it had been passed down by generations before her.

"What color do you want to be?" Beckham asked his mother, though he knew she always picked purple.

"Purple," she replied.

"Okay, I will be green." He sat on the ground by the coffee table and set the board up. He placed four, green marbles in the corner of the board by him and four, purple marbles in the corner of the board by Margaret. Then, he placed three large marbles, colored bronze, silver and gold, in the center of the board. "You can go first." He handed her the dice.

"Thanks," she said as she rolled them.

"How do you think we will be able to overthrow the government?" Beckham asked. Evidently, the game was not successfully keeping his mind from wandering.

Margaret didn't roll doubles, so she passed the dice to Beckham. "I am really not sure," Margaret sighed. "Your father worked tirelessly with Camilla to study the rules and regulations of both the government and the injections, but I am not sure if they ever found anything substantial. They were both killed before he could share any information with me."

Beckham rolled doubles and moved one of his marbles out of the home base. "Dad didn't tell you anything he figured out at all?" Beckham questioned.

"No." Margaret looked down. "Unfortunately, he did not. He tried very hard to keep everything as quiet as possible. He didn't breathe a word of it around me or the two of you in hopes they could research longer without being found out, and to keep us safe."

"Huh." Beckham exhaled. "I wish he was still around to help us."

"Me too," Margaret agreed. She offered a half smile. She rolled the dice again but still did not get doubles.

Beckham grabbed the dice off the table but stopped just as he was about to roll them. "Do you hear that?" he asked.

They sat silently, listening for a moment.

"I think it's an engine."

The rumble got a little louder and Margaret agreed with a nod. "I think you're right."

They left their game and walked to peek out the living room windows. Margaret pulled up one of the blinds slightly and they looked out. Sure enough, the people were splitting like the Red Sea as the line of cars pulled up.

The photographers started yelling.

"Vienna! Over here!"

"Mr. Howth, why her?"

"How was your hike?"

"Vienna! What's it like to be dating the most eligible bachelor in the world?"

"We love you, Copeland!"

The dark night sky was suddenly lit up with hundreds of flashes from cameras in every direction.

"Oh my!" Margaret exclaimed. She rushed to the door and Beckham followed.

By the time they got there and opened the door, they could see Copeland stepping out of the car and reaching back for Vienna's hand. A team of bodyguards surrounded them both and they pushed through the mass of people.

The bodyguards stopped at the edge of the stairs and allowed Copeland and Vienna to make their way up to the door alone.

"Good evening," Copeland greeted Beckham and Margaret. "I apologize for this disturbance on your Thursday night." He winked.

"It's quite alright," Margaret assured him.

"Thank you for a lovely hike," he said, turning back to Vienna.

"We will plan something again soon. Martin will be in touch."

Oh, Martin will be in touch? How romantic, Vienna sarcastically thought, but instead, she politely responded, "Sounds good."

Copeland lifted up the hand he was still holding and gave it a gentle kiss. "Goodnight."

"Goodnight." She smiled and with that, he was gone. He moved quickly back to his bodyguards and they pushed through the press.

Vienna walked inside and Beckham shut the door behind her.

"Wow." Vienna blinked dramatically, trying to get a grip on where she was and process the night she'd had. "That was a lot."

"Seems like it," Beckham agreed. "Tell us everything. Start from the beginning."

"Let her breathe." Margaret placed her hand on Beckham's shoulder. "Dinner is almost ready. How about you get changed and we can chat while we're eating?"

"Okay." Vienna nodded. "That sounds good." She started toward the stairs and Beckham followed.

"Beckham Penn!" Margaret reprimanded. "Let her have some space. You can wait a few more minutes."

"Yes, ma'am," Beckham sulked.

"Will you help me finish dinner?" Margaret asked. "The lasagna is almost ready. I will get the peas ready if you do the garlic bread."

"Okay," he agreed. He moseyed to the freezer and pulled out the bread. The two of them worked silently to finish preparing dinner and waited anxiously for Vienna. They placed the hot food on the table and took their seats. Beckham sat tapping his fingers repeatedly until Vienna finally came downstairs.

"Okay, spill! I am dying to hear. I need to know what comes next." He couldn't stand it any longer.

Vienna laughed. She'd always admired Beckham's steadfast determination. When he set his mind to something, he didn't stop until it was resolved.

"I wish I could say I knew." Vienna sat down at the table. "We got to the park and it was absolutely insane. The parking lot had three times as many people as were just outside our home." She kept talking as she served up a plate full of food. "We hiked and security kept everyone else out of the park, so that part was very nice. It was just Copeland, Martin and me. The biggest piece of news was Copeland's conversation with Summer. Evidently, she did not take it well when he told her this afternoon that he wasn't going to be taking her to his birthday party. I guess she threatened to go to the newspapers."

"About what? Her not getting a date?" Beckham joked.

"They're not sure," Vienna seriously replied. "Her father is head of public relations for the Howth family though, so it could be anything."

Margaret's stomach dropped.

"Oh. Are they worried?" he asked.

"It doesn't sound like it," Vienna answered. "They really have no idea what she could know, so at this point, they're crossing their fingers it's nothing."

"Let's hope so," Margaret commented.

"Okay, well, assuming Summer stays quiet and all is okay on the publicity end, what's next? How do five inept and unqualified people overthrow an entire government?" Beckham questioned.

"I wish I knew," Vienna admitted. "Turns out, Martin isn't even the one who's supposed to be running this whole thing. It was supposed to be Camilla..." She hesitated. "He's just doing the best he can, but truth be told, I don't know if he has any idea."

"Maybe, it's not the best time for all of this," Margaret casually suggested.

"What?" Vienna was instantaneously defensive. "Why would it not be the right time? You think it's okay to sit idly by while people abuse their power and kill innocent people month after month?"

"There's no need to be so aggressive, Vienna. I was simply making a suggestion," Margaret reprimanded. "Before Carnot, people died every day from terrible tragedies and the unexpected. It's really not that much different now."

Vienna refrained from stabbing her lasagna and making a scene. "I just don't think it's the same."

"I don't think so either." Beckham was now the one getting heated. "At least before, people had freedom. We have no freedom. People could choose to go skydiving and risk the parachute not opening. People could choose to not take their medication and suffer the consequences. Heck, people could choose to kill someone or take their own life. It might have been tragic but at least it was their own choice. Now, we have no say over any of it. I might live a terribly short life but it's not my choice. If I say the wrong thing or upset the wrong person with power, I'm done for. We still live in fear even though the distribution of perpetual life was intended for us to live forever without fear. The system is messed up!"

"I understand where you're coming from," Margaret calmly replied. "Your father had the same passion. I am just worried about the two of you, that's all. I want my babies to be safe and I fear there might be too much at risk."

"Too much at risk?" Vienna couldn't stay calm anymore. "Too much at risk?" She threw her fork down. "We live in fear every single day and we have an opportunity to change it. I can't sit here and do nothing. If I have to lose my life so that others can gain theirs, then that's what I will do." She stood up from the table and stormed toward the back door.

"Vienna, stop," Margaret called. "Where are you going?"

"Out!" she shouted.

"And I'm going with her," Beckham quickly stood up and followed her out the back door, slamming it shut behind him.

"Ugh!" Vienna huffed. "Where did that even come from? Last night, she's all in and then, suddenly, she has cold feet. Carnot is a mess!"

"V, keep it down," Beckham hushed. "You know it's not safe to talk negatively about the government, especially out here."

"Sorry." Vienna knew her brother was right. She began to whisper. "I'm so frustrated. I didn't anticipate coming home and having to defend myself to Mom."

"Me either," Beckham concurred. They walked quietly for a few seconds, each lost in their own thoughts. Beckham broke the silence. "Do you think Dad told Mom about the research he was doing?"

"I would assume so," Vienna replied. "From what I understand, it sounds like he dedicated his life to Edwin's plan. I assumed they talked about it."

"That's what I would think too."

"Why?"

"Well, before you got home, I asked Mom if Dad ever

told her anything and she said 'no.' She said he tried to keep things as quiet as possible, in an effort to never cause any disruption or raise any suspicion. But…" Beckham paused, "Ahh, I don't know. I just don't believe that. I feel like surely, she would have known at least something."

Vienna felt uneasy. She wanted to believe her mother, but for the first time in her life, she doubted her. "Remember how Copeland's letter said something about our mother?" she asked.

"Oh, yeah," Beckham replied. "What was it again? Something about—"

"How she wasn't certain she could be trusted," Vienna cut in.

"But Martin said Camilla didn't know if she could be trusted but he did," Beckham countered.

"I know," Vienna replied. "But, are we certain Martin is correct? He doesn't exactly know what he's doing."

"Do you really think we can't trust Mom?"

She shook her head. "I don't know," Vienna admitted. "We've both felt some of her comments have been a touch off. I just think we should proceed with caution."

"I guess it doesn't hurt to be careful," Beckham agreed.

Vienna stopped walking. She puffed out her cheeks and blew her lips together. "I guess being careful would require us to go back and apologize…"

"You're probably right about that," Beckham sighed.

They turned around and started walking back home.

"While we have a few extra minutes," Beckham started. "Anything more you want to tell me? Was there anything else of substance you got from tonight?"

"I wish there was, Beck... I really do. Right now, we are, unfortunately, at the mercy of Martin."

"When will you see them again?"

"Hopefully, this weekend. Martin said he wants to see how the papers look tomorrow and get the general feel of the public before moving forward."

"Makes sense," said Beckham.

"Yep." Vienna shrugged.

Chapter Thirty-Two

Margaret's stomach tightened into knots.

What if she knows, she wondered? What if Summer goes to the papers about Theodore and me? What if the kids find out about the old affair? She groaned. *Is it even old anymore? Until this afternoon, I hadn't kissed him since before he'd sent Lewis a letter and I didn't anticipate it today. Why? Why does he have such control over me?* She sat at the table, mindlessly moving her lasagna around, no longer feeling hungry. *Do I care for him? Did I ever care for him? I want to defend my kids. I want to fight for Lewis. Well... I should want those things, but I don't know if I do. How could they ever forgive me if they found out?*

Her mind continued to race, filtering through every option. *I could apologize and tell the kids the truth and that I no longer have feelings for Theodore... if that's true. Or, I could ride it out and see if that's what Summer knows. Maybe, she has no idea and I'm getting worked up for nothing,* she argued in her head. *She might know. How has it never gotten out? It's been nearly five years since the affair first started. How could no one know?*

She thought back to the night it all began. The year

was 2116 and the Howth family was hosting their annual spring party. Lewis and Margaret were invited to the party per usual and sat at a table of high honor toward the front of the banquet hall. The ballroom was beautiful, filled with immaculate flowers that hung from the ceiling in meticulous arrangements. The food was delicious, and the drinks were extravagant. The night was young. People were dancing, which was not terribly unusual, but it didn't happen all of the time by any means. Jazz music filled the air and Margaret remembered feeling particularly happy.

She was walking across the crowded room to get a drink from the bar, when she noticed Theodore staring at her. She shook it off, thinking he must have been looking elsewhere. However, as the night went on, everywhere she looked, it seemed, Theodore was looking back at her. With each drink, Margaret began to feel freer. She twirled and spun on the dance floor for what felt like hours. Late in the evening, while Lewis was still dancing, Margaret sat at the table and sipped on a drink. She watched as people swirled by, the alcohol in her veins running its course.

She felt a light tap on her shoulder and a voice whispered, "come with me." She was quite disoriented when she looked back to see that the instructions had come from a Howth family bodyguard. Not being in a mental state or position to say 'no,' she got up and followed the guard through the halls of Carnot. Before she knew it, she was face to face with Theodore Howth in his executive office.

"Good evening, Margaret," Theodore warmly greeted.

"Hello, Teddy," Margaret giggled like a schoolgirl.

She was too intoxicated to remember protocol.

"I've had my eye on you for quite a while now," he said. "I want you."

After that, the rest of the night was a blur. She never did figure out how she got home or if she ever went back to the party. She figured she must have because Lewis never said a word, but she still wasn't positive.

A few days later, Margaret was sitting at her desk outside of Lewis' office when the same bodyguard stopped by. Margaret hadn't been sure if the night had been real or a nightmare, but she knew in that moment it had really happened. Somewhere along the way, between the lunch breaks and afternoon meetings spent at Theodore's request, the nightmare turned into a dream. She found herself longing for Theodore and soon, she was the one summoning him.

As Margaret thought back to the first night, she wanted to be mad at herself. She wanted to regret the drinking and the trip to Theodore's office. She wanted to say it was all a mistake, and in the few years since Lewis' death, when she'd vowed to never see Theodore again, she'd almost convinced herself it had been. But now, with the taste of Theodore's lips still lingering on hers from earlier in the day, she couldn't convince herself.

If Vienna and Beckham find out, they'll never forgive me, she thought. *But I can't lose Teddy. I already lost Lewis; I can't lose him too.* Her mind argued both sides, over and over again. She felt like an angel and devil were literally standing on her shoulders, fighting hard for each side, and she wasn't entirely sure which one was which. *I didn't have Theodore for years; I could give him up again... maybe... I just got him back. But the kids. My babies. They need me. How could I choose my affair over them?* Margaret's stomach swirled. *Maybe, it wasn't that big of a deal. Maybe, I am reading into it all too much. Maybe... Maybe, I won't even need to choose. Who is Summer Nile to ruin my life? Maybe, she knows nothing.*

The back door opened, and Margaret's thoughts were cut off. In a matter of seconds, her mind raced through all of the ways she could handle the situation, but before she could decide on one, Vienna apologized.

"I am sorry for getting upset and storming off," Vienna started. "I know you're just trying to keep us safe and do what's best for us."

Vienna kept talking but Margaret was no longer listening. Her mind raced with relief. *Thank goodness they aren't mad at me. I have to make sure they trust me. As long as Summer doesn't know anything, I should be in the clear.*

"Uhm, hello." Vienna waved her hand in front of her mom's face. "Are you listening?"

"Sorry, yes." Margaret tried to rack her brain for the last comment she'd heard Vienna say. "It's okay, sweetheart. I know you have a lot on your plate right now and I want to help but you're also my baby girl, so sometimes, my motherly instincts take over and I prioritize keeping you safe. I'm on your side." She didn't know whether that was the truth or not.

"Thanks, Mom." Vienna smiled, though she didn't fully believe her mother.

"Let's start over," Margaret suggested. "Have a seat," she gestured, "and we will take it from the top."

Vienna and Beckham walked back to the table and took their seats once again.

"So, where were we?" Margaret furrowed her brows pensively. "We're hoping Summer doesn't have any dangerous information," she summarized and deeply hoped it was true. "What else did you find out?"

Not wanting to give away too much information and not having much more to say anyway, Vienna replied, "I think we're just waiting to see what the papers say in the morning. We need to see how the public responds to our date and whether or not Summer releases anything. Martin is certain she'd share information in the next day or two if she really has anything, so, it's kind of a waiting game at this point."

"I see." Margaret nodded. "I guess that makes sense."

"Yep." Vienna shrugged. "We'll just wait and see if everyone hates me tomorrow."

"Vienna Marie," Margaret spoke seriously. "They will not hate you. No one could hate you."

Chapter Thirty-Three

Icy Roads Ahead as Summer Ends
A Ploy for Power
An Airhead for an Heir
Aiming High, Looks Low

Copeland's stomach dropped as he scanned the newspaper headlines. He sat at the large oak table in the main dining hall, eating his breakfast, as he flipped through the pages. He tried to keep his orange juice and toast down as the stories got increasingly worse.

"Vienna Tunston, a no one from nowhere, catches Copeland Howth's eye, but the real question is why? Is it a ploy for power? A hate for Summer? Or an unlikely case of true love?"

Copeland read the start of the article and threw the paper down.

"Where do they get this stuff?" he huffed to himself.

"I have no idea," Martin said as he walked in the room.

"Oh." Copeland looked up, slightly embarrassed by his talking to himself. "I didn't see you there."

"I just walked in," Martin explained. "From what I've gathered, it's about nine to one out there." He wasted no time jumping into the updates. "For every nine negative articles, we've got one good one to work with. I was hoping for more like five to one, but it could be worse, so we're doing okay." He sounded positive. "Don't waste your time reading those." Martin walked over to Copeland and grabbed the newspapers from the table. "The comments of irrelevant fools will be of no help to us." He got quieter. "Our mission is not to please everyone. It's to save everyone."

"I hope Vienna is okay," Copeland commented. "I'm sure she's never had to face such opposition."

"If Vienna is anything like her father, I'm sure she's more than okay," Martin replied. "Lewis was tough as nails."

Copeland unconvincingly nodded. He finished his glass of orange juice.

"Alright." He licked his lips. "What's next? What's on the agenda today?" He changed the subject now that he had nothing else to read.

"Nothing," Martin replied. "I took the liberty of clearing your schedule, since we knew the press reports could be overwhelming."

"Oh, thank you." Copeland was genuinely pleased and surprised. "I don't remember the last time I had a day off."

"It was December 31, 2117. The day before your fifteenth birthday."

Copeland was shocked Martin knew the exact date.

"But, unfortunately, you don't have the day off."

"What?" Copeland was confused.

"You might not have imperial duties today," Martin explained, "but we have a lot of research to do."

"Research?"

"Yes, those who do not study what happened in the past are likely to bring it about again in some form," he quoted his grandfather, a line that stuck with him after the fall. "We must have a better understanding of what has happened, what we know, and what needs to be done before we take any further steps."

"How can we do that?" Copeland asked. Most of the historical and cultural information that existed before the creation of Carnot had been destroyed; only a select group of non-fiction books were widely available in the city.

"You'll see," Martin replied. "Come with me."

Copeland left his half-eaten toast and followed Martin out of the dining hall. Martin tossed the newspapers in the trash on the way out and then walked purposefully down the hall. They took a right and then a left and then another right and Copeland was confused because they were headed back to his room.

"Where are we going?" he asked.

"You will see." Martin opened the door to Copeland's room to allow him to walk in first. Copeland assumed they'd grab something and be on their way, so he was surprised when Martin shut the door and followed him in.

Martin walked through the main living space of the room and into the small sitting area that housed hundreds of books on shelves lining the walls. A wooden ladder leaned on tracks which allowed every book in the room to be reached and a brown, leather chair sat in the center of the room to create the perfect reading nook.

Martin walked to the back wall and went to pull out

a book.

Copeland let out a big laugh. "You know they're not real, right?" He chuckled. "It's all for show." He gestured to the book-lined shelves. "No one is allowed access to this much old literature." He added, "Not even me."

Ignoring him, Martin traced his hand along the spines of books and meticulously pulled some out and pushed some in further.

"Martin," Copeland tried again. "They're all empty." He pulled out a book and flipped through the pages, trying to show Martin that they were all blank, but Martin paid no attention. He continued to move the books, climbing up and down the ladder and moving it to various spots in the room.

Has he lost his mind, Copeland thought to himself? He took a seat in the chair and sighed. *This man, who is obsessively touching every empty book in this room, is the man destined to help me save humanity?*

After what seemed like an eternity, Martin climbed down the ladder and scanned the suite. He walked into every room to make sure no one was around. He walked back to the sitting area and directed a sly smile at Copeland.

"Are you ready?" Martin asked.

"Uh, I've been ready." Copeland pressed his lips together, annoyed at Martin's seemingly strange behavior.

Martin moved toward the shelves on the right-hand side once more and pulled another book out of line ever so slightly.

Before Copeland could sigh again at his strange tweaking, the center of the back wall of books began to silently move. Like a door, it opened and swung back to the left, leaving a little more than a foot of space to walk through.

"Woah." Copeland stood in awe. He'd lived in this very room his entire life and never once had he imagined the nook to be anything less than a useless library filled with blank pages.

"Hurry now," Martin instructed as he motioned for Copeland to enter first.

Copeland walked through the narrow door and into a black room. He heard Martin moving quietly around and after a few seconds, the light flickered on and Copeland stood mesmerized by the secret library. The expansive room was more than fifteen feet tall and shelving lined the walls. Books of all shapes and sizes filled every space on the shelves. Along the edge of the walls were stacks of books that didn't fit on the shelves. In the center of the room was a wooden desk piled high with papers and more books.

Copeland spun slowly in a circle, admiring every square inch of the spectacular room.

"This was your mother's study," Martin explained. "With the help of a few loyal servants, myself included, she was able to find this place. It had always been rumored Carnot was built with secret doors and hidden spaces. Camilla made it her mission to find them and when she found this spot, she made it her own."

Copeland didn't know what to say. "How?" was all he could get out.

"Well, once she cracked the code, it was quite simple."

"Where did you enter a code?" Copeland was confused.

"The books," Martin answered. "The books are the code."

"But that was so complex. You moved so many books."

"Yes... but your mother figured out the code and now it's easy."

"But how?" Copeland was nervous. Suddenly, his mother's wit seemed unattainable to him. "She could crack harrowing codes to unlock hidden rooms and I can barely handle an ex-girlfriend showing me a touch of hostility," he doubted himself. "I'm not cut out for this."

"Yes, you are," Martin encouraged. "You are smart; just like your mother. She knew you could handle it."

"You don't know that," Copeland nearly shouted. His heart was racing. He wanted nothing to do with this whole charade anymore. "I thought I could do it. I thought with your help I would be able to live up to my mother's wishes for my life but..." Copeland paused. "I can't do it. I'm not prepared for this." He moved back to where the door had been but now it was shut, and he didn't know how to exit the room.

Knowing he couldn't go anywhere, Martin slowly moved toward him. He placed his hand on his shoulder and waited for Copeland to look up. Once he met his gaze, he said encouragingly, "She knew you could do it. Please, don't give up yet. Read her notes. Read her letters. She worked so hard for you. Don't let her work go to waste."

Martin started to walk to the desk in the center of the room, with his hand still on Copeland's back, he followed. Copeland tentatively took a seat at the desk.

"I've read these notes and letters over one-hundred

times and I don't understand what they mean. Like I said, I am not the one who was supposed to lead this revolution. Your mother was supposed to be here for you and the least I can do to pass on her legacy is give you everything she left. Please, I'm begging you, take a look."

"But what am I looking for?" Copeland was still overwhelmed.

"I wish I knew." Martin sighed. "I wish I knew."

For a few moments, neither of them said a word. Martin knew he'd said all he could say, and he waited patiently for Copeland's response. Copeland ambivalently started moving papers around on the desk. He rubbed his temples, scratched his head and ran his hands through his hair.

"Okay," he finally exhaled. "I will take a look."

Chapter Thirty-Four

Vienna awoke from a sound night's sleep but instantly remembered the fears that had kept her awake for far too long into the night. She jumped out of bed and walked quickly to the door, her silk nightgown blowing behind her. She walked down the stairs and opened the front door, desperate to read what the papers were saying.

"Vienna! Over here!" a deep voice yelled.

"Vienna, how are you feeling today?" a woman shouted.

"How does it feel to be the most hated girl in Carnot?" someone else yelled.

Before Vienna could process the situation, she was yanked backwards into the house and the door shut rapidly behind her.

"Sorry, V," Beckham apologized. "I wanted to intercept you before you got to the paper, but I was a second too late."

Vienna leaned against the wall, her eyes still blinded by the flashes, and slouched down to the ground. She blinked rapidly, trying to get rid of the white spots in her vision.

"I take it the papers aren't good?" she asked, replaying the harsh comments she'd just heard in her head.

"They're not great." Beckham was shaking. "Let's get you some coffee and we'll look at them together."

She grabbed his hand, stood to her feet, and followed him to the kitchen.

"How long have they been here?" She asked as she looked back and saw the reflection of camera flashes on the front windows.

"At least since I've been up." Beckham motioned to the barstools at the kitchen counter. "Sit down."

Vienna followed his instructions and took a seat. She watched as Beckham got out a mug and poured her a cup of coffee. His hands were shaking violently and only half of the coffee he poured made it into the cup; the other half spilled onto the counter.

"How much coffee have you already had this morning?" Vienna asked, concerned.

"Four cups," Beckham spoke quickly, "or maybe five."

"What time exactly did you get up?" Vienna asked, realizing he hadn't answered the first time. She glanced at the clock on the wall to see it was only seven.

"Oh, I've been up since about five." He slurped a drink of coffee.

"Maybe you should cool it with that," Vienna suggested, pointing at his coffee. "Are you alright?"

"My mind has been racing." Beckham's face twitched. "That's all. Just firing on all cylinders this morning, I guess."

Vienna had never seen Beckham so wired.

"Have you figured anything out?" she asked.

Before Beckham could answer, Margaret came

walking into the kitchen.

"Good morn—"

She didn't finish her greeting, due to the soft shouts outside catching her attention.

"They've been here for hours," Beckham answered the question he knew was on his mother's mind.

"Oh my," she commented. "How do the papers look?"

"We haven't gotten there quite yet," Beckham replied. "Well, I have taken a glance, but I was about to bear it with Vienna. Maybe, it's best if we all take a look," he spoke quickly.

"Are you alright?" Margaret asked.

"Yep, just wired," Beckham's eyes were wide.

Vienna and Margaret exchanged concerned glances.

"Okay," Margaret unconvincingly replied. "Where is the paper?"

"Right here," Beckham grabbed it from behind him. Margaret took a seat next to Vienna and Beckham leaned on the counter next to them.

"Icy Roads Ahead as Summer Ends," Margaret read aloud. "Vienna Tunston, a no one from nowhere, catches Copeland Howth's eye, but the real question is why? Is it a ploy for power? A hate for Summer? Or an unlikely case of true love?"

"Ouch," Vienna commented with a grimace.

"Ouch is right," agreed Beckham taking another large slurp from his coffee.

"Last night, Copeland Howth took Vienna Tunston to Mickinley Park for—" Margaret continued.

"Could we maybe not read this aloud?" Vienna cut her off. "It's already worse than I imagined it would be."

"Of course. But you know it's not true," she

encouraged, though even she could hear the falsehood in her voice.

"It's okay. I don't need to be cheered up," Vienna replied. "I am going to go to school." She got up from the table and walked toward the stairs.

"It's barely after seven A.M.," Beckham said. "School doesn't start for another two hours."

"I'll walk slowly."

"Let me come with you at least," he offered.

Vienna shrugged. She was already too far into her head to respond. She went upstairs, got ready quickly and headed out the back door with Beckham in tow. Thankfully, the back alley was narrow and difficult to access, so no reporters were there. Vienna was especially thankful because in her haste, she'd nearly forgotten about them. Had they been at the back door, she wouldn't have been prepared. She pulled up the hood of her coat and walked with her head down. They walked in silence for a few blocks; their minds both racing.

"I have a theory," Beckham finally said.

"I'm all ears," she replied.

"I've been brainstorming the best ways to start the uprising."

Vienna refrained from rolling her eyes. *Isn't that what we've all been doing,* she thought to herself?

"I think we need to expose the government for their corruption," Beckham explained. "Right now, we don't have enough people on our side to revolt; they would easily kill us all next month. However, if we were able to expose them, and then they killed us, it might raise a red flag and we might be able to get more people to unite with us."

"That's great in theory," Vienna replied. "But how can we possibly expose them?"

"Dad," Beckham replied as if the answer was obvious.

"Dad?"

"Yes! We use his story."

"But we don't know his story," Vienna countered.

"True... but I might know someone who does." Beckham grinned. "We have time before school. Follow me."

Beckham started to run down the street, his backpack, slung over one shoulder, thumping against his side with every step. Vienna took off after him, trying hard to keep up with his long strides.

They ran quickly, and Vienna would have been tired except for the fact that she felt free. Her hood blew back and the wind whipped against her face, blowing her golden hair, and for the first time since her father had died, she felt truly alive. A sense of calm rushed through her veins and she couldn't put words to her feelings. In that simple moment, everything felt right.

They turned down a road and the serene feeling quickly escaped Vienna. Up ahead, she saw the Carnot mansion. Before she'd even realized it, she stopped in her tracks.

Beckham ran a few more steps before noticing he'd lost his sister. He jogged back to her.

"V, we're not going in."

She pulled her hood back up tightly. "I don't care if we're going in or not." Vienna was upset. "You heard the reporter this morning, I'm 'the most hated girl in Carnot,'" she quoted. "Why on earth would I go to the center of the city?"

"No one will recognize you," he lied.

"Beck, my face is blasted on every newspaper in town," Vienna argued.

Beckham had to admit he really hadn't done the best job of thinking this plan through. "We need to talk to Santi."

"Why?" Vienna asked.

"Santi," Beckham replied. "He's the head gate guard and he knows everyone."

"I know *who* Santi is." Vienna remembered her mother talking about him many times. "But why?"

"I remember Dad telling me a story about him just before he died. I thought about it this morning and I now wonder if it was more than just a story. I almost think it was a clue."

"A clue?" Vienna questioned. "What are you going to do? March up to him and see if he knows about the secret project Dad was supposedly working on before he died? Are you insane?" Afraid they were drawing too much attention, Vienna grabbed Beckham's arm and pulled him off the road and into an alley.

"Well, when you say it like that, it does sound insane," Beckham whispered. "But, what else can we do? I have one lead. At this rate, we're going to die next month anyway, so why don't I play the one card I have?"

Vienna wanted to argue but she really didn't have anything to say. *He makes a good point,* she thought. *We really don't have anything else to work with.*

"V," Beckham pleaded, sensing her hesitation. "Please."

Vienna sighed. "I can't go with you."

"I realize that now," Beckham said. "That was my mistake and I'm sorry." He paused. "But do you trust me to go?"

Vienna breathed in deeply. "Yes. I think we need to follow any leads we have, and you have one, so who am I to stop you?"

"Thanks, V." Beckham offered a soft smile.

"Well, what are you waiting for?" Vienna asked. "Go on. I'll meet you back at school."

"Okay." Beckham breathed in a nervous sigh. "Good plan, good plan."

"Good plan, good plan." Vienna grinned. They'd repeated that saying to each other countless times over the years and neither of them knew exactly where it came from but it made them feel confident.

Without another word, Beckham left the alleyway and started making his way quickly toward Carnot while Vienna pulled the strings of her hood a little tighter and started walking to school.

Chapter Thirty-Five

Beckham walked with eager confidence down the cobblestone road. He recalled the story his father told him three years earlier and tried to remember every minute detail.

A few weeks before his death, Lewis asked Beckham to run some errands with him one night. On the way, Beckham noticed his father was extra talkative. Lewis had always been a storyteller, but that particular November night now stood out in Beckham's mind. Beckham wanted to follow in his father's footsteps and work for the government, so it wasn't surprising to him that he was sharing anecdotes from work. He told him about a couple of big projects he was working on and shared stories of some of his co-workers. The one story that stuck out in his mind all these years later was about the guard at the gate known as Santi.

Beckham couldn't remember everything he said about him, but he did recall his father stopping in the middle of the road and turning to face him. With seriousness in his eyes, he said, "Santi has a kind soul. He is the type of young man you can trust *in* anything and *with* anything."

As Beckham replayed his father's comments, his confidence waivered. *A clue*, he thought to himself? *It was pretty generous of me to explain that comment as being a clue to Vienna.* His heart pounded. *But why would he have stopped like that and looked at me so intensely?* Beckham threw up his arms and looked to the sky. "Couldn't you have at least winked or something, Dad?" he asked aloud and realized he'd caught the attention of a few strangers walking the opposite way down the road. Embarrassed, he put his hands back in his pockets and continued walking. *It must have meant something*, he continued the debate in his head. *He would have known he was about to die, but he couldn't risk putting us in danger. Maybe that was his way of trying to communicate information.*

He became increasingly more anxious with each step to the guard shack. He had no idea what he was going to say.

With a few feet to go, he took a deep breath and approached the window.

"Good aftern— I mean, good morning," Beckham nervously corrected himself.

Santi, who had been shifting some papers on his desk, moved to the half-opened window and slid it open all the way.

"Good morning," he greeted with a wide, tender smile. "What can I do for you, bud?"

Beckham really hadn't gotten this far in planning the conversation. *Should I just ask him about my dad? Or for help*, he wondered to himself? Then, he remembered a quote his father often repeated and went out on a limb. "A wise man once said, 'the only way to find out if you can trust someone—'"

"'Is to trust that you can,'" Santi finished the quote. "You must be Lewis Tunston's son."

Beckham nodded with great relief. "Yes, I'm Beckham."

"It's nice to finally meet you, Beckham. I have heard nothing but the best things about you."

Beckham smiled. He didn't know what to say next.

"So, how can I help you today?" Santi asked.

Beckham had unrealistically hoped he wouldn't need to explain anything further. He took a deep breath and put the quote into action. "I think you may have some knowledge that could be useful to me," he said. "I am going out on a limb here, but I believe my father may have entrusted you with some classified information."

Without saying a word, Santi moved quickly to the back of the small guard shack and started sifting through a stack of papers. After a bit of searching, he grabbed a letter-sized white envelope and walked back to the window. He handed the envelope to Beckham and he immediately recognized the handwriting on the front of it. In his father's penmanship, it read, "Beckham Penn."

Beckham didn't know what to say. He couldn't believe his plan actually worked. "Thank you," was all he could get out.

Santi gave one nod of his head. "I am always happy to help a friend... and Lewis was one of the best. I think it would be better if you get out of here before anyone sees you."

Beckham could only manage to nod. He tucked the envelope under his arm and began to head toward the school. Snow began to fall lightly as he walked. He shivered as a chill wind whipped through the air. The snow started falling harder and he walked with his head down, trying not to get it on his face. In his haste to get back to Vienna and open the envelope, he ran into someone and dropped it on the wet ground.

"I'm sorry," he said as he hurried to pick it up.

"What are you doing in this area?" a familiar voice asked.

Beckham's stomach dropped. He quickly tucked the envelope into his jacket and crossed his arms.

"Oh." Beckham exhaled. "I was... uhm, stopping by my friend's house," he lied. "He has been sick, and I told my teacher I would pick up his homework for him, and Vienna went straight to school."

"I see." His mother smiled. "That was very nice of you. You should have said something. You could have ridden the train with me."

"Thanks, but it's quite alright," Beckham quickly replied. "It's a lovely day, so I enjoyed the walk."

Margaret looked around in disgust as the snow swirled in the air.

"You know I like the snow," Beckham added.

"No," Margaret plainly replied. "I didn't think you did."

"Well, anyhow," Beckham was really panicky now. "I better get to school. See you later." He waved as he started running away.

He ran faster back to the school than he had to the capital. Wet and breathing heavily, he approached Vienna in the cafeteria.

"You don't look good," she commented.

"I'm not." Beckham furrowed his brow. "Well, I kind

of am. I don't know." He pulled the envelope out of his jacket and it was surprisingly dry. "Santi gave me this envelope from Dad." He set it on the table in front of Vienna.

"Are you serious?" Vienna excitedly asked. "Truthfully, I didn't think your plan stood a chance... I mean, a random conversation with Dad years ago and you expected the security guard to have information? Never in a million years did I think it would work but that's amazing!"

Beckham took off his coat and sat down next to Vienna. It was still early to be at school, so the cafeteria was nearly empty, and they didn't need to worry about others overhearing them.

Beckham huffed. "Yeah, I guess it is."

"Beck, I feel like this is huge." Vienna was confused by his lack of excitement. "Why aren't you more excited?"

Beckham tensely rubbed his hands on his forehead. "After I spoke with Santi, I was in a hurry and it started snowing pretty heavily, so I was walking with my head down and I ran into someone and dropped the envelope."

"Okay?" Vienna still didn't understand Beckham's concern.

"It was Mom, V." Beckham shook his head. "Of all people, I ran into Mom."

"Did she see it?" Vienna now understood the severity of the situation. "It's clearly Dad's handwriting." She gestured toward the envelope with scribbly letters, in all caps, spelling Beckham's name.

"I don't honestly know," Beckham said. "She saw me pick up the envelope, but I told her it was my friend's homework."

"Did she buy it?"

"I don't know!" Beckham was overwhelmed by all of Vienna's questions. "I doubt it. You know I am a terrible liar and I was supposed to be with you." He let out an exasperated sigh. "I'm sorry, V." Beckham's cheeks were flushed, and he rubbed his hands on his face. "I tried but I might have messed it up. Surely, she is suspicious and that's my fault."

"Beck," Vienna interrupted. "It's okay. You did great. Let's not worry about what Mom may or may not be thinking. We can't control that." Vienna flipped the envelope over and started gently peeling back the seal. "Instead, let's focus on assessing the information you successfully got from Santi. You did a great job! I never would have known that Santi could have information for us. Like, this is honestly so crazy and exciting!"

Beckham breathed slowly. Vienna had always been able to speak some sense into him.

"You're right," he finally agreed. "Maybe, Mom really did buy it and I'm just overthinking it."

"Exactly," Vienna agreed. She finished opening the seal and reached into the envelope. She pulled out a thin stack of papers and set them on the table.

Chapter Thirty-Six

Margaret walked purposefully toward the gates of Carnot.

"Good morning, Margaret," Santi called in his usually chipper voice.

"Morning," Margaret mumbled. Wasting no time on small talk, she flashed her badge, Santi opened the gate and she sped up the sidewalk. Once inside, she raced to the right and started winding through halls she wasn't allowed in. There was little security stationed throughout the residential side of Carnot because crime and safety were not concerns for the city. People who worked in the government building knew better than to impose on the Howth family, but Margaret did not care. She needed to get to Theodore as soon as possible.

She approached the door to Theodore's bedroom and banged wildly on it.

"Theodore." she said as she knocked.

"Ma'am!" A security officer came around the corner. "You can't be back here!" He started running down the hall toward her.

To Margaret's great relief, the bedroom door opened,

and Theodore stepped out.

"It's quite alright, George," he assured the guard who was now standing next to them both. "I asked her here."

"Oh," the guard replied, his cheeks turning a faint red. "I'm sorry."

"It's alright. Off you go." Theodore spoke to the guard like a kindergartener.

"Have a nice day," the guard politely offered but neither Margaret nor Theodore returned the well wishes. They walked into Theodore's room and he closed the door behind them.

"I think we're in trouble." Margaret didn't waste a breath. "I saw Beckham this morning with an envelope and it had Lewis' handwriting on it," she continued. "I have no idea where he got it from, but he was quite flustered when he ran into me."

"I thought they trusted you," Theodore replied. "Why wouldn't he want to consult you about the envelope?"

Margaret sighed. "I made a comment yesterday about it possibly not being the right time to make any moves."

"You what?" Theodore looked at her with contempt.

"I was trying to protect you. It really was a casual comment and the kids seemed fine last night," she fibbed. "It wasn't until our run-in this morning that I truly became worried."

Theodore huffed and began pacing the room.

"But," Margaret added, "I have an idea."

Theodore looked intently at her, waiting for her to explain.

"We leak a story," she said.

"About what?" Theodore asked.

"Lewis and Camilla."

"What about them?"

Margaret didn't answer. She raised her eyebrows, waiting for him to catch on.

"Oh." Theodore nodded slightly, finally understanding. "Like us, but about them." He pointed his finger gesturing at the two of them and then to an empty space to represent the other two.

"Exactly." Margaret grinned. "If we sever the trust between our children and their oh-so-perfect other parents," she rolled her eyes, "we might be able to create enough doubt that they stop their pursuit."

"Do you really think that would work?" Theodore was uncertain. "How could we even get the story out? Why would either of us go to the press to uncover a story like that years after our partners have passed?"

Margaret smiled a sly and fiendish smile. "We won't be the ones to share the story."

"Who will?" Theodore questioned.

"Summer," Margaret straightforwardly replied.

"Summer Nile?" Theodore's forehead wrinkled into disordered lines.

"Yes."

"Why would she do that?"

"Because your son didn't ask her to be his date to his birthday party and from what I hear, she is pretty upset about it," Margaret explained. "Supposedly, she already threatened to go to the press about a story I am assuming she doesn't have. So, I suggest, we swoop in and give her one."

Theodore began to pace again, his mind analyzing the proposal. After a few moments, he turned with an evil grin.

"That just might work," he agreed. "But how do we get the information to her? How do we know she won't turn on us?"

"You're the leader of Carnot." Margaret was slightly annoyed she needed to explain his power to him. "Bribe her or something." She threw up her hands. "Plus, if she receives direct orders from you to expose the story, she's not going to do anything but oblige."

"Hmm," Theodore hummed. "Do you think fifty years of guaranteed life will be enough?"

"I think that plus a VIP invitation to Copeland's birthday party would be plenty," Margaret suggested.

"What would a VIP invitation be?" he asked.

"I don't know." Margaret shrugged. "But who cares? Make something up."

"How are we going to know she shares what we want her to share with whom we want her to share it?" Theodore was a detail-oriented man and he didn't like loose ends.

"Hmm." Margaret tapped her fingers together, thinking hard. "What if you hand deliver it to her?"

"Maggie, you know I cannot show up to her house unannounced like that. It would cause tremendous attention."

"What if I delivered it on your behalf?" she quickly suggested.

Theodore thought aloud, "It's unlikely she'll know who you are... though it is possible."

"Doubtful," Margaret replied. "Plus, the city we live in is not supposed to house corrupt people." She winked.

He wanted to find a flaw in her suggestion, but he couldn't think of one big enough to say 'no.'

"Annnd," Margaret added one final point to help convince him, "from what I understand, Summer can't turn down even the smallest piece of gossip."

Theodore breathed in heavily. "I think we may have ourselves a plan," he proclaimed.

"Now, we just need the details." Margaret grinned. "Do you have time now?"

"I always have time for you." Theodore moved toward her and wrapped her tight in his arms. He ran his hand slowly down her spine and onto her butt.

"But we don't have time for that." Margaret winked as she looked up at him.

He kissed her lips. "It's always worth a try." He let go of her. "I guess we should get to work."

They spent the next hour drafting up fake details, information and sources about the affair. They ensured every attribute was buttoned up with no flaws to make the story one-hundred percent believable and accurate.

When they were finished, Margaret took the drafted press release and placed it in an official government envelope; complete with the official ivy leaf seal of Carnot. The emblem was slightly different than that which was placed on Ivy Letters. This one was, of course, not edible. The official seal featured golden ivy vines that formed a nearly complete circle around a single, green ivy leaf.

Margaret gave Theodore a kiss goodbye and left for Summer's house. It was likely too early for Madison to be in the office anyway, but Margaret didn't care to notify her about possibly being late. After all, she had all the job security and protection she needed with Theodore.

Summer was supposedly homeschooled, though it

was no secret that she typically spent her days home alone. Her father's job kept him busy nearly 24/7 and her mother spent most of her time at the bar in the Rastler Hotel.

It was only a few blocks walk to the Niles' home. The residential street they lived on was perfectly manicured with a median that ran down the center full of horse-chestnut trees. Though it was winter, and the trees had no leaves on them, the grass in every yard was still emerald green. Margaret had never been to the Niles' house. She looked down at the piece of paper Theodore had scribbled the address on.

"638," she read. She looked up to see she was passing a house numbered 580. A *few more to go*, she thought to herself. She continued to walk quickly down the road with her scarf wrapped over the bottom half of her face, at the off chance anyone would see her. Luckily for her, the street was quiet, and the only person she saw passed on the opposite side of the road pushing a stroller.

Finally, she approached the house numbered 638. The walnut features of the Tudor style home perfectly contrasted the white and gray stone. Although the architecture was vintage, it was clearly well kept.

Margaret had not been nervous about speaking with Summer until she went to knock on the front door. She paused, with her hand in the air, halfway to the lion door knocker and took a deep breath. She knocked three times with the metal handle and waited patiently. She heard movement inside and the doorknob started rattling. After a few seconds, the door opened, and Summer stood, perfectly made up, staring back at her.

"Hello." Summer's brows were knit. "How can I help you?"

"Hi, Summer," Margaret started. "My name is Mar-a," she corrected herself mid-sentence. "I am here on official business on behalf of Theodore Howth." She tried to sound professional. "He has sent me with confidential information he believes you have reason to be interested in."

"Oh." Summer was shocked, but she couldn't hide her sheer delight at the idea that Theodore thought her worthy of such information. "Come on in," she invited.

Margaret gawked at the immaculate entryway. The wooden stairs to her left rounded extravagantly to the second floor and the hardwood floors had to be original. The living room opened up with high wood-beamed ceilings and two chandeliers made of three layers of candle lights that would have looked out of place anywhere but in this home.

"Your home is beautiful," Margaret complimented as she took a seat on the light gray sectional. Summer sat down, her posture as straight as a board, a few feet away from Margaret on the couch.

"Thank you," she replied.

"Theodore is in need of some help with the press," Margaret began.

"Then, why doesn't he ask for the help of my father?" Summer questioned.

"Confidential and discreet help, darling," Margaret elucidated. "In exchange for this envelope," she rubbed her hand over the top of the letter sitting in her lap, "and you following the instructions step by step, Theodore will grant you fifty years of guaranteed life—"

"Oh my," Summer gasped.

"As well as a VIP invitation to Copeland's birthday party," Margaret finished.

"Wow," Summer replied. "That is quite the offer." She managed to stay calm and collected on the outside but inside, her heart was pounding. She hadn't been so excited since the first time Copeland kissed her and nothing turned her on more than a juicy piece of gossip.

"It is," Margaret agreed. "So, do we have a deal?"

"Yes," Summer reached out to shake her hand. Margaret grasped hers and gave one firm shake. "We have a deal."

"Wonderful," Margaret replied. She let go of her hand and grabbed the envelope off of her lap. She passed it to Summer and in no time, she was on her knees, over-looking the envelope's contents spread out on the cof-fee table.

"Is this true?" Summer asked as she scanned the pages. "Why would Theodore want this story exposed?"

"I am not permitted to speak on any of the content or motives," Margaret answered. She didn't want to outright lie, so she figured that was a good answer.

Summer sighed and continued to read through the information. "So, I simply need to contact the press and send this release," she picked up a piece of paper, "and keep my mouth shut?" She wanted to make sure she understood everything correctly.

"Yes," Margaret confirmed. "As long as the press receives all of the information in that packet and runs the exact story as it is written there," she pointed, "then you will fulfill your end of the bargain, assuming you never tell a soul."

Summer nodded slightly.

"Of course, should it ever be found out that you do tell someone, you will be killed in the next round of Ivy Letters," Margaret threatened.

Summer gulped. "How... I mean, the Ivy Letters are random—"

Margaret thickly interrupted, "We don't want to find out that the Ivy Letters can be tampered with, do we? I surely wouldn't want to take that chance, per these specific instructions. I was told to relay the information to you, and you are to do with it what you must. Although I must say a deal including your silence seems to be in your best interest."

Summer breathed in heavily, weighing her options. "When does he want me to release the story?"

"Ideally, he would like it to be on the front page of every newspaper tomorrow morning," Margaret answered. "You know better than me what needs to be done to make that happen."

"Okay," Summer agreed. "I can do that."

"Wonderful!" She was pleasantly surprised with Summer's uneasy mix of motivation and fear. *She's right where we want her*, she thought to herself. "Can I trust you with handling the rest? Or do you need any of my help?" she asked aloud.

"I think I can handle it." Summer stood up. "Thank you for the opportunity."

Margaret followed her lead and stood up. She reached out her hand and Summer eagerly shook it.

"You're very welcome," Margaret replied.

"Let me walk you out."

"That's quite alright. You have a lot of work to get done."

Summer nodded and Margaret gracefully walked toward the front door, an ingenious smile sweeping across her face.

Chapter Thirty-Seven

Copeland awoke suddenly to light streaming in from the door. He picked up his head and, for a moment, couldn't remember where he was. He sat up and a piece of paper remained stuck to his face. He pulled it off, shut his eyes tight and rubbed them.

"Sir," Martin said sounding alarmed. "We have a situation."

Copeland's back hurt from the way he'd been sleeping. He didn't remember falling asleep in the library or Martin leaving, but he knew both of those things must have happened.

"What's going on?" Copeland stretched his arms as high as they would go.

"I'm afraid Summer has reached out to the press." Martin walked to Copeland and set the newspaper he'd been carrying on the desk in front of him.

Copeland's jaw dropped. He stared at the page, blinking slowly, over and over again, hoping what he was reading would change. He pinched his arm. "Please tell me this is just a dream, Martin. Tell me I am still sleeping."

Martin rubbed his hand on his forehead. "I wish I

could, sir."

"Is it true?" Copeland asked, desperately wishing for the answer to be 'no.'

"I..." Martin paused. "I don't believe so, but if I am being honest, the only reason I don't think so is because I regard my sister," he admitted. "I have no concrete evidence to say otherwise."

Copeland inhaled slowly. "'An affair for the ages,'" he read the headline aloud. "'Nearly three years ago, we lost our beloved Camilla Howth. Although she may have died peacefully in her sleep, it seems her past did not die with her. Inside sources of the Howth family confirmed the suspicion earlier this week that she was indeed having an affair during the year prior to her death with a man named Lewis Tunston. Lewis had been a lifelong friend to Camilla, and she'd hired him to work for the family soon after her marriage to Theodore. Coincidence? We think not.'" Copeland slammed the paper onto the desk. "This is garbage!" he exclaimed. "It simply cannot be true!"

"I agree." Martin, though fuming on the inside, tried to stay calm.

Copeland rubbed the bridge of his nose. "Where do we even go from here?" Copeland asked. "Is any of this even true?" He gestured to his mother's papers he'd been combing through scattered all over the desk.

"Yes," Martin confirmed. "I know this has to be true. This was more than just Camilla. This was, and is, my family's seminal work." He was desperate for Copeland to believe him.

"I need to talk to Vienna." Copeland couldn't sit and think about things any longer; he needed to get out and do something. He stood up and walked to the small button on the wall, which he now knew opened the door, and pressed it.

Martin followed him. "Sir, if you leave Carnot, it's going to be a mess out there. You will be inundated with reporters and photographers."

"Oh my gosh." Copeland slowly ran his hands up his face and through his hair. "I didn't even think about what this looks like between Vienna and me now. I asked the daughter of my mother's supposed lover to be my date to my birthday party." His hands were now wrapped around the back of his neck and he strained to look up at the ceiling.

Martin knew the situation was bad, but until Copeland had spelled it out like that, he hadn't quite grasped the weight of it all.

"Just give me a second to think," Martin said. He walked through the library door and began to pace in Copeland's bedroom. "You're right; you do need to talk to Vienna, but the question is, how to make that happen. You could meet her at the theater I took you to, but you'd have to get there without being seen and we'd have to get the message to her without it being intercepted. I am in the clear because no one cares about me, so I can get the message to Vienna," he concluded. "But you... you." He closed his eyes tightly. "How do we get you there?" he thought aloud.

"The whole fake-worker switcheroo thing worked last time," Copeland reminded him.

"Yes," Martin agreed. "But it's Saturday and barely anyone is here." He scratched his head. "A car is definitely not an option. It would cause too much attention."

He sighed. "Maybe, you're right. Maybe, a switcheroo of sorts will be our best bet. Give me a few minutes. Let me see if I can gather some supplies."

Copeland nodded and Martin left the room in a hurry. Copeland paced, thinking about what he would say to Vienna.

Do I think it's true? Does she think it's true? Does it make it weird for us to date? I actually quite liked her. He shook his head. *Not our focus right now, Copeland,* he reprimanded himself. *If it is true, does that affect our plans or can we still move forward? Why would it matter if our parents had an affair? The government is still corrupt. Will she feel the same?*

Martin swung the door open and came back into the room empty handed.

"That doesn't look like a disguise," Copeland commented in a failed attempt to lighten the mood.

"I've got an idea! No disguise needed."

"What?!"

"We'll go to Tellmen's," Martin replied. "We were supposed to have a meeting next week with them to discuss arrangements for your party, but I can say it got moved up. Then, we can take the car, be out in public, and no one will suspect a thing. It's going to be much easier to get Vienna to Tellmen's without causing a scene than it would be to sneak you out of here."

"I like it," Copeland agreed. "Well done, Martin."

"Thank you, sir. I'm going to arrange for a car and call Chelsea to ensure it's alright if we stop by today. I am sure she can arrange for us to meet in a room without any windows for privacy. Once that's settled, I'll work on getting Vienna there to meet you."

"Wait." Copeland had an idea. "You should get Vienna there first. The second I get there, you can guarantee it will be surrounded by press, but if she gets there before me, they won't have any idea she's already inside when I arrive."

"Great point!" Martin exclaimed. "Wonderful! I will head over to the Tunston's now and explain the plan. You stay put in here and don't talk to anyone. I'll be back to get you as soon as possible."

"Sounds good," Copeland agreed, and Martin excitedly left the room.

Chapter Thirty-Eight

Margaret was sitting on the couch in the living room when she saw the shadow of a man pass by the windows. She knew if someone was walking in front of the house, they were one of two things: a neighbor or government official. In their instructions to Summer, they'd asked her to arrange for the block in front of the Tunston home to be barricaded for privacy purposes. When Margaret got the paper earlier in the morning, she was pleased to see it was successfully being guarded.

She heard a knock on the door and got up to open it.

"Archie!" she beamed.

"Hi, Margaret," he replied. "Can I come in?"

"Of course." She opened the door a little wider.

"Where are Beckham and Vienna?"

"They're still sleeping," Margaret replied. "I think they were up pretty late last night."

The day had already felt extremely long to Martin, so he was surprised to see that his watch said it was only eight in the morning.

"Oh, I see. I am sorry about the article. Did you have any idea?"

"Did I have any idea my husband was having an affair?" Margaret pretended to be offended. "No, I wasn't aware my husband of over sixteen years had been having an affair with Carnot's paramount lady," she spoke with disgust.

"I'm sorry. I shouldn't have asked." Martin was nervous. "If it makes you feel any better, I didn't know about my sister either."

"Oh, my apologies," Margaret genuinely replied. She'd momentarily forgotten he was related to Camilla. "I should have known this hurts you as much as it hurts me."

"It's quite alright." Martin never liked being vulnerable. He cut straight to the chase. "Copeland asked me to relay a message to Vienna. He would like to meet with her as soon as possible."

"What for?" Margaret asked.

Martin wore a puzzled expression. *Isn't it obvious?* he thought. "The article," he answered aloud.

"Oh, of course." Margaret offered a fake smile. *You knew this would happen,* she reminded herself. *You knew they wouldn't suddenly give up.*

"Do you think you'd be able to get Vienna to Tellmen's in about an hour?" Martin asked. "I didn't anticipate the insane amount of press when we came up with this plan."

Margaret tapped her finger on her face and thought about the options. "I think I could get her out the back and maneuver through some alleys," Margaret thought aloud. "Yes, I know just the path and with a large coat and winter hat, we should be able to make that happen."

"Wonderful!" Martin was ecstatic the plan was

coming together. "I will head back to Carnot now to get Copeland ready. We will plan to be there thirty minutes after you, as to not arouse any suspicion."

"Sounds like a plan," Margaret agreed and with that, Martin was quickly out the door, and on his way back to Carnot.

Margaret took a sip of the coffee she'd been drinking before Martin's arrival and was disappointed to find it was already slightly lukewarm. She dumped it out in the kitchen sink before grabbing her winter coat and scarf from the coat tree by the front door. She put on her coat and wrapped the plaid scarf around her neck as she picked up the newspaper from the coffee table.

She folded the paper in half, perfectly displaying the front page headline, and set it on the kitchen counter before quietly leaving the house out the back door.

Chapter Thirty-Nine

Copeland sat on the brown, leather bench in front of his bed and anxiously tapped his foot. He'd calculated Martin's trip to the Tunston's at least fifteen times in his head and he knew Martin should be back any second. He heard the doorknob turn and with great relief, he saw Martin walking into the room and excitedly stood up.

"All is well and going according to plan, sir," he announced. "I spoke with Margaret and she is going to get Vienna to Tellmen's in an hour." Martin looked at his watch. "Or actually about forty minutes now."

"Great." Copeland was pleased. "So, we'll leave in about twenty?"

"I think we should leave in about forty-five," Martin corrected. "We don't want to arrive too closely; on the off chance someone would spot Vienna walking in."

"Touché," Copeland agreed. He sat back down and restlessly started tapping his foot again.

"Did you find anything in your reading last night?" Martin tried to make conversation to pass the time. He grabbed an accent chair and turned it to face Copeland. A week ago, he would never have dared to casually sit and chat with Copeland; their relationship had been strictly formal and followed all of the official protocols. But now, so much had changed, and though he'd always been Copeland's uncle, he could actually act like it.

Copeland sighed deeply. "I wish. It seemed that most of my mother's and," Copeland paused, not particularly wanting to say Lewis' name, "it seemed most of *their* research was focused on how to start an uprising. They spent a lot of time thinking about how they could get people to join their side and prove that the government was acting corruptly."

"And?" Martin prompted, seeing that Copeland was done with his statement.

"And I'm just not sure that's the best way to go about it," he admitted.

"Well, how do you think it should be done?"

"I'm not exactly sure... but I don't know that violence should be fought with violence," he explained. "You see, before we had eternal life, people were able to choose between good and bad. On a basic level, they could choose to help an old lady cross the street or opt to scream at her to move faster instead. Whereas now, our only real option is to help her cross the street. We're forced to do good because choosing bad isn't an option."

"That is sort of true," Martin agreed. "But don't we know choosing bad really is still an option? If it wasn't, how would people like your father be able to choose to kill people out of hate?" He didn't want to say the next part, but he worked up the courage. "Or my sister be able to cheat on her husband? If this world is perfect and only allows good, why is there still misconduct?"

"That's precisely the question," Copeland agreed. "There were a number of books regarding psychology in there," he pointed toward the library, "a subject I'd never heard of before. The books are full of information about the science of the mind and human behavior. In Carnot, we're not able to think for ourselves, or so it seems." He was pacing again, deep in thought. "I think we're suffering from false consensus effect," Copeland explained. "I don't think we need to fight our way out... I think we need to think our way out."

"False consensus effect?" Martin had never heard the term and hardly could repeat it back.

"The tendency to see one's behavioral choices as relatively common and appropriate to existing circumstances while viewing other responses as uncommon, aberrant or inappropriate." He sounded like he was quoting a textbook.

"Okay," Martin tried to process the definition, "but what does that mean?"

"Honestly, I am not exactly sure," Copeland confessed. "I am really hoping Vienna can help."

Martin nodded in agreement. "I am hopeful she can."

The next forty minutes ticked by ever so slowly. Copeland was starving but didn't want to risk seeing anyone, so Martin went to get him some breakfast. He ate a bagel with strawberry cream cheese and drank his coffee as leisurely as possible, but it still wasn't time to leave.

After a couple games of checkers, Martin finally said, "I think we can head out now."

"Great!" Copeland jumped up. "Let's do it."

He followed Martin out to the porte-cochère on the

backside of the mansion and into the black town car. They rode out through the main entrance and Copeland was relieved to see that a relatively normal number of journalists were waiting at the gates.

"I figured there would be more," he commented.

"The rest are at the Tunston's," Martin explained.

"Oh." Copeland felt less relieved.

They rode through the city streets and the press followed them. Copeland was thankful the ride didn't take long. They pulled up to Tellmen's and his security detail forged a path for him to walk to the door.

The reporters shouted at him from every direction.

"Copeland, how do you feel about your mother's affair?"

"Copeland! Does this change your relationship with Vienna?"

"Over here!"

"Copeland, look this way!"

Copeland made it inside and inhaled. "Phew, guess it could have been worse."

"I suppose so," Martin agreed.

"Hello." Chelsea was waiting right inside the door. "How are you doing today?" She curtsied.

"Great," Martin replied. "Thank you for allowing us to meet here on such short notice. We appreciate your hospitality and confidentiality."

"Of course." She smiled. "We appreciate your business. Follow me." She gestured and turned around. "She is already here."

Martin and Copeland followed her up the stairs while the security officers stayed down by the doors. They walked up two flights and took a left. They entered an expansive room with high ceilings and wooden floors. The only supports were white, metal columns spread evenly throughout the space. Copeland imagined the room was once full of life with instrument makers building and designing grand pianos.

In the center of the room was a round table with five chairs. Martin had asked for five in case Beckham and Margaret decided to join Vienna, but only one was occupied.

"I'll leave you to it," Chelsea said. She closed the door and left the room.

"Hello." Margaret stood to greet them. She curtsied slightly to Copeland.

"Where's Vienna?" Copeland asked, concern filling his face.

"I'm so sorry, Copeland," she apologized. "I couldn't get her to come. She was absolutely mortified at the article and she said she didn't want to see you."

"What?" Copeland was upset. "I need to talk to her. I asked her to be here. No," he corrected, "I sent her orders to be here. I am Heir to Carnot; she must follow my orders." Copeland only played the imperial card when he was really upset.

"Sir," Martin tried to calm him down. He placed his hand on his shoulder. "It's okay. I am sure Margaret can help us."

"No," Copeland jerked his shoulder away from Martin's hand. "It's not okay. I need Vienna, not Margaret. This is ridiculous. We went through all this effort to meet her here and she doesn't show." Copeland rolled his eyes. "What did you tell her?"

"I told her Martin stopped by and asked if she'd meet

you here in an hour. She said she didn't care to meet with you anymore. She's angry at her father, not you," Margaret explained. "She doesn't believe anything he's said now, and she doesn't care to live out his," she lifted her hands to make quotes in the air, "'silly plans for a revolution.'"

Copeland angrily ran his hands through his hair, pulling at it. "What?" he yelled. He gritted his teeth. "I don't believe this. She is the only one who can help me. How dare she ignore a request to meet the Heir of Carnot? Doesn't she think there's a possibility the news could be fake?"

He's so full of himself, Margaret thought as she restrained from rolling her eyes. "I'm sorry," she sounded sincere. "I begged her to come but she wouldn't listen. I don't think she's going to be leaving the house for a while now. She's utterly embarrassed."

"This is a nightmare." Copeland rubbed his head. "Without her, I can't move forward. It was essential to my mother's plan that I find her."

I was hoping you'd say that, Margaret thought to herself and held back a grin. "Again, I am truly sorry. Maybe, she just needs some time to cool down," she said aloud.

"There's no time to cool down," Copeland huffed. He shook his head with frustration. "I'm done here." He walked out of the room and Martin shrugged hopelessly at Margaret; he didn't know what to say.

Martin chased Copeland down the hall. "Copeland!" he called. "Copeland, calm down."

"I can't calm down, Martin. Everything is falling apart. It's over. I've let my mom down. She's let me down. Vienna hates me. There's no point in keeping up this charade anymore. Our country is broken, and it always will be." By now, Copeland had walked down the steps and he stopped at the bottom. "Please cancel my birthday party," he instructed. "It would be embarrassing to show up without a date and I'm in no mental state to celebrate." He walked to the door and back outside.

Chapter Forty

Vienna walked downstairs, stretching her arms and neck from a relaxing night's sleep. She'd managed to make it through school yesterday with attention like nothing she'd ever received. Despite the negative press, for once in her life, she had been insanely popular. Evidently, high school girls care less about what the newspapers say and more about what it's like to kiss Copeland, and she didn't dare correct them on the fact that she hadn't actually kissed him. Even though the relationship was fake, Vienna relished every moment of flattery, and Beckham didn't seem to mind the extra attention either.

Everything was going well. They'd worked late into the night paging through the envelope of research their father had left them. They couldn't wait to meet up with Copeland and show him what they'd found. The envelope was filled with pages of research and a note, that looked as though it had been hastily scribbled, addressed to Beckham.

Beckham,

If you've somehow received this envelope, I sincerely commend you on your intuition. I've run out of time to present this information to Camilla and I think it could be critical to the research.

We all know I will die this month and I couldn't risk this information getting intercepted by anyone, not even your mother. Please take a look at everything I have compiled here.

I believe in you both.

I love you,

Dad

"Mom," Vienna called as she walked down the stairs. It sounded oddly quiet. She looked at the clock on the wall and saw it was 9:45 A.M. *Wow, I guess I was tired,* she thought to herself. Hearing no response, she walked into the kitchen to fix herself a cup of coffee. She didn't care to read the newspaper after yesterday, but the perfectly folded print caught her eye.

"'An affair for the ages.'" She read the headline. *Ohh, scandalous,* she thought to herself. She unfolded the paper and read it silently. "'Nearly three years ago, we lost our beloved Camilla Howth. Although she may have died peacefully in her sleep, it seems her past did not die with her. Inside sources of the Howth family confirmed the suspicion earlier this week that she was indeed having an affair during the year prior to her death with a man named Lewis Tunston.'"

Vienna closed her eyes and shook her head, assuming she'd read it incorrectly. She tried again, reading more rapidly this time. "'Nearly three years ago, we lost our beloved Camilla Howth. Although she may have died peacefully in her sleep, it seems her past did not die with her. Inside sources of the Howth family confirmed the suspicion earlier this week that she was indeed having an affair during the year prior to her death with a man named Lewis Tunston.'"

"What?" she exploded aloud. "What?" She couldn't handle reading another word. She ran upstairs, paper in hand, and stormed into Beckham's room.

Beckham, who had been sound asleep, sat up with a great startle. "What's going on? Are you okay?" he asked.

"No!" Vienna fulminated. "I am positively not okay." She threw the newspaper on top of Beckham's comforters. He sat up quickly and scanned the paper.

"What?" Beckham asked. "What is this?"

"I don't know," Vienna replied. "Do you think it's true?"

Beckham thought about all of the information they'd gathered in the last week of their lives. He sighed, distracted by his thoughts.

Remember how easy life was ten days ago? Not a worry in the world, he thought to himself, then snapped out of it.

"I guess it could make sense," he replied aloud. "It sounds like they did spend a lot of time together... plus, both Camilla and Dad made notes about Mom's trustworthiness or lack thereof... but maybe, they were the ones who couldn't be trusted. It's hard to spend that much time with someone and share the same interests and not fall in love."

"What do you know about falling in love?" Vienna was worked up. "Dad would never have done that to Mom. I just don't see it happening... Mom on the other hand, I wouldn't be surprised." She rolled her eyes. "But Dad, no way." She sat down on the edge of the bed.

Beckham wanted to respond but he didn't know what to say. He knew she was right. They sat quietly for a few moments.

"Well, what do we do about it?" he finally asked.

"That's what I am trying to figure out. If we could talk to Copeland, then maybe, we could come up with a plan... maybe, he knows more."

"Do you think Summer leaked the article?" Beckham wondered aloud.

"I would assume it had to have come from her."

"How are we going to get to Copeland?" Beckham asked. His mind was spinning like a top.

"I really don't know." Vienna sighed. "I'm guessing he'll want to talk to me too, but I don't know. We were originally waiting to see how the papers responded to our first date... which wasn't great," she added, "and now, with this, I'm not sure he'll want to be seen with me anymore."

"He needs you, V," Beckham encouraged. "Plus, he likes you."

"Number one, you don't know that," Vienna corrected, "and two, can you even date someone if your dad and their mom had an affair? Is that even allowed? Who cares?" Vienna moved on. "It's not about dating him anyway. It's about restoring Carnot. Let's just think things through. If he asks me on another date, we're golden. No problem. We can talk about everything then. But, if he doesn't, what do we do?"

"Surely, he will reach out, even if he doesn't want to go on a date. I don't think he would go on such a public date with you and never call. Plus, this," he motioned toward the paper, "has to be a lot for him to process as well."

"That's true." Vienna scratched her forehead. "I know we're not exactly trusting Mom at the moment... but if this is true, it's probably a lot for her as well."

Beckham was annoyed. He'd been so frustrated with his mother, the last thing he wanted was to feel bad for her. "I guess you're right. Is she here?"

"I don't think so. I called for her when I went downstairs, and she didn't answer."

"Where would she go?" Beckham asked. "I feel like the last thing I'd do if an article was written about an affair my late husband had would be go out in public."

Vienna raised her eyebrow. "That's a really good point." She jumped up from the bed and quickly made her way down the stairs. Beckham followed. They made it to the bottom of the steps, and she was shocked to see her mother sitting at the dining table, casually sipping a cup of coffee and eating a warm cinnamon roll.

"Mom, when did you get here?" Vienna asked.

Margaret looked back at her, confused. "Uhm, what do you mean?"

"I was down here like five minutes ago and I called your name, but you didn't answer," Vienna replied.

"Strange... I've been up since 7:00. I must not have

heard you from the bedroom," she lied.

"How are you holding up?" Beckham asked as he took a seat at the kitchen table.

Vienna wasn't totally sold on her mother's story, but Beckham had already moved on, so she joined them at the table.

"I'm alright," Margaret sadly replied. "I'd always had my doubts about your father and the late nights he spent at the office, but he told me it was about his research and, silly me, I believed him."

"I'm sorry, Mom," Beckham sincerely replied.

"It's okay," Margaret said. "Honestly, I'm more upset about the drama it caused Vienna. How unfortunate."

"Yeah," Vienna apathetically agreed. "How unfortunate."

"The worst part is, you don't even know the half of it." Margaret dramatically put her hands to her face.

Beckham and Vienna exchanged perplexed looks.

"What are you talking about?" Vienna asked.

"Martin stopped by this morning with a message from Copeland," Margaret began. *At least that part is true*, she laughed to herself. "He said Copeland was very upset and no longer wants to take you as his date to his birthday party."

"What?" Vienna was in disbelief. "Did he say anything else?"

"Not really." Margaret pretended to be disappointed. "It sounded like Copeland was upset with his mother, not you. I think he feels betrayed. Martin said he doesn't know if he can believe anything she said anymore."

Vienna slouched down in her chair. She hadn't thought about this scenario. An option in which she'd never get to speak with Copeland again. "I can't believe he wouldn't talk with me directly." Vienna was mad. "I mean, seriously, he sent his assistant to do it for him? What a joke."

"I'm sorry, sweetie," Margaret comforted.

"Sorry, V," Beckham added.

"It's alright." Vienna stood up. "I think I just need some fresh air."

"Uhm, I'm afraid that might not be possible," Margaret replied. "Due to the article, the government has closed our block. I don't think there's any way you can get out and not be seen."

"Seriously?" Vienna angrily pulled her ponytail. "Ugh!" She stomped up the steps and slammed the door to her room.

She paced back and forth, recalling all of the information she'd received. She replayed every conversation, from her first run-in with Copeland to the present moment.

"What am I missing?" she asked herself over and over again. "What am I missing?"

Her mind raced, questioning whether or not the affair was real, questioning why Copeland would give up so quickly, and more than anything, questioning why she'd gotten involved in the first place.

Chapter Forty-One

Beckham sat in his room, with the pages his father left him sprawled across the floor. After his sister had stormed out of the kitchen, he grabbed a cinnamon roll, a thermos of coffee and locked himself in his bedroom.

He read and re-read every ounce of information, trying desperately to piece it together. Over and over again he read. He read and then paced, then plopped onto his bed and read again. He didn't know what he was searching for, but he wanted desperately to find it. Something felt off but he couldn't quite put his finger on it.

"Beckham," his mother called. "Dinner's ready."

"Dinner?" Beckham looked up at the clock on the wall and saw it was nearly 6:00 P.M. *Oh my*, he thought. He'd been working all day and had very little to show for it.

"Coming," he called back. He gathered all of the papers and neatly stacked them together. He lifted up the edge of his mattress and placed the stack under it.

He walked downstairs and saw Vienna and his mother were already seated at the table. Vienna appeared as though she'd spent most of the day crying. Her skin looked dry and her eyes were red.

"What are we having?" he asked. He grimaced when he saw the vegetable stew staring back at him from the pot. He cleared his throat, forcing a smile. "How delicious."

"Considering I couldn't really go outside today, this was the best I could do," Margaret replied.

Beckham took a seat and they all served up their food.

"Are there at least crackers to put on top of it?" he asked.

"There should be," Margaret answered. "Check the cabinet."

Beckham stood up and walked to the kitchen. He opened the cabinet furthest to the left and was pleased to find a box of saltines. He took the box back to the table. No one was talking but then again, no one really had anything to say.

"What have you been up to all day?" Margaret finally asked.

"Nothing," Beckham lied. "I slept for most of it. I think I am tired from schoolwork."

"Me too," agreed Vienna.

"Well, I am glad you got some much-needed rest. Maybe, it was a blessing in disguise to have our house swarmed by press today," Margaret suggested.

Neither Vienna nor Beckham felt like responding.

They ate the rest of their meal in silence. The room was an odd mix of passive aggressive anger and distrust.

After dinner, Beckham went back to his room and studied the pages again.

He'd easily read the snippet about false consensus effect one-hundred times but the one-hundred-and-first, something clicked. He wanted to scream with excitement, but he couldn't risk his mother hearing him. He assumed she was downstairs, drinking her normal evening glass of wine and reading her illegal book. He opened his door as quietly as possible and tiptoed down the hall. The house was darker than he'd expected.

What time is it, he wondered? He successfully made it to Vienna's door and right when he reached for the knob, she opened it. She opened her mouth in fear but before she got out a sound, Beckham covered it. He grabbed her and walked her quickly back to her bed. He let go of her mouth and she started breathing rapidly. Beckham quickly moved to shut the bedroom door.

"I'm sorry," he whispered. "I didn't mean to scare you."

"It's okay," Vienna assured him; she'd nearly caught her breath again.

"I think I figured it out," he spoke in a whisper.

"Figured what out?" Vienna had spent the entire day moping about everything; she didn't really care to think about their pointless plans anymore.

"What Dad was getting at with the papers," Beckham replied. "False consensus effect."

"False consensus what?" Vienna asked.

"False consensus effect," Beckham repeated himself. "It's a pervasive cognitive bias."

"Beck, English please."

"Sorry," he apologized. "I read Dad's notes over and over, but it suddenly clicked. In the midst of all of his notes, there was a small paragraph about psychology.

At first, I didn't really think it made sense with the rest of the information but now it does. False consensus effect, in layman's terms, is essentially an effect that says people see their own choices as relatively normal and appropriate. For example, it's like believing all people like chocolate more than vanilla because you feel that way."

"So?" Vienna wasn't following.

"So, I think Dad thought this concept played a role in Carnot, the effect leads people to assume others think and act the same way that they do, even when that might not be the case," Beckham explained.

Vienna considered the information. "So, you mean to say you think everyone in Carnot thinks and acts the same because of a psychological bias and not because of an injection?" Vienna tried to understand.

"In a way, yes," Beckham replied. "Don't get me wrong, I do believe the injection allows our bodies to live forever and not get physically sick but mentally, I am not sure it does anything."

"Interesting... but how does that help us?"

"We need to talk to Copeland. We need to see if he has any other information and find out if he knows anything that could help us prove or disprove this theory."

"How are we going to do that?" Vienna doubted. "You heard Mom; it sounds like he wants nothing to do with us."

"Yeah, I did hear Mom," Beckham replied. "But yesterday, we didn't trust her and now suddenly, we're taking everything she says at face value? I'm not really on board with that."

"Well, what do you suggest?"

"We need to get into Carnot."

"HA!" Vienna let out a large laugh. "And how do you possibly suppose we do that?"

"Santi." Beckham smiled.

"Oh, because you guys are besties now or something?" Vienna sarcastically asked. "You really think Santi, the guard who is notorious for never letting an unidentified soul into Carnot, the man who didn't let Mom in a few days ago because she forgot her badge after getting in like an hour before and working there for fifteen years, is randomly going to let us in?"

"Yeah," Beckham seriously replied. "I do."

"You're out of your mind," Vienna laughed.

"I don't think so."

"Fine. Say we do get into Carnot," Vienna played along. "What do we do next? How do we find Copeland's room without being seen?"

"Easy," Beckham answered nonchalantly. "I know where it is."

"What? How?"

"V, I've known since I was three what I wanted to do when I grew up," he corrected himself, "Or I guess what I used to want to do. I think that's changed in the past week but that's a conversation for another time... anyway, I've spent years studying the ins and outs of the government and Carnot. I basically know the floorplan by heart."

"Really?" Vienna never had a clue what she wanted to do when she was older, and she couldn't fathom spending so much time studying a subject from such a young age.

"Yeah, the residential side is to the east and

Copeland's bedroom is on the first floor," Beckham explained.

"So, you're telling me that if we, by some stroke of incredible luck, actually get into Carnot, then you could quickly lead the way to Copeland's room? And then what? We just knock?" Vienna used her questioning as a defense mechanism. She didn't want to get her hopes up for a plan if it had no real chance of succeeding.

"That's exactly what I'm saying," Beckham confidently replied. "It would be easy."

"Well," Vienna sighed. She flopped into her desk chair. "You might actually be onto something." After a few seconds of mulling it over, she asked, "But what do you think happens if we get caught?"

"Most likely, we'll," he raised his hands to make air quotes, "randomly be selected to die next month."

"Hmm," Vienna hummed. "Is that all? If I were to guess, I'd say we already have targets on our backs for next month, so really, if you're thinking logically, that's not too big of a risk after all."

"That's what I'm saying." Beckham was glad she was finally getting on board.

"When do you think we should go?"

"I don't know," Beckham admitted. "There are pros and cons to every option. For instance, if we went at night, it would be easier to talk to Santi but harder once we were inside. However, if we went during the day, it might be easier inside to blend in but harder to talk to Santi."

"What if we talked to Santi first?" Vienna suggested. "We could make a plan with him and go from there. He would surely know what would be best for us."

"That's a good idea... but when would we do that?"

"Why not now?" Vienna replied. "There's no time like the present."

"Right now?" Beckham laughed. "That seems a little intense."

"You're the one who came in here all fired up with theories and plans, and now you don't want to actually execute them?" Vienna taunted.

"I guess you're right," he confessed. "If I want to lead, I can't be afraid to act on my plans. If we're going to do it, we might as well do it now."

"Exactly!" Vienna jumped up from her chair. "Wait..." she hesitated.

"What?" Beckham questioned. "You just got me on board and now you're the one hesitating?"

"Would Santi even be working right now? I thought he worked mornings."

"Shoot," Beckham sighed. "I doubt he works fourteen-hour days." He couldn't help but chuckle a little at the fact that neither of them had thought about this issue earlier.

"Ugh." Vienna was bummed. "We could go first thing in the morning?"

"Yeah, we'll just have the issue of Mom allowing us to leave the house."

"You really think she'll keep us here? We could tell her we're going hiking. We always go hiking," she reasoned.

"It's definitely worth a shot," Beckham agreed. "We can get up early and hope she's not up and then, if she is, we can try the hiking thing."

"I think that's our best bet," Vienna concurred. "But isn't tomorrow Sunday? Do you think he works weekends?"

Beckham put his palm to his face. "This is not the easiest plan to execute," he laughed. "I don't know... but there's no harm in checking. Right?"

"True."

"Then, it's settled. Set your alarm for 6:00 A.M."

"Will do," Vienna agreed.

Beckham stood up and started toward the door. Halfway there, he turned around. "Hey, V."

"Yeah?"

"It's going to be okay," he encouraged.

"Thanks, Beck." Vienna sincerely smiled. Beckham didn't act like a big brother too often, but in moments like these, she was thankful he could be protective of her.

After a restless night of sleep, Beckham's alarm sounded. He quickly turned it off, hoping the noise hadn't been too loud to wake his mother. It was still dark outside, and he didn't want to raise any suspicion by turning on the lights. After all, he was never up this early for school, let alone on a Sunday. He successfully got dressed, without too much hassle, into dark gray sweatpants and a black hoodie. He silently crept down the hall to Vienna's room. She was waiting for him in the doorway, dressed in dark colors as well.

They made eye contact and without saying a word, they were on their way. They tiptoed down the stairs and managed to avoid the creaky step. Luckily, there was no sign of movement. They silently walked to the backdoor and opened it as slowly and quietly as possible. It creaked loudly one time and they paused in fear.

A faint moan was heard from their mother's bedroom, but they quickly exited and closed the door behind them. Streetlamps served as the only light against the dark sky and the twins blended in well with their dark clothes.

They ran fast down the empty streets and though they hadn't talked about it, they both knew their best bet was to get home before their mother woke up.

In what felt like no time, Beckham and Vienna were only a block away from Carnot. With the building in sight, they slowed their pace and began to walk. Beckham didn't know if it was the adrenaline or nervous energy, but he didn't feel tired at all. Vienna on the other hand was huffing and puffing.

"Alright, you good with doing the talking?" Vienna asked. She didn't realize she hadn't spoken all morning until the words felt almost strange coming out of her mouth in the sleeping city.

"I guess," Beckham hesitantly agreed. "Let's just hope he's working this morning."

"I hope so."

The guard shack sat to the left of the main gate and they were coming up on the backside of it.

"Let's walk past and make sure it's Santi before we walk up to it," Beckham suggested.

"Sounds good."

They walked past the shack and Beckham looked back. He couldn't quite make out his face but could tell by the silhouette shining in the window that it was him.

"Bingo." Beckham was relieved. "Let's do it."

They turned around and purposefully walked to the window.

"Do you ever not work?" Beckham lightheartedly teased.

Santi, who had been looking down reading the newspaper, jumped slightly.

"Sorry," Beckham apologized. "We didn't mean to startle you."

"That's alright." Santi smiled, recognizing his familiar face. "I'm just not used to people being here this early on a Sunday. And no, I am pretty much always on duty." He shifted his gaze. "You must be Vienna Tunston."

"Indeed, I am," Vienna replied. "Pleasure to meet you."

"You as well. How can I help you two this morning?"

"We have a favor to ask you," Beckham started. "And it's kind of a big one."

"Well, I promised your father I'd do everything I could to help his children. As long as it's not access to Carnot you need," he teased, "I am happy to help."

Beckham and Vienna exchanged uneasy looks.

"Oh no." Santi sighed, seeing their faces. "Is that what you need?"

"Yeah," Beckham decided it was best to cut straight to the chase. "We need access."

"Oh my." Santi threw his head back. He put his hand over his eyes, frustrated with the dilemma.

"It's our last hope," Vienna chimed in. "If we don't get in, it's all over. Every ounce of progress our father made will be negated. Please," she begged. "We need your help."

Santi repeatedly rubbed his hands over his coarse, black hair.

"Right now?" he asked, concern filling his tone.

"No," Beckham quickly answered, thankful to share

some good news. "Whenever you think would be best, we can make work for us."

Santi nodded. He was visibly torn between the decision to follow rules and his desire to help.

Beckham and Vienna stood still, anxiously awaiting his answer. They knew they couldn't do or say anything more.

After what felt like an eternity, Santi took a deep breath and said, "Tomorrow morning. Mondays are the busiest at Carnot, and you'll have the best chance of sneaking in. I'd aim for about 9:00 A.M., which should work well because your mother always gets here earlier than that. Take these," he grabbed two plain white, plastic cards off of his desk and handed them through the window. "When you get here, flash them to me and it will look like you're normal employees."

"Thank you so much," Beckham exclaimed.

"Once you're inside, I can't help you," Santi sounded discouraged.

"It's alright," Vienna assured him. "You've already done more than enough. Thank you!"

"You're welcome." He smiled. "Your father was a good man. I'm glad I can be of some assistance."

"He was the best," Beckham agreed. "Thank you, again! We will see you in the morning."

"See you tomorrow," Santi replied as they walked away. *I sure hope they come up with something...* he thought to himself, *or this will likely be the end of my road.*

Chapter Forty-Two

A sliver of sunlight crept in from between the curtains and caught Margaret's eyes. She rolled over in bed and let out a yawn. She was surprised to hear the sound of the coffee maker in the kitchen.

What time is it, she wondered? She rolled back over to look at her alarm clock and saw it read seven A.M. *Are the kids already up?*

She was confused. She sat up on the edge of the bed and slipped her feet into her worn, gray slippers. She stood up, wrapped her white, fluffy robe around her and walked out of the bedroom.

"What are you doing up so early?" she asked when she saw Vienna was pouring a cup of coffee in the kitchen.

"Couldn't sleep," Vienna casually answered. "Lot on my mind."

Beckham and Vienna had decided it would be more believable if only Vienna was up. Considering Beckham was rarely seen before 9:00 A.M., they worried it would have been too suspicious.

"I'm sorry, sweetheart," Margaret empathized. "I know you had a rough day yesterday."

"It's okay." Vienna acted upset. "I'm sure it's all for the best."

"I'm sure it is."

"How did you sleep?" Vienna asked, trying to change the subject.

"I slept pretty well. It's a lot for me to process too," she lied.

"Yeah," was all Vienna could offer. She couldn't get herself to give any empathy until she knew the truth.

The rest of the day went by without any trouble. It felt like every other Sunday; there was no talk of revolution or the Howth family or anything else of substance.

Margaret awoke the next morning and got ready for work per usual. She walked the same three blocks she always did before catching the train downtown. The train ride took the normal eight minutes and she got off on the fourth stop at Station One. She waved at Santi, walked inside the building and sat down at her new desk on the third floor. She hadn't spent much time at her desk the past week and she was oddly thankful to be sitting there again.

"Good morning," Madison greeted her.

"Morning." Margaret turned around.

"Big news," Madison announced. "Copeland's birthday party has officially been canceled, so I guess you can go back to your old job."

"What?" Margaret was shocked. "He," she corrected herself, "They canceled it? Why?"

"I have no idea. It's quite the story today." She almost stopped mid-sentence, remembering what the story had been over the weekend. "I'm sorry about Lewis," she added.

"It's alright," Margaret lied. "Truthfully, I should have known."

Madison didn't know how, and didn't want to, continue that conversation, so she opted for an offer. "Do you need any help carrying your stuff back downstairs? I am sure Elton has missed you terribly."

"I think I am good. Thanks though."

"Of course." Madison was rather relieved she didn't have to work with Margaret anymore, given the scandal.

Margaret packed up her desk in a matter of minutes and made her way to the elevator.

Canceled, huh, Margaret thought to herself. *Well done, Margaret. You got him to cancel the party altogether.* She shook her head slightly, overly pleased with the outcome. *Silly boy. He'll never be able to talk to Vienna now.*

Chapter Forty-Three

Copeland was awake but not yet moving. He rested in his bed, the room still dark, and breathed heavily in and out. A few days ago, everything was looking up; his birthday party was at the venue of his choice, he was working on fulfilling his mother's last wishes, and he'd met a girl he quite fancied. But now, it had all fallen apart; the party was canceled, his mother, whom he'd trusted more than anyone, had had an affair, and the girl he liked didn't even want to see him.

He let out a big yawn and stretched his arms widely. He didn't really feel like getting out of bed, but he didn't feel like staying in it either, so he figured he'd get up.

He walked to his dresser and opened a drawer. He had no idea what was in the top, left drawer because he'd virtually never opened it. Martin always set out his clothes but since the meeting with Margaret, Copeland had only seen Martin a couple of times, which was odd, considering he'd seen him every single day of his life before that. Martin was defeated and not hiding it well. His grandfather's life's work had all come tumbling down and it was his fault; or at least that's how he viewed it.

As Copeland opened each dresser drawer, trying to find clothes, he heard a rush of footsteps down the hall.

What is that, he thought to himself? Before he could make any guesses as to what the noise was, his bedroom door flew open.

Copeland, who was in the middle of changing, wearing only black socks and red, plaid boxers, couldn't believe his eyes. He stared at the door as Beckham and Vienna tumbled through.

A security guard quickly came up behind them and grabbed the back of their shirt collars. Vienna flung her arms violently, trying to break free, but never took her gaze off Copeland's abs. Beckham grabbed the front of his shirt off his neck, trying to relieve the choking sensation.

"It's okay," Copeland assured the guard. "They're with me."

"Sir," the guard argued, "they have no documentation and they were running wildly down the halls."

"It's no problem at all. I was expecting them," he lied.

"Yes, sir," the guard replied, still looking unconvinced. "Next time, please follow the proper visitor guidelines."

"You got it." Copeland gave him a thumbs up. He spoke with an arrogance that sounded pleasing on the surface but encompassed a deep layer of attitude.

The guard let go of their collars and Beckham let out a very loud and unpleasant, cough-like breath. Vienna on the other hand didn't appear too fazed.

"Thank you." Vienna sneered at the guard.

Without saying another word, the guard left and Beckham closed the door behind him.

"Thank you," Vienna said sincerely to Copeland.

"What are you doing here?" Now that security was gone, Copeland could express his real concerns.

"I think this conversation might be a little more comfortable for us all if you put some clothes on." Beckham's voice was raspy. He rubbed his neck. It was still hurting from the guard's tight hold.

Copeland's face turned a bright red as he looked down, realizing for the first time he was only in socks and boxers.

"Oh my." He blushed. "I'll be right back." He quickly walked around his bed and into a door which they assumed must have been his closet. Soon after, he emerged wearing a pair of dark blue jeans and a maroon, short sleeve button down shirt.

Vienna had never seen him look so casual before. His hair was unkempt, and his eyes looked a particularly bright blueish-green. *Not what we're focused on today,* she reminded herself.

"Again, I'll ask," Copeland started as he walked toward the twins. They had made themselves comfortable in his sitting area. He sat down. "What are you doing here? I thought you didn't want to see me." He was only looking at Vienna.

"You thought I didn't want to see you?" She was confused. "I thought you didn't want to see me?"

"What in Carnot are you talking about?" Copeland questioned. "I sent Martin to your house yesterday morning to arrange a meeting at Tellmen's. I went to Tellmen's and only your mother was there. She said you didn't want to meet with me. She told me you no longer believed anything your father said, and that you didn't care to live out his," he lifted his hands to make quotes in the air just as Margaret had done, "'silly plan for revolution.'"

"What?!" Vienna was furious. "Wait! Let me guess. Did she also say I was upset at my father and not you?"

"Yes, she did."

"Ugh! The nerve! Why did you believe her?" Vienna started to pace the room.

"I had no reason not to believe her," Copeland defended himself.

"Yeah, V," Beckham added. "We hadn't gotten the chance to tell him about our concerns with her comments."

"Wait, how did you know she said the thing about being upset at your father?" Copeland asked.

"Because she told me the same thing about you," Vienna explained. "She said Martin came by with a message from you to let me know that you were upset with your mother, not me, and that you felt betrayed. She said you couldn't believe anything your mother said anymore and that you no longer wanted to take me as your date to your birthday party."

"What? Where is this coming from?" Copeland rubbed his head.

"I have no idea!" Vienna exploded.

"I think we need to walk through everything," Beckham, the only one still emotionally calm in the room, suggested. "It sounds like a lot of false information has been spread, so let's just take it from the top and compile everything." He looked at Copeland and added, "Of course, that's only if you're still up for working together?"

"Certainly," Copeland quickly replied, suddenly

feeling a sense of hope again.

"Wonderful!" Beckham declared. "Let's get to it."

"Let me call for Martin." Copeland walked to his nightstand and pressed a small red button that made no audible noise. "He can let us in."

"Let us in where?" Beckham asked.

"You'll see." Copeland liked the fact that he was on the other end of the teasing now. He couldn't wait to see Beckham and Vienna's faces when the library door opened.

In what seemed like no time at all, Martin opened the door. He did a double take at the twins.

"What?" He was happy but confused. "What is going on here?"

"It seems there's a crack in our foundation," Copeland explained.

"It's our mother," Beckham continued.

"But we're here to get to the bottom of it," Vienna added.

"I was worried about that," Martin sulked.

"What?" they all three objected at once.

"Let's get to a more private spot," Martin started to walk toward the library.

Vienna and Beckham followed and stood at the edge of the nook.

"Wow," Beckham commented. He walked up to a bookshelf and grabbed one. He opened it and was not surprised to see the blank pages. "Pretty to look at but worthless to learn from."

"Just wait." Copeland grinned. "Put that back, please." He pointed to the book still in Beckham's hand.

Meanwhile, Martin was running his hand along the

spines of books and diligently pulling some out and pushing some in further.

"What is he doing?" Vienna whispered to Copeland.

"You'll see." He softly smiled at her.

Vienna couldn't stand the way it felt like a million butterflies took flight in her stomach at the sight of his inviting smile. She gave a slight nod and looked away, pretending to stare intently at Martin.

After a few more minutes of fastidious tweaking, the back wall of books began to move. Beckham and Vienna stood in awe.

"Follow me," Copeland instructed.

The four of them filed into the expansive, secret library. Beckham opened book after book, shocked to see each one filled with words and knowledge of particular subjects.

"This is incredible," he complimented.

"Indeed, it is," agreed Martin.

"Alright," Vienna said; her stomach feeling like most of the butterflies had landed again, "let's get to it. Do you want to start or should we?"

"You can start," Copeland answered.

"Sounds good. You go ahead." Vienna looked at Beckham to begin.

Beckham reached into the waistband of his jeans and pulled out a few folded papers. "We'll get to these in a second," he said, setting them on the desk. There was only one chair in the room, so the four of them stood in something that resembled a circle. "Our concerns with our mother started on Thursday, after your date." Beckham gestured to Vienna and Copeland.

A few thousand more butterflies took off in Vienna's

stomach. *Ugh*, she thought to herself, annoyed at the feelings.

"When we were talking after it, she made a few comments about it not being the right time for a revolution and concerns about our safety... and something felt off," he explained. "It seemed like out of nowhere she wanted us to forget about it all together."

"What?" Copeland furrowed his brow. "Why?"

"She claimed it wasn't that big of a deal," Beckham replied.

"What wasn't?" Copeland didn't allow him any time to further explain.

"The way Carnot is being run," he continued. "She said that before Carnot, people died every day from tragedies and the unexpected and that it's really not that different now."

"Are you kidding?" Copeland was getting angry.

"No," Beckham plainly replied as if the question was not rhetorical. "So, needless to say we had our doubts. We decided we would do everything we could without her and share the bare minimum for the time being. In the midst of all our thinking and analyzing, I remembered a conversation I'd had with my father not long before he died. He'd mentioned Santi—"

"The guard?" Martin interjected.

"Yes," Beckham continued, trying not to get annoyed at all of the interruptions. "Something in me felt that the conversation was more than just a conversation, so I went out on a limb. I approached Santi early Sunday morning and lo and behold, he had an envelope of information from our father for me." He picked up the papers he'd set on the desk. "It was pages of notes and thoughts he'd scribbled down on what I believe was the last night of his life, or close to it."

"Read the note," Vienna instructed.

Beckham unfolded the papers and flipped through them carefully, trying to find the note. He found the paper, moved it to the front of the stack and began to read, "Beckham & Vienna, if you've somehow received this envelope, I sincerely commend you on your intuition. I've run out of time to present this information to Camilla and I think it could be critical to the research. We all know I will die this month and I couldn't risk this information getting intercepted by anyone, not even your mother. Please take a look at everything I have compiled here. I believe in you both. I love you, Dad."

"I'm sorry!" Martin was suddenly hysterical. "I'm so sorry. I told you Margaret could be trusted, and I thought she could be. I thought your mother," he looked at Copeland, "did not know, and I thought I did, but now, I see I was wrong." He pointed to the letter. "I messed everything up and I apologize sincerely."

"Martin," Copeland spoke assertively, leaving no room for him to worry, "you did nothing but help us start what we know will be a successful rebellion. There is no need to apologize. We are where we need to be right now and that's thanks to you."

The room fell silent at Copeland's words. Martin, who was trying his hardest to keep the water from spilling out of his eyes, nodded slightly.

"Thank you," he whispered.

"What did you learn from his notes?" Copeland asked, trying to shift the conversation back to the topic at hand.

"He'd written about a pervasive cognitive bias called false con—"

"—sensus effect," Copeland finished the words with him.

"Are you familiar?" Beckham raised his brow, shocked he'd been able to finish his sentence.

Copeland laughed a surreal laugh. "That's precisely what I discovered in here." He threw up his hands, gesturing to the library.

"Seriously?" Vienna was in disbelief.

"Wow," Martin commented.

"I have absolutely no idea what it means," admitted Copeland, "but I was hoping Vienna would know."

Beckham cleared his throat. "I'm actually the one who figured it out," he corrected.

"Great," Copeland replied. "As long as someone has figured it out, I don't care who. What does it mean?"

"False consensus effect is essentially an effect that says people see their own choices as relatively normal and appropriate. For example, it's like believing all people like pancakes more than waffles because you feel that way."

"Sorry, I know what it is," Copeland apologized. "My question is why does it matter? How does it apply to Carnot?"

"I think what my dad was trying to get at was that the effect leads people in Carnot to assume others think and act the same way that they do, even when that might not be the case. In other words, I think he thought, and I agree," he added, "that people here think and act the same because of a psychological bias and not because of an injection. Which would explain why some people are able to act differently, like your father for instance."

"So, what you're saying is that everyone acts and thinks one way because everyone else acts and thinks the same way and everyone is just assuming everyone else is acting and thinking like them, so it's an endless cycle?" Copeland rationalized.

"Exactly," Beckham replied.

"So, how do we stop the cycle?"

"That's precisely what we need to figure out."

"Gotcha." Copeland was caught up. "But what about our parents? How does that play into everything?"

"I have no idea," Beckham spoke up quickly.

"I—" Martin was interrupted.

"Do you even believe it?" Vienna asked.

"I'm not sure," Copeland replied. "I want to assume it's just fake news Summer made up, but I don't know why she'd do that. I feel like with everyone and everything she knows, she wouldn't have had to make anything up..." Copeland trailed off. "Which makes me wonder if it really is true."

"I think—" Martin patiently tried to start again.

"Does it matter if it's true or not?" Vienna questioned. "At the end of the day, aren't we just trying to save the people of Carnot? Why does it matter if our parents made a mistake?"

"It matters if we can trust them or not," Beckham, who had always been a stickler for the truth, countered.

"I think I—" Martin interjected.

"I guess." Vienna shrugged. "But, why wouldn't we be able to trust all of their research? Surely, they didn't send us on this wild quest of a revolution for no reason.

Maybe, they were just victims of breaking the mold of the effect," she reasoned. "Maybe, they found out they could do bad, so they did. They were only human."

"I have something to say," Martin suddenly shouted. The domineering tone sounded foreign coming from his mouth.

They stopped their jabbering immediately and turned their attention to him.

"Thank you." Martin spoke quieter now. "I think I may have a theory but it is pretty far out there, and I might be completely off."

"That's okay," Vienna encouraged. "We're brainstorming right now, which means there are no bad theories."

"Okay," Martin took a deep breath. "I think it's possible that Lewis and Camilla were not the ones having the affair." He paused and breathed again. "I think it could be Theodore and Margaret."

"What?!" Copeland spoke with incredulity.

"No way!" Beckham objected. "Maybe there is such a thing as a bad theory."

"Rude!" Vienna called her brother out. "Why is that a bad theory?" She jumped to Martin's defense. "Why couldn't that be possible?

"There's just," Beckham argued, "there's no way... and why would it even matter?"

"It matters because we think Mom has been undermining us and this would give us a reason as to why," Vienna explained. "What makes you think that?" She turned to Martin, annoyed at her brother's skepticism.

"Well, years ago, there were rumors about Theodore's love life, but no one was ever named. In fact, it wasn't long before your mother died that the rumors really picked up speed. After she died, the rumors stopped completely, and things were very quiet around your father's office."

"Seems rather convenient that when the rumors became more troubling, Camilla suddenly received a bad Ivy Letter." Vienna raised her eyebrows.

"Yes, it does," Martin agreed.

"Recently, there seems to have been an increase in traffic to Theodore's office." He continued, "The other day, when you spoke with your father about the party plans," he looked at Copeland, "I saw someone down the hall."

"Is that why you stopped?" Copeland asked, remembering Martin's sudden halt outside of the office.

"Yes, I tried to follow the woman, but I lost her. I couldn't tell for certain, but from the back, it very much looked like Margaret."

"Why didn't you tell us sooner?" Vienna wondered aloud. "If you thought it was her, why did you still trust her?"

"I wasn't certain," Martin replied. "It could have been anyone. I didn't really think about it being Margaret until the article came out."

"Even if it was her," Beckham argued, "maybe, she was just working on something."

"Regular government employees are not allowed on our side of Carnot unless invited," Copeland countered. "And those invites are few and far between."

"Exactly," said Martin.

"Okay, fine." Beckham was still on the defense. "Then, why the article about Dad and Camilla? What does that have to do with Theodore and Mom?"

"I think it could be their attempt to derail our plans," Martin explained. "Think about it. The same day your mother got defensive with you both is the day I thought I saw her leaving Theodore's office. Then, two days later, a story which could have been published years ago, if it was true, suddenly makes an appearance. I don't think it's coincidence. I think it was Margaret and Theodore who planted the article, not Summer."

The room fell silent as Vienna, Beckham, and Copeland processed Martin's theory.

"That is not a bad theory," Vienna finally complimented.

"You really think they would plant a fake and embarrassing news article like that just to sabotage our plans?" Beckham still wasn't convinced.

"I wouldn't put it past them," Martin reasoned. "In the grand scheme of protecting the nation of Carnot, I don't think something like a petty news article would be that devastating to them."

"We could ask Summer," Copeland suggested.

"What?" the three of them simultaneously replied.

"Why not?" Copeland asked. "She's the one who threatened to leak an article. I think it's only right if we know whether or not she did."

"Actually, he makes a good point," Martin was the first to agree. "If we know she didn't plant the article, it's relatively safe to assume that Margaret and Theodore did."

"Again though, I'll ask, why does it really matter?" Vienna questioned. "How does knowing who leaked the article impact our plans? At the end of the day, we want

Carnot changed and our parents left us huge resources to help us do that; why does it matter if they had an affair or if Mom and Theodore did or if Summer leaked the article?"

"It matters because it matters," Beckham retorted with an edge to his voice Vienna had never heard before.

"Can I ask why it matters if we *do* find out?" Copeland attempted a more diplomatic approach. "Obviously, we want to know the answer but how does finding out negatively impact anything?"

"It…" Vienna swallowed hard, realizing the answer Beckham had alluded to, fighting back tears. "I guess it matters because he wasn't a cheater. My dad was the best man I've ever known and if he did have an affair, I… I don't know how we could move forward." She wiped her eyes which now overflowed with tears. "I want to restore Carnot, but how can we do that if our beliefs about him are tainted?"

"I understand, V," Beckham placed his hand on her back. "I feel the same way about Dad. I don't think he would have done something like that but even if he did, we can't control it. What we can control is doing our best each day, and right now, doing our best is fighting for the people around us, regardless of our parents' choices. We have to do our best and we're getting really close to figuring out what our next steps should be. Finding out if it was Summer who shared the article could actually help us," he reasoned. "If we find out it was fake, that only fuels our fire. If we find out it was real—well, we can be better than our parents. I know you don't want your memories of Dad to be tainted, and I don't want mine to be either, but I think it's important we find out one way or another."

Vienna wiped her eyes and she looked at Beckham. "Okay," she hesitantly agreed with a laugh. "And when did you get so smart?"

"Always have been." Beckham winked.

"Alright, now that we're all on board," Copeland started, "what's our plan of attack?"

"I think we should ask Summer to come here," Martin proposed. "It won't be overtly suspicious if she is seen arriving here and you won't have to leave to speak with her."

"Just me speak with her?" Copeland questioned.

"Yes," Martin plainly replied. "She'll be the most honest with you and there's no need for all of us to be there. In fact, there's something I want to try." He walked over and pressed the button to open the door out of the library. "Stay there," he instructed. The door shut automatically behind him. "Can you hear me?" he asked, standing near the bookshelf.

"Yes," they replied.

Martin took a few steps back and spoke at a normal volume. "How about now?"

"Yes," they replied again.

"And now?" he asked, standing further still from the bookshelf.

"A little quiet but yes," Copeland could be heard above Vienna and Beckham's replies.

"Splendid!" Martin exclaimed. "Will you please press the button?" When the library door was opened, all of the books reverted back to the normal alignment. Martin felt it was easier for them to press the button to let him back in, rather than rearrange all of the books.

"Yep," Copeland replied, as he walked to push it.

"Thank you," Martin said as he walked back in. "If you can get Summer to speak with you in the library, then we should be able to listen in on your conversation."

"Really?" Vienna asked. "That would be great!"

"Yes," Martin confirmed. "I wasn't speaking that loud and you guys could still hear me from the edge of the room."

"Wow," Beckham commented. "That's perfect."

"It is," Martin agreed. "Now, we just need Summer."

"Will you call for her?" Copeland asked.

"Of course, sir." Martin's tone suddenly changed from friendly to professional. "I'll be right back." He gave a bow, along with a small wink.

Chapter Forty-Four

"She should be here any minute," Martin commented, looking down at his watch. "Two minutes to eleven."

"Perfect." Vienna paced the room the way she always did when she felt anxious.

When Martin called Summer, she eagerly agreed to meet with Copeland. Vienna assumed she thought she'd be getting an invite to his party, but she couldn't be certain.

After his call, they spent the next thirty minutes drafting what Copeland would say. Although they didn't have much time, they felt confident in what they'd come up with, and all they could do now was wait for her to arrive.

"Was that the door?" Beckham asked.

Vienna and Martin moved to the edge of the library door to join Beckham and placed their ears against the wall.

After a few moments, they heard light chatter but couldn't make out the words.

"Sounds like she's here," Martin whispered.

"Do you want to sit?" was the first audible sentence

they could hear.

"Sure," Summer replied.

"I'm sorry about how things went down the other day." Copeland wasted no time in starting the script. "With Vienna and all."

"It's okay," Summer refrained from being overexcited, she didn't want Copeland to think she cared too much.

"It was a silly fling and it was selfish of me and I'm sorry," he continued.

Even though Vienna knew he was speaking from the script, she couldn't help but feel hurt. *Maybe that's really how he feels*, Vienna thought to herself. *He sounds so believable.* She groaned aloud. "Ugh."

"What?" Beckham whispered.

"Sorry, nothing," Vienna whispered back, embarrassed she'd made the noise out loud. *We don't care about him*, she silently reminded herself. *He was only using you.*

"The article made me realize how important it is to trust people in my life." Copeland went on, "Especially, when I hold such a position of power. How can I trust some commoner off the streets?"

That one felt like a dagger in Vienna's chest.

"I can't even trust my own mother now," Copeland sighed. "I can't trust anyone."

Summer's stomach turned. She could tell the article had really hurt him.

"Well, almost anyone," he added. After a long pause, he looked into Summer's eyes and said, "I can trust you."

"That's really flattering." Summer smiled.

"And since I can trust you," Copeland started, "I have a question to ask you."

Summer's heart raced. *Yes, I'll be your date to your birthday party*, she rehearsed her response in her head.

"Is it true?" he asked.

"Ye—," she began instinctively responding. "Wait, what? Is what true?"

"The article. Is it true about my mother and Lewis?"

Summer laughed a frustrated laugh. "You asked me here today to find out if the article was true?"

"Yes," Copeland answered. "When I was at your house, you threatened you'd leak an article, but I didn't think you'd actually do it. Let alone leak an article that would hurt me so badly. I thought maybe something about the way I eat spaghetti or that I sometimes wear pink underwear, not that my deceased mother, whom I loved more than anyone, had an affair with the father of the girl I *was* dating."

"Perfect," Beckham whispered, pleased with Copeland's delivery. They were banking on Summer focusing on the term "was dating."

"Was dating?" she questioned.

"Bingo," Martin whispered.

"Yes." Copeland's tone was sad. "I can't date her anymore, not as the heir. It's too undignified."

"I'm sorry." Summer sounded sincere. "I didn't mean to hurt you."

"So, it is true?" Copeland asked again.

After what felt like an eternity of silence, Summer finally answered, "I'm... I'm not sure."

"She's not sure?" Beckham whispered with disgust.

"You're not sure?" Copeland raised an eyebrow.

"I'm not and I—" Summer began to breathe rapidly. "I can't say." She was hyperventilating now.

"Why not?" Copeland asked. "Are you okay?"

"I will surely die," she finally said through what sounded like tears.

"You will die?" Copeland didn't understand. "What are you talking about?"

"I can't say." Summer was distraught.

"I will protect you. You will not die. I need to know the truth."

"I don't know that you can protect me," Summer explained. "I don't think you can."

"I can," he assured her. "Summer, so many things depend on this; more than you even know. Please, I am begging you, tell me what you know."

After a few seconds, Summer finally replied, "I don't know if it's true."

"How does she not know?" Martin frustratingly whispered.

"But I didn't choose to run it," she added. "Well... I am the one who ran it, but I didn't want to."

"What?" Copeland asked, wishing she'd explain further.

"A woman came by and offered me a deal," Summer began.

"Who?" Copeland interrupted.

"I don't remember her name. She gave me an envelope and said it was from your father. She said if I followed the instructions, I'd be granted fifty years of guaranteed life and..." she trailed off.

"And what?" he prompted.

"And," she was completely embarrassed to say, "and a VIP invitation to your birthday party."

"Oh," Copeland sighed. "I see."

"I had to agree," Summer defended herself. "I couldn't say 'no' to a request made by your father. I didn't know what was in the envelope when I agreed and when I read the article, I felt awful. She told me she couldn't disclose whether or not the information was true."

"Why didn't you come to me?"

"She said if I told a soul, I'd be killed in the next round of Ivy Letters."

"So, why are you telling me now?" Copeland didn't understand her sudden shift.

"Because," Summer solemnly replied, "I do love you. I love you and I can't stand to see you love someone else. I would rather die than hurt you and now, seeing your face, I know I've done just that."

"I don't love anyone else."

"Yes," Summer countered, "you do. I saw the pictures. I've never seen you look at anyone the way you look at Vienna; especially not me. I'm sorry I don't know more and I'm sorry I hurt you. Truly, I wish I could offer you more, but I have nothing."

Copeland tried to process the conversation. He'd played out a lot of scenarios beforehand, but this was not one he'd guessed. Summer loved him and thought that he loved Vienna, so she leaked the article but not by her own choice and she had absolutely no idea if it was true or not.

"It's okay. I know you didn't have another choice."

Summer was silent, unsure of what to say next.

Copeland scratched his forehead; they'd gotten very far off script. "Could you describe the woman in any more detail? Like her hair color or skin tone?"

"She was elegantly beautiful. She had shoulder-length

brown hair and fair skin," Summer started.

"Come on," Martin whispered. "Let's go."

"Go where?" Vienna questioned.

"Out there," answered Martin. "He needs help."

"Sounds like he's doing just fine," Beckham nervously countered. He did not want to leave the safety of their hiding place.

But before Beckham could argue any further, Martin had pressed the button. The door slowly opened and natural light streamed in. Martin was the first to walk out, followed by Vienna and lastly, Beckham.

Summer was clearly uneasy. She stood up and started backing away from them. "What's going on here?" she timorously asked.

"We are here to help you," Martin assured her. "We want to protect you. But, in order to do so, we need your help in return."

"My help with what?" Summer was defensive. "I'll scream. I'll tell everyone you forced me in here."

"Please don't scream," Vienna calmly raised her hands.

"Please hear us out," Beckham added.

Summer tilted her head and looked at Beckham inquisitively, taking in his features. "The woman looked like him," she pointed, speaking to Copeland.

"Really?" Copeland asked. "Are you sure?"

"I'm positive," she answered. "Their eyes are almost identical, and they're built the same. The only difference is their hair color."

"It's true," Vienna chimed in. "Everyone always says Beckham looks more like our mom and I looked more like our dad."

"Well, if it's true that Margaret delivered the article to Summer, then we can safely assume Theodore was in on it." Martin paced, thinking out loud. "However, that still doesn't help us in determining whether or not it's true."

"Doesn't it though?" Copeland questioned. "Why would Dad and Margaret be working together if they weren't trying to cover up their own secret? Why would they even know each other if they weren't the ones having the affair?"

"What?" Summer was so confused.

"We're going to need to catch her up," Vienna said. "That is, only if we really can trust her?" She looked to the others for confirmation.

Before anyone could answer, Summer spoke up. "At this point, I'm better off dead and you're my only hope of protection." She sounded like she wished that wasn't the case. "Whatever you need, I'm here to help. You can trust me."

"Great." Beckham took no time to make sure the others were on board. "I'll get her caught up."

"Okay." Summer looked up at his blue eyes and couldn't help but marvel at his perfect smile.

Beckham worked to fill Summer in on everything from the fake run-in at Rich or Pour to the letters from their parents to the secret library door and everything in between.

As they spoke, Copeland, Vienna, and Martin sorted through all of the information they'd gathered. They threw out notes and papers that weren't helpful and managed to dwindle it down to a small stack.

"If I wasn't ready to help before, I most definitely am

now," Summer declared after Beckham had finished filling her in.

"Awesome." Copeland was thankful the morning had gone so well. Besides the fact, of course, that his ex-girlfriend and the girl he went on one date with (who he now wondered if he loved) were both working with him to help save humanity. "Now all we need is to figure out how to restore Carnot."

"Easy-peasy." Summer let out a half-hearted laugh.

"I actually have an idea," Vienna announced.

No one answered; they all stared back at Vienna, waiting for her to continue.

"Let's go back in there." She pointed to the secret door.

Martin immediately began moving books in and out.

"What is the code?" Summer asked.

"The books are the code," Martin explained. "I have to pull some out and push some in for the door to open."

"I know," Summer replied. "What I mean is what does the code mean? How did Camilla figure it out?"

Copeland couldn't believe he hadn't thought to ask.

"I guess I don't exactly know," Martin admitted.

"I thought you said you helped her?" Copeland questioned.

"I did," said Martin, "But my job was to find seams in Carnot and predict where hidden rooms could be. She was the one who was able to actually solve the code."

"So how do you open the door?" Vienna asked.

"I simply know which books need to be moved," Martin explained.

"We need the books," Summer concluded.

"Yes," Vienna agreed. "Once it's unlocked, you guys

go in and we will gather them."

"I don't think we can take them off of the shelves while we're in there," Martin worried. "I don't know if the door would re-open."

"These books are empty anyway," Beckham gestured to the shelves. "We only need the titles."

"Good point," Martin complimented. "I have those."

"Great," Copeland agreed. "I'm all for analyzing anything we think can help."

Martin continued to move the books, and in no time, the door swung open. Summer stood in awe of the secret door the way the others had the first time they'd seen it. Although it had opened earlier, she'd been overwhelmed and hadn't been able to take it in.

They went into the library and Martin walked to the desk. He opened the top drawer and pulled out an old, faded piece of paper.

"Here you go." He set it on the desk.

Recognizing what it was, Beckham asked, "Doesn't it seem a little counterintuitive to keep the code to the room inside the room?"

"I have it memorized," Martin confidently replied.

"Better hope you never forget it," Beckham mumbled to himself.

"It looks like there are about forty books on here," Vienna declared after a quick count. "Let's see if we can find them in here. We'll look for books on the top half of the list," she gestured to Summer. "And boys, you take the bottom."

Everyone agreed and began to search the seemingly endless and unorganized shelves. After an hour of searching, Summer and Vienna had found all of their books.

"Girls rule." Summer high-fived Vienna when they beat the guys.

After another couple of hours spent helping the guys search, they deemed the remaining five books missing.

"It's okay," Vienna decided. "We have a lot of material here and I am sure we can get something out of it."

"Is that the time?" Beckham looked over Martin's shoulder as he checked his watch.

"Yes, it's nearly three in the afternoon," he answered.

"We don't have much time," Beckham looked at Vienna. "We have to make it home before Mom."

Vienna sighed, disappointingly. "You're right," she agreed. "When are we going to meet? I don't think there's any chance Beck and I can get into Carnot again."

"Yeah, especially not after that security guard nearly choked me," Beckham added.

"Would you be able to sneak out late tonight?" Martin looked at Summer. "I know a place we could meet."

"For sure," she replied. "My parents don't care about me. It would be easy."

"What about you guys?" Martin looked at the twins.

"Maybe," Beckham sighed. "It's always a toss-up when Mom will go to bed."

"But we're willing to try," Vienna added.

"It's an old theater off of Philmore Street," Martin explained.

"Oh, I know right where that is," Vienna replied.

"Me too," Summer said. "I thought it was all boarded up?"

"It is," Martin responded, "But you can still get in."

"Meet at midnight?" Copeland suggested.

"Sure," Vienna agreed.

"Take as many books as you can hide, and we'll report back tonight." Martin started handing out the books they'd piled on the desk.

Vienna could fit one into each coat pocket and another in her waistband; Beckham managed to find spots for four in his coat, and Summer fit three in her pockets.

"See you tonight," Summer called as she left the library first.

"She's got it so easy," Beckham commented on her ability to walk worry-free through Carnot.

"Yes, she does," Vienna agreed.

They waited a few minutes and then went on their way. They walked purposefully with their heads down and without any hassle, they made it outside.

"Phew." Vienna breathed a sigh of relief.

"I wouldn't 'phew' so fast," Beckham grabbed Vienna's arm and pulled her behind one of the pillars.

"What?" Vienna asked.

"Shh," Beckham hushed. "Theodore is walking up the sidewalk."

"Do you think he saw us?" Vienna asked.

Before Beckham could answer, they heard the uninviting voice of Theodore.

"Good afternoon, Tunston twins." He turned to look at them after he'd made it up the steps.

"Hello, Mr. Howth," Vienna spoke and they both obligatorily bowed.

"What are you two doing at Carnot on this beautiful day?" He gestured toward the uncommon, blue, winter sky.

"We were having lunch with our mother," Beckham quickly lied. "We thought since we were out of school now, it would be nice for us to spend a little time with her."

"I see," Theodore clearly was not sold but didn't care to press further. "I hope you had a lovely time. Have a nice day." He turned back toward the door and walked inside.

"Oh no, oh no, oh no." Beckham pulled his hair.

"Come on." Vienna grabbed his arm again. "We can't do this here."

They walked as quickly as they could without running off of the property.

"Thanks, Santi," Vienna said as she set the badges on the edge of his windowsill.

Before he could turn to acknowledge them, they were gone. He stood up, walked out the side door of the guard shack and saw them running at an all-out sprint down the road.

Chapter Forty-Five

Theodore sat with his feet up on his desk, tapping his fingers and patiently waiting. The door swung open and Margaret walked in.

"Hello, Maggie." Theodore smiled a sly smile. "How was lunch with your children?"

"Lunch with my kids?" Margaret was confused. "What are you talking about?"

"Well, I just ran into them outside and they said they brought you lunch today. Honest as they may appear, I thought it would be best to fact check their information," Theodore explained.

"They most definitely did not have lunch with me today."

"I was afraid you'd say that," Theodore sighed. "But if they didn't have lunch with you, who were they with?"

"And how did they get in?" Margaret questioned.

"I thought you said the news of Lewis and Camilla's affair would keep them apart."

"I did." Margaret was very frustrated. "They seemed defeated."

"Did you speak with both of them?" Theodore doubted Margaret's efforts.

"Yes, I met with Copeland and Martin, and told them Vienna was upset and didn't want to see them and I told Vienna that Copeland didn't want to meet with her," Margaret defended herself. "I was certain everyone bought it."

"Well, what are we going to do now?" Theodore rubbed his temples with his hands. He had been very calm but the frustration began to show on his face.

"I don't know." Margaret shrugged. "Hope they don't figure it out?" she suggested.

"Hope they don't figure it out?" Theodore was furious at the absurdity of her suggestion. "Hope they don't figure it out?" He stood up and walked around the desk toward Margaret. "This nation is only holding on by a thread right now and you want me to just 'hope they don't figure it out?'" he repeated her words back to her with rage.

"I'm sorry," Margaret apologized. For the first time, she realized how alone and powerless she was in the room with Theodore. She thought back to the party, the first time he had called her to him.

He breathed a heavy and airy sigh. "They're all gone next round," he declared. "And so is Santi. He must have let them in."

Margaret's first instinct was to scream. It was as if a veil had been lifted from her eyes. The years of her adulterous schemes suddenly cut deep with a guilty knife to her soul. *How could you do that?! How could you possibly plan to kill your own son so casually? And my kids*, she thought to herself? Her stomach spun violently, and she felt like she could hurl. *How did I end up here?* She felt as though her life was in shambles. Then, out of the blue, it came to her. "I think that's the only option," she lied aloud. "I agree."

"Then, it's settled," Theodore replied. "I doubt they'll make enough progress this month to do any major damage but just to be sure, we'll need to do everything we can to keep them apart."

"Understood," Margaret spoke seriously. "I think it would be best if Copeland still had his birthday party."

"Still had?" Theodore questioned.

"Uhm," Margaret did not want to be the one to tell him the news. "He canceled it."

"He what?" Theodore asked.

"I heard it from Madison," Margaret explained. "She must have gotten word from someone. I assumed you knew."

"I didn't," he admitted. "Thank you for bringing this to my attention. I think you're right. Copeland should have his party and he will bring Summer. All will appear well in Carnot." He grimaced.

"Sounds like a plan." Margaret forced a smile, feeling sick.

She turned to leave, and Theodore called, "A kiss before you go?"

She turned back around and grinned.

"Of course," she said as she walked around his desk. She rested her hand on his shoulder, leaned down and kissed him. As her lips touched his, with every fiber of her being, she realized how in the wrong she truly had been.

Chapter Forty-Six

Once they were a few blocks from Carnot, Beckham abruptly stopped running.

"We can't go home," he declared. "There's no way. If Mom is really working with Theodore, she'll surely find out we were there, and she won't let us leave."

Though she didn't want to believe it, she knew he was right. "I know," Vienna sighed. "But what do we do? Where do we go?"

"Do you think we'd have time to stop at home?" he questioned. "Just to grab a few things. If we get blankets and clothes and the basics, we might be able to hide out somewhere for a while."

"Maybe," Vienna agreed. "If we run into her though, it's over... but it would be nice to grab some stuff."

Beckham started talking through the timing aloud. "Say Theodore went directly to Mom's desk and she left immediately, it would still take her a minimum of fifteen minutes to get home and more likely twenty. We're already ahead of her. If we run the rest of the way and hope she doesn't time the train perfectly, we could be in and out before she gets there."

"Alright." Vienna took off. "We can plan on the way. If we're doing it, we don't have a second to waste."

Beckham started running. "What should we grab? We need to know exactly who's grabbing what before we get there."

"Water bottles, blankets, toothbrushes," Vienna started rattling off essentials.

"Extra layers, some food," Beckham added.

"Yes, food, water, and clothes are the basics," Vienna said. "I'll go upstairs and grab us a bag with blankets, clothes, our toothbrushes, and toothpaste. You stay downstairs and get some food and water for us."

"Okay," Beckham agreed.

No longer needing to save their breath for talking, they ran faster. If it hadn't been for their pumping adrenaline, it would have taken them five minutes longer to run home.

They entered through the back door and Vienna ran up the stairs. She grabbed a duffel bag from her closet, threw the books from her pockets and waistband in it and then began tossing in long sleeve shirts and pants. She ran to Beckham's room and did the same; grabbing whatever clothes she could find (luckily, he kept most of them on the floor). She ran to the bathroom, collected their toothbrushes and toothpaste and finally, stopped at the hall closet to grab some blankets.

She ran downstairs where Beckham was filling up a second water bottle in the sink. "The food is in the bag," he said gesturing with his head toward the counter. "I put my books in there too."

"Perfect," Vienna replied. "Mine are in the duffle."

Beckham screwed the top on the water bottle.

"Ready?" he asked.

"Yep."

Beckham grabbed the bag of food, placed one water bottle under his arm and opened the back door with his free hand. He walked through first and Vienna followed, her arms stuffed full of blankets. Beckham shut the door behind her and without saying a word, they both took off running again. They looked like mad people running down back alleys with their arms packed full.

After a couple of blocks, Vienna slowed, finally feeling the rush of her exhaustion.

"We made it," she breathed heavily.

"We did. Hopefully, they will be able to help us come up with a better plan tonight."

"Hopefully, so." Vienna rearranged some of the items she was carrying to make it easier to walk. "I think we should go to the theater now."

"Agreed," said Beckham, also shifting some of the things he was carrying. "Sounds like it will be a good place to hide out."

Vienna had a better sense of direction than Beckham, so she led the way. After all of the running, the walk to Philmore Street didn't seem too taxing. Once they were inside the theater, they set down all of their stuff and made themselves comfortable on the stage.

"Home sweet home," Beckham laughed.

Vienna laughed as well but also felt anxious about the unfortunate truth of his comment.

The hours passed surprisingly fast as they dove into the books they'd taken. They took turns skimming each one and tried to make sense of them.

"Do you think these books even mean anything?"

Beckham asked. "I mean, we don't know who designed the hidden rooms at Carnot, so how do we know they even relate to our mission?"

"We don't," Vienna admitted, "but we're trying to learn anything we possibly can from them."

"I have no idea what the common denominator is between our seven books," he commented. "Some are long, some are short, some have female heroes, and some have male, some are fantasy, and some are romantic, some are really old, some are less old…"

Vienna giggled at his attempt to joke in the midst of their stress.

"I'm just saying, I see no correlation," Beckham finished.

"And maybe, there isn't one." Vienna shrugged. "But, what else do we have to do right now? We might as well read while we wait and see if anything comes to us."

Beckham couldn't argue, so he started to read again.

As the night grew later, the theater grew darker around them.

"A flashlight would have been a good idea," Beckham commented when he could no longer read the pages.

"Yeah." Vienna had never been fond of the dark. "Maybe we should try to get some sleep until they arrive," she suggested.

"Good idea."

They spread out their blankets and tried to fall asleep. At first, Beckham felt restless, but he must have fallen asleep because a few hours later, he was awoken by a light shining in his eyes and hushed voices.

"What are you two doing here?" Martin asked, seeing their spread of blankets, books, and more.

Beckham, who was still groggy, rubbed his eyes. "We couldn't go home," he said through a yawn.

"Why not?" Martin was suddenly concerned.

Vienna, who had woken up and was now stretching her arms high, answered, "We saw Theodore on the way out. We were worried he'd talk to our mom and we wouldn't be able to meet you, so we decided to pack our bags and leave."

"You left for good?" Copeland questioned. He admired their dedication, but given the life he'd grown up with, he couldn't fathom being homeless.

"Guess so," Vienna replied.

"Wow," Copeland sighed in admiration. He set down the lantern he'd been carrying near Vienna and pulled out a box of matches from his pocket. He struck a match and lit the candle inside, illuminating the space around them.

How can someone still look so good in this poorly lit space, Vienna thought as she saw Copeland's face?

He took a seat next to her and Martin sat down next to Beckham. They formed a circle and left space for Summer between Martin and Copeland.

"Hopefully, Summer gets here soon," Martin commented.

"Have you found anything?" Vienna couldn't wait for Summer. She wanted so badly to know if anyone had noticed anything about the books.

"No." Copeland was the first to answer. "We haven't found anything yet. What about you?"

"No," she replied. "Maybe, it's pointless to be spending so much time on this. We don't even know if the code means anything."

"True," Martin said. "But we also don't know how to successfully start an uprising, so while we're thinking on that, we might as well read."

They heard movement coming from the front of the building. Copeland quickly blew out the candle in his lantern and Martin flicked off his flashlight. A deep darkness encompassed them all.

"Shh," Martin quietly instructed. "In case it isn't her."

They saw a faint light moving into the theater and then walking down the center aisle.

From the other end of the room, Vienna could easily see the grace and poise with which the person was walking. "It's her," she whispered.

Just then, Summer nervously called, "Are you guys here?"

"Yes," Copeland called back as he started fumbling for the matches. "We're on the stage." He found them and lit his lantern again.

Summer's figure became clearer in the soft glow of her lantern as she made her way onto the stage.

"Am I late?" she asked as she sat down in the space they'd left for her.

"No," Martin answered. "We just got here, and they've been here awhile." He motioned toward the twins.

"We couldn't stay at home," Beckham filled her in. "We ran into Theodore on our way out of Carnot and we were certain he would tell our mother. We stopped at home to grab some supplies and came straight here."

"Wow... Do you need a place to stay?" Summer offered.

Vienna and Beckham exchanged glances.

"You definitely don't have to do that," Vienna replied.

"I want to," Summer insisted. "You can't stay here." She gestured around the theater with a look as though something rather foul smelling was right under her nose.

"Would it be safe?" Beckham asked, looking to Martin for assurance.

"I don't see why not. As long as you don't leave the house during the day and stay away from windows," he reasoned.

"Easy," Summer responded for them. "My parents redid our attic years ago and I don't think I've ever seen them step foot in it. There's a half bath and queen bed up there. We can hide you away. No problem."

"Wonderful." Vienna couldn't help hiding her relief that she wouldn't have to sleep in this dark and dank building.

"Have you come across anything in your books?" Copeland asked. He was now the anxious one in the group.

"Unfortunately, nothing solid," Summer replied. "I read them all and I found—"

"You read them all?" Beckham interrupted. "Already?"

"Yes," Summer was suddenly embarrassed. "I learned how to speed read when I was quite young. Even though we didn't have access to many books, my mother felt it was important to teach me. I think I've read *The History of Carnot* at least a million times," she exaggerated. "Anyway, as I was saying, I found they all have an element of loyalty to friends but that seems like a general theme of like... life."

Beckham let out a chuckle and Vienna shot him a look.

"What?" Beckham defensively asked. "She's funny."

Summer grinned at Beckham. If it had been lighter in the room, a faint blush could have been seen on her cheeks.

"She's right though," Vienna replied. "Loyalty to friends is great but I'm not exactly sure how we're supposed to use that for a revolution." She quickly defended herself, before anyone could construe her words incorrectly. "Of course, I know we need to be loyal to one another but what I am saying is we already knew that."

"True," Copeland agreed. "So, what do we do next?" He didn't like to talk in circles about things. Copeland had never cared much for thinking; he had always been more of an action taker.

"We should switch books," Summer suggested.

"Or shift our focus back to how we want to lead a revolution," Vienna proposed.

"I think we should keep reading," Beckham agreed with Summer.

"I'm with Vienna," Copeland added. "Looks like it's up to you, Martin. Do we keep reading or start planning?"

Martin sighed. He never liked to be the one making decisions. He thought about it for a moment and then declared, "I think we should keep reading. I know books are valuable and I think regardless of whether or not we find they have a correlation to the task at hand, reading them will help us learn and be more prepared."

"You really think reading this children's book is going to help us take control of Carnot?" Vienna questioned as she held up a very old and tattered copy of *Charlotte's Web*.

"I don't know," Martin replied. "But I don't think it can hurt."

"Okay," Vienna hesitantly sighed. "I guess I don't have anything better to suggest."

"Perfect. Everyone, pass your books to the left," Summer instructed.

"Yikes," Beckham commented, seeing that Martin had handed him a large stack of twelve books. He'd only successfully scanned through two of the four books he'd passed to Vienna.

"Looks thrilling," Copeland sarcastically commented on the book at the top of the pile Vienna had passed him. The green tinted cover depicted an old man with a long beard and a small boy holding a wand.

"Actually, it was pretty good," Vienna admitted. "At least the parts I read."

"I'll take your word for it." Copeland winked.

Did he just wink at me, Vienna curiously wondered, her cheeks suddenly feeling warm?

"Alright, it's settled," Martin said taking charge. "We will each read our next set of books and meet back here tomorrow night. In the meantime, of course, we should all still be thinking of the best way to move forward with our mission."

Everyone nodded in agreement.

"And needless to say," Martin added, "we all hope Theodore and Margaret don't pull anything over on us."

"Let's hope not," Beckham exhaled.

"Are you good to take them with you?" Martin asked Summer.

"Yes," she replied. "It shouldn't be a problem. When I left, my parents weren't home. I doubt they will be now."

Vienna felt an unfamiliar twinge in her stomach. She almost felt bad for Summer, the girl who appeared to have everything.

"Great," Martin replied. "Why don't you three go first?"

"Okay," they all agreed. Vienna and Beckham worked to fit as much as they could in the duffel bag. Summer grabbed the bag of food they'd packed and added her stack of books to it. Beckham put the duffel bag on his shoulder and wrapped his books in a blanket. Vienna grabbed the other two blankets and wrapped her books in them.

"It's amazing how much easier it is to carry this stuff when you're not running for your life," Beckham laughed.

"True," Vienna chuckled.

"We'll see you tomorrow night," Summer said as she started walking down the steps off the stage.

Copeland waved and Martin called, "See you!"

The three of them took the least populated roads on their walk to Summer's house and in the dark of the night, they didn't see anyone else.

There were a few lights on in the house as they walked up the driveway to Summer's front door.

"Good," she commented. "They still aren't home."

Vienna had no idea how she possibly knew that, but she was thankful she did.

They walked in and Beckham's jaw dropped at the stunning décor and architecture. Summer was walking in front of them and Vienna lightly tapped his chin, signaling him to pick up his jaw before it hit the floor.

"But look," Beckham mouthed as he pointed to the space around them.

"I know," Vienna mouthed back.

"So, this is our humble abode," Summer said as she turned on a few more lights. "We should probably get upstairs quickly. We don't want to press our luck."

They both nodded and followed Summer as she started up the wooden steps. They made it to the second floor and walked down a wide hallway. At the end of the hall, Summer opened a door that looked like it would lead to a closet, unveiling more wooden steps.

"Sorry, about the narrow stairs," she apologized.

For one moment, Vienna thought the sleeping quarters might not be as nice as she'd hoped, but then, she made it to the top of the steps.

"It doesn't really fit the theme of the rest of the house," Summer said. "But I think it's a cool space."

The back slanted wall of the room had two large windows that took up nearly all of it. The floor was a light wood color and on the left side of the room were matte black stairs. Beckham took a few steps in and turned in a circle to take a look at it all. He set the duffel bag on the floor and even Vienna didn't comment on his dropped jaw this time.

The platform bed to the right was made of an intricate wood design that reached all the way up to the "V" of the ceiling. The white walls and sleek furniture worked perfectly to create a beautifully modern space.

Beckham walked up the black staircase and exclaimed, "There's another bed up here!"

"Really?" Vienna questioned and she followed him up.

"Oh, it's just a mattress," Summer commented as she followed them. The small loft space had a futon-like mattress covered with a plethora of blankets. "My mom designed the space for her 'meditation,'" she made air quotes with her fingers, "but she's never once used it. I didn't think either of you would want to sleep on a mattress without support."

Oh, heavens no, Vienna thought in a posh accent. *How could we possibly sleep without support?*

"I call dibs." Beckham raised his hand.

"Where's the bathroom?" Vienna asked, realizing suddenly she needed to go and not caring about sleeping in the loft.

"If you walk downstairs, it's to the left of the stairs we came up," Summer answered.

Vienna walked back down the steps and into the bathroom. A huge shower took up the back wall and the room was almost bigger than the loft, with a large soaking tub on the left side and a toilet and vanity on the right.

"I thought you said it was a half bath?" Vienna questioned when she walked out of the bathroom.

"It is," Summer replied. "It only has one sink."

Beckham's face displayed everything Vienna wanted to. He let out a hardy laugh. "Is that what you think a half bath is?"

"Uhm, yes." Summer nervously bit her lip.

"A half bath is when there's no shower or bathtub," Beckham explained. "Like, when it's just a toilet and sink."

"Oh, well, sorry for the confusion." Summer was clearly embarrassed. "I hope it will do."

"It will more than do," Vienna reassured her. "It's great."

"Wonderful." Summer smiled. "I must admit I am rather exhausted. I am going to get some sleep. I'll come back in the morning to check on you and bring some food."

"Thank you," said Vienna.

"Sounds good," Beckham added.

After Summer had left the room, Beckham sat down on the side of the bed and Vienna joined him.

"I hope Mom's not too worried about us," he commented.

Even though Vienna was still furious at her mother, she agreed. She didn't like the thought of her agonizing over them. "I'm sure she's fine," she fibbed in an attempt to help calm both her and her brother's nerves.

Chapter Forty-Seven

After her conversation with Theodore, Margaret wanted to run home. She wanted to run screaming, "I am sorry" the whole way but she knew she couldn't. She knew trying to convince Theodore of anything but killing their kids would be an impossible task and would only make him question her loyalty. She knew if she left work early, he would also question her loyalty.

Her mind would have raced uncontrollably the last two hours of the day if it hadn't been for the fact that the birthday party, which had previously been canceled, was now back on. She packed up her desk for the third time and moved up to the third floor again. Theodore no longer cared about Copeland's opinion. He sent one of his men to tell Madison that she had free rein over the entire party and could plan whatever she wanted. Madison spent the rest of the day brainstorming and Margaret pretended to listen while her mind wandered.

How have I let things get so far out of hand, she wondered? *I need to apologize. I need to let them know I am on their side.*

After what seemed like an eternity, it was finally five o'clock. She hurried home as quickly as she possibly could. When she arrived, she flung open the front door, ready to beg for forgiveness for all she'd done wrong.

"Vienna!" she called. "Beckham!"

She caught sight of the disastrous kitchen; cabinet doors were flung open; food was half opened and the counters were slightly wet.

No, she thought to herself.

She ran upstairs and into Vienna's room. It looked like a tornado had blown through with clothes strewn across her floor. She went to Beckham's room to disappointingly find the same result. She sat on his bed and buried her face in her hands.

"They left," she sighed. I *don't blame them*, she mused, once again replaying all of the terrible things she'd done. *Should I run after them? Where would they even go? There's no telling how far they've made it by now.*

She absentmindedly stared up at the ceiling.

My only option is to help them succeed before the first of January, she concluded. *But how can I find them?* Her mind raced and after a while, she yelled, "Aha! How did I not think of it sooner?" she answered her own question. "Martin. I need to get to Martin."

Knowing Martin would have already left for the day, she reasoned her best bet was to catch him at work in the morning, ideally, first thing.

I'll schedule the earliest meeting possible with him tomorrow, she thought. *That way, I can get some time alone with him and explain myself.*

The rest of the night dragged on. Margaret couldn't remember the last time she'd spent the night alone.

When the twins were younger, they'd occasionally spend the night at their friends' houses, but Lewis had always been there, and since he'd passed away, they hadn't slept anywhere but home.

Margaret tossed and turned in bed all night. She was thankful when the sun began to creep into her bedroom. She got ready quickly and decided to walk to the office, instead of taking the train.

Unsurprisingly, she was the first one to arrive on the third floor and immediately, she dialed Helen Felton.

"Good morning, this is Helen." The woman on the other end picked up in a tone most would feel was much too chipper for eight in the morning. Helen had worked at Carnot for over forty years as assistant to the assistants. As she liked to say, "I'm in charge of keeping track of and scheduling each assistant's calendar, as they schedule the important people's calendars."

"Hi, Helen, it's Margaret. I'm looking to schedule the first available meeting with Martin. It's urgent regarding Copeland's birthday party."

"Okay," Helen replied. "Let me take a look for you," she hummed to herself as she looked through his schedule. "It looks like he has an opening at 9:30 this morning."

"That would be perfect."

"And is it just you for the meeting or will others be joining?"

"Actually, I won't be attending," Margaret lied. She wanted to ensure Martin would show. "It will just be Madison."

"Oh, okay then, dear. Does the Aphrodite Suite work?"

"That's great."

"Okay. Perfect! I've got her down for 9:30 A.M. today

in the Aphrodite Suite," Helen declared. "Is there anything else I can do for you?"

"No." Margaret's smile could almost be heard through the phone. "You've been a tremendous help."

"Have a lovely day," said Helen.

"Thank you! You too." She hung up.

Margaret was surprised how quickly the next hour and a half passed. In no time, she found herself standing outside of the suite. She walked in and made herself comfortable at the large table. She tapped her foot nervously, waiting for Martin, desperately hoping he'd come.

A few minutes later, the door opened, and Copeland walked in. He quickly halted when he saw Margaret's face.

"What is she doing here?" He looked at Martin, appalled.

"What are you doing here?" Margaret asked Copeland.

Martin quickly shut the door behind them and answered Margaret's question first. "I told him I had a meeting about his birthday party, and he asked to join. Considering it's his party, which he is now being forced to host against his will, I obliged," Martin answered, an air of vexation in his voice. "As for her," he looked at Copeland, "I have no idea. I was under the impression this meeting was with Madison."

Copeland and Martin stayed standing, close to the door. Margaret stood up and began to walk toward them. Instinctively, they both took a step back.

"Please, let me explain," she begged.

"Explain what?" Copeland was very defensive. "We

already know you planted the article. We assume you're sleeping with my father. And we know you're a traitor. What would you possibly want to explain? Did you just come here to gloat?"

"No." She sounded sincere. "I'm sorry. I'm sorry for everything. I was wrong. I was so very wrong, and I know that now. I need to speak to Beckham and Vienna."

Copeland let out a loud and obnoxious laugh. "Yeah, right! As if we'd ever tell you where they are."

Martin didn't feel as defensive as Copeland did. He could see the hurt in Margaret's eyes. He could tell her pain was running deep.

"Maybe, we should hear her out," Martin suggested. "Would it really hurt anything to hear what she has to say?"

"Are you serious?" Copeland was still very guarded.

"Right now, we have a plan without Margaret, and we are fine." Martin spoke to Copeland as if she wasn't in the room. "If we don't believe her, we leave and she's on her own to find the twins. No harm done really. However, if for some reason, we do believe her, we gain an ally and possible knowledge," he reasoned. "We can only gain by listening to what she has to say."

Margaret pleaded, "Please."

Copeland huffed. He couldn't argue with Martin's logic. "I'll give you three minutes," he said as he held up three fingers and walked to take a seat in a chair.

"Oh, thank you," Margaret replied. "Thank you, thank you."

"The time has already started." Copeland looked down at his watch. He didn't care for her gratitude.

Martin joined Copeland at the table as Margaret

began explaining herself. She didn't take a seat with them but instead paced along the opposite side of the room.

"I'm going to give you the fastest summary I can," she began. "Years ago, when Lewis was still alive, I met your father at a party and things escalated rather quickly from there." She didn't want to get into the details. "We both knew our significant others were working to overthrow Carnot, so Theodore put an end to it. He ordered them to be killed in the next round of Ivy Letters. After that, I didn't see him for years. Actually, I didn't see him until last week. I mean, of course, I did in passing but we hadn't spoken in all of that time. I hated that he took my Lewis and I hated more that part of the reason was because he wanted me. When you guys came over that first night and read your mother's letter," she looked at Copeland, "I was truly on board with helping you. Your father is a sick man and I wanted revenge for Lewis... but then, the next day he called me to his office out of the blue. He hadn't done it in years, but because you asked Vienna to be your date, he wanted to speak with me." She was holding back tears now. "I don't know why he has such power over me. When I was with him, it was like everything else faded away again and for the first time since Lewis' death, I felt something... I felt loved."

Copeland wanted to laugh or make a gagging sound like an immature boy but truthfully, down in his soul, he knew what she meant.

"I helped him formulate a plan to publish the article about Lewis and Camilla. We hoped it would discourage you all from meeting again and after I met with you at Tellmen's and spoke with Vienna, I really thought it had. It wasn't until yesterday afternoon, when Theodore told me that he ran into Beckham and Vienna at Carnot, that I realized it hadn't." She sighed. "And it wasn't until my conversation with him that I realized how far off course I'd gone. He..." she trailed off.

"He what?" Copeland prompted.

Margaret took a deep breath. "He told me yesterday afternoon that he plans to kill you all in the next round of Ivy Letters."

"What?" Copeland blinked rapidly. "He said that?" He'd always known his father was cold, but still, this news was almost too much to bear.

"I'm afraid so," Margaret replied. "It was my breaking point. I know my breaking point should have been much sooner and I deeply regret that it wasn't, but all I can do now is make the next right decision and it's this. It's helping you. It's helping my babies."

Martin sat speechless. He'd known he'd wanted to hear Margaret out but even he hadn't thought she'd provide such valuable information.

"But what if this is a lie?" Copeland countered. "How can we trust you after all you've done?"

"You can't." Margaret spoke honestly. "I've done absolutely nothing to earn your trust but I am giving you all I have to offer right now, and I do hope you'll consider it. Lewis always used to say, 'the only way to find out if you can trust someone is to trust that you can.' So, that's what I am doing. You have all of the information you need now, and I understand if you want nothing to do with me."

Martin mulled over her words. "Could we have a minute?"

"Of course," she replied.

Martin stood up and Copeland followed. They stepped out into the hall and spoke quietly.

"I'm not so su—" Copeland started.

"We can trust her," Martin interrupted.

"You're sold that quickly?" Copeland was shocked.

"You can see it in her eyes. She's desperate. She messed up and she's at our feet, begging to fix it. It's a matter of her children now."

Copeland wanted to argue. He wanted to say Martin was wrong. He wanted to protect Vienna and he worried allowing her mom back in would put that protection at risk, but he knew Martin was right. He could sense Margaret's desperation in every word, and he felt deep in his bones that what she was saying was true.

"Okay," he finally sighed. "I agree."

Chapter Forty-Eight

Copeland spent the rest of the day reading. He had three books to get through: the sixth novel in a series about wizards, *Romeo and Juliet*, and *My Sister's Keeper*.

When Vienna had handed him the stack of books, he'd complained about the wizard one, but after looking closer at the other two books, he realized it looked the least girly of them all. He tried to read *Romeo and Juliet*, but it was hard to understand, and the last book seemed boring to him. He ended up opting to switch back and forth between them all. He was a good reader, but he hadn't had much of an opportunity to practice his skill, so he read rather slowly.

What in the world do these books have in common, he wondered? He read and then thought and then read again and then thought some more. *How can we overtake Carnot? Even with Margaret, there are only six of us and there are so many of them.* He thought of all of the guards in Carnot. Even though the city had never seen a war, or really even a simple street fight, Copeland knew they had more power prepared than they let on.

Around seven o'clock, Copeland's stomach rumbled,

and he realized he hadn't eaten all day. He didn't know where Martin was, and even though he normally left around five, he assumed he was still in the building. He pressed the button by his bed and sure enough, a few minutes later, Martin arrived at his door.

"Good evening, sir," he greeted. He bowed out of respect for protocol, even though it was no longer necessary for their relationship.

"I just realized I haven't eaten all day," Copeland said, "and I don't think I can read another word right now. I need to pass some time before tonight. I am getting anxious."

"I understand," Martin replied, and Copeland could now see the bags underneath his eyes. He looked exhausted. "Shall we go to the kitchen and see what we can find?"

"Yes. Let's do that."

They walked together through the empty halls of Carnot. It was times like these when Copeland realized just how big his home was. The halls went on and on when no one was filling them and the whole place was eerily quiet.

They entered the large kitchen and Copeland went immediately to the freezer. He pulled out a gallon of mint chocolate chip ice cream.

"Is that your dinner?" Martin asked.

"Nope." Copeland walked to the refrigerator and pulled out chocolate syrup and whipped cream. "This is my dinner," he declared.

Martin laughed, "That actually sounds pretty good."

Copeland opened a cabinet and got out two bowls. "I'll serve you up some." He prepared two large bowls of ice cream topped with a generous amount of whipped cream and chocolate syrup. "Yum," he commented to himself as he sat on the counter and took his first bite.

"Yum is right." Martin joined Copeland on the counter.

"I hope tonight goes well."

"What's tonight?" a familiar voice asked and the hair on Copeland's back stood up.

"Father." Copeland turned to see Theodore walking in the kitchen. "How are you?" he asked. He had managed to avoid seeing his father since their conversation regarding his birthday party.

Martin quickly stood to his feet before Theodore saw him and set the ice cream down. It was not acceptable protocol for him to be acting so casually while he was with Copeland.

"I'm well," Theodore plainly replied, not forgetting his original question. "What's tonight?"

"I'm taking Summer on our first date since we've been back together," he quickly lied.

Wow, Martin thought to himself. *That was good.*

"I didn't realize you two were back together."

"Well, since I'm being forced to still have my birthday party, I figured it was best to show up with a date," Copeland replied. "And I didn't feel like Vienna was a viable choice anymore."

"I see," said Theodore. "I think that's a wise decision." He walked to the refrigerator and pulled out a plate with a metal lid. He set it on the counter and uncovered a delicious looking meal of chicken, rice, and vegetables. He placed it in the microwave and waited in silence until it was heated.

Awkwardly, Copeland continued to eat his ice cream while Martin stood, watching his melt.

"Good luck," Theodore wished Copeland. "Oh… One more thing, Martin. You might want to wipe that whipped cream off your upper lip," he smirked as he walked out of the kitchen.

Martin's stomach dropped and he wiped his mouth. Once the sound of his footsteps faded down the hall, Copeland let out a sigh.

"Oh my. What are the chances?" he asked.

"Good save," Martin complimented.

"Do you think it was believable?"

"I don't think you could have come up with anything better."

They finished their ice cream and spent the next few hours reading and twiddling their thumbs in Copeland's room. When the clock hit 11:15, they started on their way to the theater. They'd planned to meet Margaret at 11:40 at the corner of Philmore and 14th Street.

Carnot was even quieter than before. They took the quickest route out of the building, which was out a side exit a few doors down from Copeland's room. The guard at the gate was sworn to secrecy in service to the Howth family, so they didn't have to worry about him telling a soul. They quietly made their way off the property and down the city streets. Carnot was a quiet town and few people were ever out in the faint glow of the streetlights.

They arrived at their meeting place a couple minutes early. They could see the outline of a person walking toward them a few blocks north.

"I bet that's her," Copeland commented. He was right;

a few minutes later, Margaret approached them.

"Hello," she said.

"Hi, Margaret. Follow us," Martin instructed, wasting no time. He felt it would be best for them to be inside the theater before the others. If Beckham or Vienna got upset, it was less likely they'd be heard in the theater. Plus, they still needed to fill her in on everything they'd figured out.

Martin climbed through the small opening between the wooden boards and Margaret hesitantly followed. Copeland went through last, scanning the street around them for any followers. He still was on his highest defense with Margaret joining them.

Margaret stuck up her nose at the smell of rotting wood. It was hard to see in the dark, with only the glow of flashlights, but she could see the walls, covered with chipped paint and the velvet chairs coated with thick layers of dust.

"How did you find this place?" she asked.

"Camilla found it." Martin didn't care to explain further.

They made their way up to the stage where they'd met the previous night and made themselves comfortable.

Martin began catching Margaret up to speed. He started with their theory on the false consensus effect and filled in everything up to Summer and the books they were trying to understand.

Margaret wanted to be upset at Summer for betraying her, but she knew she had no right to be mad.

Just when he'd finished explaining, they heard a rustling noise coming from the lobby. They turned off their flashlights and sat silently.

A few moments later, they could see three figures carrying flashlights, walking toward the stage.

"Hello," Vienna called as she shined her flashlight on the stage. She shined it back and forth until she caught three people in the light. "Who's there?" She stopped in her tracks. She could swear it was her mother, but she hoped her mind was playing tricks on her.

"It's okay," Copeland quickly replied. "She's on our side."

"What is she doing here?!" Beckham exploded before Vienna could even process what he'd said.

"Beckham, please keep quiet," Martin begged. "It's okay."

"I don't know why you think it's okay," Beckham argued at a slightly quieter decibel.

"We promise," Martin replied. "She came to us this morning and told us everything."

"She can help," Copeland added.

Margaret spoke up for the first time. "Please hear me out." Vienna didn't want to listen but something in her made her take another step toward the stage.

Beckham and Summer, who also had every right to be upset at Margaret, followed Vienna's lead.

They sat down on the ground and formed a circle, just as they'd done the previous night. Neither Beckham nor Vienna made eye contact with their mother.

"I'm sorry," Margaret started. "I know you have no reason to trust me but please, hear me out."

Beckham waved his hand, still not looking up, signaling her to continue.

Margaret dove into all of the gritty details she'd shared earlier in the day with Copeland and Martin.

She told the kids of her affair and her relationship with Theodore. She explained why she'd gone to Summer to sabotage their plans. She told them she'd realized how wrong she'd been when Theodore said he planned to kill them all.

"In that moment, I realized everything I'd done wrong. I realized how far off course I'd gotten, and I knew I needed to do everything I could to reach you and help save your lives. We don't have much time. He will surely order you all to be killed on January first. We have to find a way to change things by then."

The harsh reality of her words hung in the air as Beckham and Vienna analyzed everything she'd said.

Vienna was the first to speak. "How could you betray Dad like that?" she questioned. "First with the affair and then with the article?"

"I don't know." Margaret's eyes began to well. "I made huge mistakes and I don't have any way to justify them. If I could undo them, I would, but I can't and for that, I am forever sorry."

"It's okay, Mom," Beckham said forgiving her. "Thank you for your apology."

Vienna was angry at her mother, and though she could hear the sincerity in her voice, she still wasn't sold.

"Just like that?" she questioned Beckham, a little angrily. "You're going to forgive her just like that? After everything she's done?"

"Yeah, I am," Beckham confidently replied. "She has nothing to gain in coming to us but everything to lose. If Theodore finds out, she's dead too. People make mistakes, V."

Vienna sighed and threw her head back.

"He's right, you know," Copeland added. "I had a hard time believing her earlier, but I know he's right. Plus, even if we're wrong and she's still lying, which I don't think she is, we're going to die next month anyway, so what do we have to lose?"

Vienna might not have trusted her mother, but she did trust Beckham and Copeland. She bit her lip and sighed heavily. After a few silent moments, she finally answered, "Okay. I forgive you."

Margaret excitedly stood up and went to hug them both. She stood between them, leaned down and squeezed them tightly.

"Thank you! Thank you!" she beamed. "I promise I won't let you down."

"I forgive you, too," Summer quietly added, though no one acknowledged her.

"I guess we should get her filled in," Beckham suggested.

"We already did that," Martin informed him.

"What if we hadn't agreed to work with her?" Vienna questioned, annoyed at their moving forward without the approval of everyone.

"We had a feeling you would," Copeland half-heartedly laughed.

Vienna rolled her eyes. "Good. Then, I guess we can get down to business. Any thoughts?"

"Martin just filled me in on your theory of false consensus effect and I think that's a great one," Margaret started. "I think you see the truth of that in people like Theodore and myself. If the injection really made people and all things good, then we wouldn't be sinful."

Summer added, "And my mother wouldn't be an alcoholic."

"Exactly," Margaret agreed slowly, feeling the awkwardness of Summer's confession. "I think how our society functions is also a result of groupthink. There is no creativity or ability to think differently, leaving everyone acting the same."

Vienna had never heard her mother speak so intelligently before.

"Where did you learn about groupthink?" Beckham questioned.

"Your father may not have told me everything he worked on but that didn't mean I didn't have access to his books," Margaret explained.

"She makes an excellent point," Beckham was now talking to everyone. "I think we can all agree the injection does not change the mold or thought process of our minds but only our physical bodies. It's our society and environment that has changed our minds. With the elimination of all bad things in Carnot, we've only learned how to be good," Beckham explained, "but the cracks in this foundation are starting to show at a rapid pace."

"We have to expose it," Copeland responded.

"But the question is: how?" Vienna asked.

"If we simply tell people, they won't believe us," said Summer.

"And even if they did, the government would still be in control," Margaret added.

"We have to do something so powerful it leaves no room for questioning," Vienna reasoned.

"But we don't know what that is," Martin said.

"Not yet," Vienna replied. "But we still have plenty of time. We have twenty-one days until the first of the month. The government is utterly powerless during that time."

"That's true," Margaret concurred.

"If we work together, I know we can come up with something," Beckham encouraged.

"We all need to be on the same page in the meantime," Copeland instructed. "As far as everyone out there knows," he gestured to the city around them, "Martin is my assistant and nothing more, Margaret is planning my party and on my father's side, Vienna is a girl I can no longer date due to the article on Lewis and Camilla, Beckham is… well, sorry, but you're still just Beckham as usual, and Summer is my now-steady girlfriend."

Vienna's stomach twinged at his words.

"Precisely," Beckham agreed. "From the outside, no one should assume anything abnormal is happening. Luckily, we have people inside Carnot who can help us communicate. We would probably be pressing our luck to meet every night, but Summer and Margaret can always get into Carnot and communicate for us. And then, when we need to discuss big things, we can all get together."

"I like it," Martin replied. "I think that's a great plan."

"Me too," Vienna lied. She didn't like the fact that she wouldn't get to see Copeland as often as she'd hoped.

"Then, it's settled," Margaret declared. "What's next on the agenda?"

"We should switch books again," Summer suggested. "Without meeting, it will be harder to switch books so we should try to get as many books to each side as possible. We can keep half at Carnot, and you can keep half at your house."

"Perfect," Beckham agreed. "Let's do it."

They emptied their coats and bags and placed all of the books in the center of the circle. Summer announced each one and placed it in a pile where the least amount of people on the side had read it.

When she was finished, Vienna recommended they shouldn't spend too much more time reading. "I'm just saying, with our limited amount of time, I don't think we should spend too much of it trying to solve a puzzle we're not even sure has any answers, let alone, any correlation."

"She makes a good point," Copeland agreed. "I say we give it another week of reading and if we've got nothing, we move on."

"I can agree with that."

"Me too."

"Me three."

"Same."

"Great." Vienna was pleased everyone was on board.

"Well, if we don't have anything else to cover right now, I guess we should be on our way," Martin proposed.

"Just one second," Copeland replied. "Vienna, could I talk to you in private for a moment?"

"Uhm, sure." She raised an eyebrow.

A few days ago, that comment would have pierced Summer in the heart but now, with Beckham sitting next to her, she hardly heard his request.

Copeland stood up and grabbed Vienna's hand to help her to her feet. He didn't let go until he'd led her backstage to what must have been, in its prime, a dressing room.

Copeland took a deep breath and worked up his nerve. "I wanted to tell you—"

"Actually, I have something to say," Vienna interrupted.

"Okay?" Copeland tentatively replied.

"I don't know what you're going to say but obviously, I did overhear your conversation with Summer yesterday and I just don't think this would be a good time for this." She motioned between them. She spoke with a false confidence. "Before you said anything, I just wanted you to know how I felt." Vienna didn't know what came over her. *Why am I being so guarded*, she disappointingly wondered, hearing her words?

"Oh, yeah. For sure." Copeland tried to play it cool even though his heart felt like it had shattered into a million pieces. "I was just going to make sure you were okay with me pretending to date Summer," he lied. "You know, it's going to be all over the papers and whatnot, and with the news about your father, it might be hard to handle." He was instinctively defensive. "I wanted to double check you'd be okay."

"Uh, yeah. I can handle it," Vienna smugly replied. She hated that her heart beat wildly out of control when she was in the same room as him. She'd never depended on anyone other than Beckham or herself, and the last thing she needed, in the midst of their stress, was to worry about a boy. Let alone a boy who had only noticed her for his own personal agenda.

"Good." Copeland shrugged.

"Good." Vienna shrugged back.

They walked out from behind the stage to join the others once again. Martin and Margaret were standing and chatting, while Summer and Beckham were still seated.

"You two ready now?" Martin questioned.

"Yep," Vienna answered and picked up her pace to walk ahead of Copeland.

"Perfect," Martin replied. "Let's get out of here."

Chapter Forty-Nine

"Stupid, stupid, stupid." Vienna fumed aloud, lying in bed with her hand on her forehead. "Why would you tell him you don't want to be with him?" She replayed her conversation with Copeland.

Her bedroom door creaked open.

"Oh, good. You're still awake," Beckham whispered.

"Can't sleep." Vienna sat up.

"Me either."

It was nearly three A.M. They'd made it back to their house around one, and Margaret had gone to sleep right away. She'd had a big day and the immense relief of forgiveness she'd felt had helped to knock her right out. Beckham had said he was tired and went straight to bed as well, but clearly, he wasn't tired enough to shut off his mind.

"What did Copeland say to you?" he asked as he sat down next to her on the bed.

"Is that really why you came in here?"

"Part of the reason for sure," Beckham admitted.

"I think he was going to tell me he liked me," she replied.

"You think?"

"Yeah, I think... because... I cut him off," Vienna explained. "I cut him off and told him I didn't think it would be a good time for us with everything going on."

"What? Why would you say that? Don't you like him?"

"I mean, I guess so, but Beck, there's so much going on right now. I've never even had a boyfriend... let alone a famous one. You saw the cameras on our first date. I can't sign up for that," Vienna rambled.

"But he likes you and he's kind and well-mannered and rich." Beckham winked. "Why not let someone in?"

Beckham had nailed it and Vienna knew it. Since her father had died, she'd been completely closed off to everyone.

"It doesn't matter." Vienna shook her head. "I closed the door. Anyway, he said he just wanted to make sure I would be okay seeing all the news of him and Summer and Dad and whatnot." She shrugged.

Beckham sighed and rolled his eyes. "What am I going to do with you?"

"Don't know," Vienna laughed.

"Will you do me a favor?" Beckham asked.

"Depends what it is."

"Just think about it," he replied. "Consider letting someone in. You might find it's actually kind of nice."

"I'll consider it," Vienna agreed just to stop talking about it.

"Thank you." Beckham smiled. "Well, aren't you going to ask me about my love life?" he prompted.

"What?" Vienna looked blankly at him. "What love life?"

"With Summer."

"Like, Summer Nile?" Vienna was confused.

"Uhm, duh. Have you not noticed we've been completely hitting it off?" Beckham was a little offended.

Vienna laughed. "Seriously? I had no idea. Good for you, Beck. I mean, she's a little bit crazy," she made circles in the air with her pointer finger, "but she's also a catch."

"Thanks. I was really excited to be staying at her house. I thought I'd get to spend some time with her but then, Mom had to go changing to be a good person and all," he joked.

"Awe, and now she has to pretend to be with Copeland," Vienna realized the difficulty of Beckham's situation.

"Yep." Beckham sighed. "At least she knows he doesn't love her. At least I know it's all for show."

"Have you talked to her about your feelings?"

"Not yet," he replied. "But the chemistry is there for sure."

What I would give to have such confidence, Vienna laughed in her head. "Good for you," she approved aloud.

"Thanks, V! I guess it's quite the love triangle... or more like love square we find ourselves in," Beckham chuckled.

"If only I loved someone in the square." She smirked.

"If only." Beckham rolled his eyes again and with that, he stood up and left the room.

Vienna must have fallen asleep shortly after he left because she woke up to the sun shining in through her curtains and couldn't remember anything else. She put on a pair of loose-fitting, green pants and a baggy, white shirt. She wanted to brush her teeth, but her toothbrush was still at Summer's house and she didn't have a spare, so she opted for rinsing her mouth out with water. She brushed her hair and pulled it back into a high ponytail before heading downstairs.

Her mother was already up, and the pot of coffee had just finished brewing.

"Morning," Vienna greeted. She was thankful to be back in her own home with her mother to take care of her.

"Good morning," Margaret replied. She must not have heard Vienna coming because she seemed a bit startled. "How did you sleep?"

"I didn't get much of it, but I slept well when I did," Vienna answered. "And yourself?"

"I slept very well," she replied.

"Which book are you reading?" Vienna noticed the book she'd set down on the kitchen counter.

"*The Hunger Games*?" Margaret answered as if it were a question. She looked at the front of the book to confirm. "Yes, *The Hunger Games*. It's good so far."

"Nice," Vienna replied as she poured a cup of coffee. "Notice anything special about it?"

"I wish," Margaret shrugged. "Not yet. What book are you starting with today?"

"Uhm, I have to go back upstairs and grab it. It's like chronology of something or something like that." She couldn't remember.

"Nice. How many books have you read so far?"

"I've scanned seven, but I've generally only under-stood five of them."

"Good job," she complimented.

"Yeah, well, I think Summer has read like fifteen at this point so really, I'm not doing that great," Vienna deflected her compliment.

"Better than me," Margaret admitted.

Vienna went upstairs and grabbed her book. On the way back down, she announced, "The book is actually titled *The Lion, the Witch and the Wardrobe*. It's from a series called *The Chronicles of Narnia*, I guess."

"Interesting," Margaret replied.

The two of them sat in silence reading their books until Margaret had to leave for work.

Once Beckham was up, he and Vienna stacked all of the books up in her room and divided them into unread piles for each of them. They spent the rest of the morning and afternoon scanning as many books as they could.

Around four o'clock, Beckham, who was lying on the floor of Vienna's bedroom, groaned. "I am not finding anything. I don't understand how these book correlate. In this one," he grabbed *The Hunger Games*, "kids are fighting to the death and this one," he pointed to *Romeo and Juliet*, "is about star-crossed lovers a long, long time ago."

"Plus, that one's not even a book," Vienna replied. "It's a script."

"Exactly." Beckham threw up his hands. "She dies for him and he dies for her... big whoop."

"Righ—" Vienna stopped mid-thought. "Wait, say that again."

"What? She dies for him and he dies for her?" Beckham repeated himself.

"Yes," Vienna stood up. "Yes! That's it. Beck! You're a

genius! What do all of these books have in common?" she asked as she began excitedly pacing the room.

"I don't know, V," Beckham annoyingly replied. "That's what we've been trying to figure out."

"Think about it." Vienna spoke rapidly. "In that one, her sister volunteers to take her place in the games. In that one, they both die for love. In that one, the lion dies to save the boy. Sacrifice, Beck! They're all about sacrifice!"

Beckham scanned the books scattered all over the floor. He tried to remember what each one was about.

"I think you're right." Beckham's eyebrows moved inquisitively. "I really think you might be right." He couldn't believe it. "But what does that mean for us?"

"For starters, it means we can stop reading," Vienna laughed.

Beckham laughed too. It felt like they could relax for one second in the midst of all the stress.

"But as far as the revolution, I don't really know," she said when she'd finished laughing.

"We need to meet with the others," Beckham suggested.

"Yes, we do. Unfortunately, I don't think we can make that happen until tomorrow night."

"We could call," Beckham proposed.

"You know we can't do that," Vienna replied. "There are so few phones in Carnot and surely, they're all monitored."

"I know," Beckham sighed. He knew they had no safe way of pushing up the meeting, but he was bummed. "I guess tomorrow will have to do."

Chapter Fifty

Beckham was thankful the time had finally come for them to meet with the others. The day had dragged on at a dreadfully slow pace and he thought the night would never come.

The Tunstons arrived at the theater before the others. They sat on the stage and anxiously waited for them. It wasn't long before lights could be seen shining across the building. Copeland and Martin were the next to arrive. A few minutes later, Summer walked in.

"Alright, let's not waste any time," Beckham started speaking the second Summer sat down. "Vienna, go right ahead."

"As Beckham and I were reading yesterday, the connection between the books finally dawned on me," she started. "They're all about sacrifice." She stopped speaking and gave them all a moment to think about it. "It seems in each one, someone or something is sacrificed to save someone or something else."

"The question is: how does this help us?" Beckham interjected.

"Actually, Beck, I think I may have figured it out," Vienna replied.

"Oh," Beckham sighed, slightly hurt she hadn't told him earlier.

"Based on our theories of false consensus effect and groupthink," Vienna went on, "we believe that everyone can think for themselves; they've just learned not to and don't know any different."

A few people nodded in agreement.

"So, what we have to do is show them they *can* think for themselves," she paused, "by showing them *we* can think for ourselves."

"What do you mean?" Copeland asked. He feared he knew where she was going but he didn't like it.

"We have to show them we can die. We have to show everyone that we can still make bad choices," she explained. "We have to sacrifice." She took a deep breath. "I need one of you to kill me."

"What?!"

"No!"

"Absolutely not!"

"It's the only way." Vienna continued. "I've thought it through from every angle and all of the pieces of the puzzle fit this solution. We have to show everyone we can think freely. We have to show them we can make bad decisions."

"Why would we want people to know they can make bad decisions?" Summer questioned.

"It's not that we want everyone to make poor decisions," Beckham explained. He now understood Vienna's plan. "It's like I said last week, in this society, we have no freedom. Before Carnot, people could make their own choices. Though they could choose to die, at least it was their own choice. Now, we don't have any say over it. If we say the wrong thing or upset the wrong people with power, we die. Why should they get to choose what happens to our lives?" Beckham went on, "The obvious hope is that by showing people good and evil, they still choose good. But, wouldn't we rather live in a world where we have freedom?"

"Exactly," Vienna agreed. "There's no point in everyone aimlessly doing good because they know no difference, while a few people in power get to control everything."

"I actually think I understand," Copeland sadly admitted.

"Me too," Summer agreed.

"Not me." Martin shook his head. "There's no way you're dying."

"But Martin," Vienna contended, "it has to be this way. I have to die to save everyone."

"No," Martin corrected himself, "I understand where you're coming from. What I am saying is that *you* do not need to be the one to die."

The room fell silent at his words, waiting for him to explain.

"You're too young. You have too much left to live for." Martin stood up and started walking around the circle. "It all makes sense now. My grandfather knew it all along. I can see it woven through every thread of his plans. He knew the foundation of Carnot would eventually shatter but he was willing to make sacrifices. He knew his family would be willing to follow in his footsteps. Think about it, we've already been impacted by sacrifices. Lewis and Camilla knew; they just didn't have time to act on their knowledge. We've already lost loved ones to the system, but now, we can change the system by losing one of us." He paused. "It's me who has to die."

Vienna wanted to object but she knew he was right. It did make sense. He was older and well-known and loved and cared for by many people. His death would shake the walls of Carnot and if they were lucky, bring them down completely.

The room was silent, everyone's minds spinning with the unfortunate weight of his words.

"But when?" Copeland sighed. "And how?" He spoke softly and with great sorrow. He'd only just found out he had an uncle and now he had to lose him.

"Before the first," Martin answered. "We have to act before the next round of Ivy Letters goes out or who knows how quickly he will kill us all."

"It needs to be very public," Summer added. "We need as many people as possible to witness the event. The more people who see it with their own eyes, the less we will have to tell."

"She's right," Vienna agreed. "But how to do it? And who? Martin, none of us want to..." she couldn't get herself to say the words.

"I wish I could do it," Martin answered. "But doing it myself would not convince anyone. It could be written off as a fluke."

"Martin, you're going to have to choose," Margaret said. "None of us will choose how or when or who. You have to make the decisions."

"I know," Martin sighed. "Can I have until tomorrow to think about it?"

"Of course," Vienna replied.

"Definitely," Copeland added.

Summer, Beckham, and Margaret nodded in agreement.

"Alright," Martin confidently stated. "We'll meet back here tomorrow night."

With that, no one said another word and they solemnly went back to their homes.

Chapter Fifty-One

Margaret had successfully been avoiding Theodore. She hadn't seen him since their conversation about the kids and though she wanted nothing less than to see his sick face, she wasn't surprised when one of his guards approached her. He told her Theodore had scheduled a lunch date for them and asked her to go to his office at noon.

At lunchtime, Margaret walked to Theodore's office and found that the food had already arrived. The coffee table was piled high with finger sandwiches, fruit, and an array of salads.

"Good afternoon." She smiled. "Yum," she added, seeing the table.

"Hello, Maggie." Theodore, who had been seated behind his desk, stood to greet her. He walked over and planted a kiss on her lips.

She kissed him back, to keep up the charade, but even she was shocked at how quickly the flame between them had burned out. His lips tasted like a sour lemon on hers.

"Take a seat." He gestured toward the couch. "Let's catch up."

His tone made Margaret nervous. *Does he know?* She felt a sense of panic come over her. *No, he can't know,* she reasoned with herself taking a calming breath. *Stop worrying.*

"First and foremost, I want to thank you for getting things back up and running for Copeland's party. I know you've been instrumental in bringing that to life and..." he stood up and walked back over to his desk, "look at this," he grabbed a newspaper and set it in front of her.

The cover featured a posed, color portrait of Copeland and Summer. Margaret read the headline to herself, *Winter Ends, Summer is Back.*

She commented, "Wow, that's great." She hoped her tone sounded convincing, but her emotions were so mixed together, she couldn't be sure.

"I know, and it's all thanks to you," Theodore beamed. "Thank you for your loyalty!"

Margaret could tell he was being sincere now. Her stomach ached. *What will he do to me when he finds out? Will he kill me? Can he kill me?* Her mind raced. For the first time, she was playing through the possible repercussions.

"How do you think your children are holding up?" he asked.

"I think they're quite alright," she replied. She picked up a triangle-shaped sandwich and began to pick at it. She desperately needed to do something with her hands. "Vienna has been moping around, as to be expected after losing the first boy she'd ever gone out with, and Beckham seems a little down as well. I think, despite whatever they found out when they came here, they're both totally sold on Copeland's abandonment of their plans," she lied.

"Magnificent," Theodore beamed. "Only a few short weeks until we can be rid of our worries completely."

Margaret felt nauseated by his words.

"I have a question for you, Maggie."

"What's that?" she asked with a mouthful of food.

Theodore stood up from the couch and slowly walked to Margaret. "I have loved you for many years," he started, "and there have been so many obstacles we've had to overcome with one another. I know we haven't spent much time together the last three years but since we've reconnected, I can't stop thinking about you."

Margaret swallowed the bite of sandwich with a big gulp, fearing the direction this conversation was headed.

"Once our children are out of the picture, there will be nothing stopping us from finally sharing our relationship with the world." He was now standing next to Margaret, looking down earnestly at her. "Which is why, I'd like to ask you, my sweet, sweet Maggie," he moved onto one knee, "the most important question of my life." As he was kneeling, he reached into his pocket and pulled out a small, black, velvet box. "Margaret Willow Tunston, will you marry me?" He opened the box, unveiling a gorgeous white gold engagement ring with small diamonds sparking around the band and a large, glistening four-carat, round cut diamond in the center.

Margaret didn't know what to say. Actually, she did know what to say, but she knew she couldn't say it. She hoped the time that passed in real life felt much shorter than the time in her head. She felt sick to her stomach, but she pulled herself together.

"Yes!" She smiled. She stood up and hugged Theodore while he was still kneeling on the ground. He kissed her on the cheek.

"I love you," he whispered in her ear.

"I love you, too," she whispered back.

She let go of Theodore and he stood up. He grabbed her hand and placed the ring on her left, ring finger.

"It's perfect." She felt slightly relieved that she could stop lying for one moment because the ring *was* absolutely perfect. The smallest part of her was almost upset she wouldn't get to keep it.

"Of course," Theodore started, "you can't wear it right now. We will need to wait until things settle down following the events of January to announce our engagement, but I couldn't wait to ask you."

"Certainly," Margaret agreed, taking in the ring one last time.

Theodore slipped it off of her finger and placed it gently back in the box.

If he only knew, Margaret thought to herself.

Chapter Fifty-Two

"Is there some way we can fake the death?" Copeland asked.

"No," Martin replied. He sat still, fixed in thought, on the bench in front of Copeland's bed. "If we fake the death, it is not a sacrifice but only a mirage of one."

"But what will happen when you die?" Copeland wanted desperately to understand everything. "Will a war break out? Will people still live forever?" He spoke rapidly.

"Copeland, breathe," Martin calmly replied. "I do not know everything, but what I do know is this, if we only threaten my death, the theory of good and evil will be spread into the world but only the theory. It is with the sacrifice of my life and the *knowledge* of good and evil that the people of Carnot will be saved."

"But why? Why do you have to die?" Copeland questioned.

"I must lose my life so others may find theirs."

Copeland wanted to argue. He wanted to scream and cry and throw a fit, but he knew he couldn't. He knew Martin was right. He just didn't want to believe it.

"Let's go outside," Martin suggested. "It's a lovely day and I think it would be nice to spend some time in the sun."

"Okay," Copeland agreed.

The sun was shining but the air was not as warm as Copeland had hoped. When he was tired and cold, after walking for a while, he left to go back inside, but Martin spent the rest of the day walking the grounds of Carnot.

Copeland's afternoon dragged on. He took occasional trips outside to see if Martin was still walking. Surely, Martin must have thought about how strange it might look should someone else notice, but Copeland didn't dare bring it up. He simply let him continue walking.

When the clock hit 11:30 P.M., Copeland was surprised Martin wasn't at his door; he was never late.

Surely, he's not still walking, Copeland wondered? I'll give it five more minutes.

At 11:35, Copeland decided to check outside. He walked out the back door and sure enough, Martin was sitting on a bench outside in the garden. What little warmth had been lingering in the air with the sun had completely gone away with the dark night. The air was now bitterly cold but even in his light jacket, Martin didn't seem to mind.

"Are you ready?"

Martin nodded.

They walked in silence to the theater, the cold air giving their breath depth.

Once everyone was gathered, Martin began without making any small talk. "It will happen on Monday," he said. "We will spread the word as swiftly as possible, but only to people we trust not to tell those in charge.

We will meet in the street in front of Carnot and the five of you will stand opposite me." He walked to Copeland and handed him a piece of paper. "You will read this note aloud to the crowd before shooting me."

"What?"

"A gun?"

"No!" everyone opposed.

"Shooting you?" Margaret objected, "Are you out of your mind? Where are you going to get a gun?"

"I have one," Martin answered. "It was my grandfather's and he managed to hide it through the fall. I don't think it was a coincidence now. I think he knew."

"You want me to kill you?" Copeland could hardly speak through the lump welling in his throat. "I don't want to. I won't do it."

"It has to be you," Martin explained. "You hold the most power. You have the biggest influence over the nation. You can lead by example."

"Lead by example?!" Copeland was appalled. "Lead by example?" he repeated. "How is killing someone possibly leading by example? That is the opposite of leading by example!"

"I agree!" Vienna added. "That sounds absolutely ludicrous!"

"You may not understand what I am doing now but later, you will. Please follow my instructions," Martin pleaded.

"Martin," he objected again. "Martin, I can't do that." His eyes filled with tears.

"Please," Martin spoke calmly. He fixed his eyes on Copeland's and stared intensely.

After a long hesitation, Copeland exhaled, "I will do

as you wish."

"Thank you," Martin graciously replied. "Please meet at the gates at five P.M. It will be our best option in getting spectators—"

Vienna felt sick at his use of the word "spectators" as if it were some type of entertaining event.

"—because many people will be getting out of work. Plus, it gives us a significant amount of time for things to shake out before the first of January, in which, if all goes according to plan, there will be no Ivy Letters distributed for the first time in over seventy-seven years."

Copeland didn't hear a word the rest of the meeting. His heart ached for the uncle he'd lose in a few short days and ached more at the thought of him being the one that was supposed to take his life. *How can this be the way? Why me*, he asked himself over and over again?

"I am sincerely hoping that war does not break out. We should not fight violence with violence. I suggest none of you carries a weapon," Martin said.

"Really?" Beckham questioned. "But what if it does? How are we supposed to defend ourselves?"

"Use your words," Martin proposed. "I am hoping Copeland's words bring peace and understanding to all."

Sensing discussing the topic longer might not turn out well, Margaret changed the subject. "I have some good news," she announced.

"What's that?" Beckham asked.

"I had lunch with Theodore today," she paused.

Everyone stared back at her, knowing that was not the good part of the news, and waited for her to continue.

"He asked me to marry him," she finished.

"He what?" Copeland was shocked.

"He asked me to marry him," she repeated.

"How is that good news?" Copeland was too offended to think rationally.

"It's good news because we know he still trusts her," Summer answered.

"Exactly!" Margaret concurred. "It's good news because it shows our efforts have been working and no one, not even Theodore, will see our coup coming."

"That is great news," Vienna agreed, then made a face. "But, ew."

Copeland simply nodded. He understood why the news was good, but he couldn't celebrate at the moment. He couldn't think about anything except the fact that the hardest task he'd ever have to complete was only a couple of days away.

"I don't think it's a good idea to meet again before Monday," Martin said. "It seems too risky."

"I agree," Margaret replied. "No reason to press our luck."

The others nodded in agreement.

"I brought something for us." Martin reached into a small bag. Copeland hadn't noticed he'd carried anything to the theater. He pulled out a bottle and a few plastic cups. "I brought a bottle of red wine for us to drink. I know it will be a difficult few days for us all which is why, right now, I want to take time to celebrate and sit with you. We have a plan to overthrow Carnot. A plan to defeat the enemy. And that is something to be proud of."

Martin poured six glasses of wine and passed them

around. Though they didn't particularly feel like celebrating, no one wanted to go against Martin's wishes.

"Cheers!" he declared once everyone had a drink. "To us and to the restoration of our nation."

"Cheers!" they replied as they raised their glasses and took sips of wine.

Chapter Fifty-Three

The next three days dragged on more slowly than Vienna could have imagined. Overall, the house was extremely quiet. Vienna didn't have anything to say and unsurprisingly, Margaret and Beckham didn't either.

She spent most of the time reading or better yet, attempting to read. She never got further than a few pages without her mind wandering to thoughts of "what if" and "what next."

The newspapers made her more upset than she'd anticipated. She told Copeland she didn't want to be with him and that the timing was all wrong but now, seeing him smiling with another girl, she knew she'd made a mistake.

Vienna couldn't sleep on Sunday night; she tossed and turned for hours and hours but didn't get a wink of sleep. In some ways, she was thankful. The lack of sleep helped the day go by faster than she'd expected and before she knew it, as is always the case when waiting, the time had finally come for her and Beckham to leave. They planned to meet Margaret outside the gates, as she'd had to work.

"Are you ready?" Vienna called from downstairs.

"As ready as I'll ever be, I guess," Beckham replied as he walked down the steps and met Vienna at the bottom.

The twins walked nervously together, neither of them saying a word. When they were about a block away, Beckham broke the silence.

"Hey, V," he started, "it's going to be okay."

Vienna looked at Beckham as they continued to walk. "You really think so?"

"I do," Beckham confidently replied. "I have an odd sort of peace about it."

"I hope so," she unconvincingly responded.

It was 4:55 P.M. and they were surprised to see a few people already congregating by the gates. Summer, who was standing in front of the guard shack, waved to them and they walked over to her.

"Hi," she greeted.

"Hey," Beckham replied.

"Have you been here long?" asked Vienna.

"Only, like, two minutes," she answered.

"Nice," Vienna replied. That was all the small talk she could muster.

Beckham and Summer chatted about nothing while Vienna anxiously watched the doors of Carnot.

As people began trickling out, Vienna saw her mother and Martin emerge together.

I wonder where Copeland is? Then, it suddenly dawned on her how hard it might be for him to get out; he would likely be swarmed by people. She was surprised Martin didn't wait for Copeland, but she figured they must have talked it through.

Martin and Margaret walked down the long sidewalk

and joined them next to Santi's shack.

Martin looked remarkably calm but his slightly shaking hands gave away his true, nervous energy.

"Copeland will be here right at 5:05 P.M.," Martin informed them. "He couldn't be out here sooner than that without causing too much commotion."

"Makes sense," Vienna replied. No one else had the courage to speak to Martin. His presence had brought on a sudden sense of sorrow.

Vienna continued to watch the doors of Carnot and sure enough, when her watch ticked to 5:05 P.M., the doors opened and out walked Copeland, surrounded by guards.

Where's Theodore, Vienna thought to herself?

Copeland made his way to the gates and people started closing in on the guards.

"Back it up!" they shouted. "Make way!"

After a few minutes of chaos, with guards paving the way to make a sort-of oval surrounding them on the street, the time had come for Copeland to speak. The crowd was large and surrounded them on every side. As Martin had instructed, the five of them stood opposite from him, about ten feet away. Copeland stood in the center with Vienna and Margaret on his left and Beckham and Summer on his right.

"Good afternoon," Copeland greeted.

At his words, the murmuring crowd hushed. He reached into his pocket and pulled out a folded piece of paper. He unfolded it and Vienna could see how intensely his hands were shaking. "Thank you for coming," he started, reading from the letter. "I have asked you here today for a very important reason. Across from me stands a very kind and gentle soul." He gestured to Martin. "Martin Pluto has served as my assistant for as long as I can remember and has made immense efforts to give me the best life possible."

Martin was focusing on his breathing, trying to keep it steady.

"Many of you remember my mother," he chose the word 'many' as to not sound assumptive, but he knew everyone standing there knew her. "She was also a kind and gentle soul, so I don't think it would be surprising to you if I told you the man standing before me is indeed not only my assistant but also, my uncle, Archie Beckett, and the brother of my dearest mother."

The crowd collectively gasped and a hum of whispers broke out.

"The Beckett family has been working tirelessly for many years," Copeland continued at a louder volume, trying to speak over the buzzing crowd, "to uncover the workings of Carnot and the way our government has been run since its creation. You see, with the discovery of perpetual life came an immense opportunity to hold control over it, and that is what my family, the Howth family, has done for many years. My family has used and abused power to control every aspect of our lives. From the moment we are born to the day we die and every second in between—"

"What on earth is going on out here?!" Copeland heard the familiar voice of his father shouting from the steps of Carnot.

"Today, it is my privilege to release us all from the grip the government has held on us, the mirage of goodness we've believed we live in and more than anything, introduce us to a life of true freedom: a life without Ivy Letters." Copeland spoke with increasing urgency as his father ran down the long sidewalk. "We live in a mirage of freedom. We live in this nation where we believe we are safe and have eternal life, but the truth is, while most people believe there is only goodness here, there are a few people who have learned of the opportunity to do bad. There are people in charge who know we are able to choose between good and bad, but for years, they have kept that information to themselves. It's important—"

The sound of a gunshot filled the air and Copeland let out an agonizing cry. He grabbed his left arm and fell to his knees; blood dripping down his body.

Horrible gasps filled the crowd as everyone stared at Theodore. His hands were shaking slightly as he still held the gun pointing at Copeland.

"Copeland!" Vienna cried hysterically as she kneeled down on the ground next to him. She took off her scarf and held it to his wound, trying to stop the bleeding. She had never seen so much blood before but it didn't appear the bullet had cut too deeply. From what she could tell, it looked like it had grazed the edge of his arm and didn't get lodged in it.

Everyone stood eerily still for what seemed like an eternity. No one wanted to move toward Theodore, for fear of what he might do next.

After a few seconds, Martin made the first move. He started slowly walking toward Theodore.

"Please, Mr. Howth, hear me out." He spoke softly but before he could get out another word, Theodore pulled the trigger again and shot Martin in the right side of his chest.

Martin immediately fell to the ground and Margaret and Summer ran to him. Before Theodore could make another move, bodyguards came up behind him and tackled him to the ground.

"You conniving hypocrite!" Theodore screamed as the guards were holding him down. "How dare you lie to me, Maggie!"

Santi, who had been watching anxiously from the guard shack, ran to the pile of guards with handcuffs.

"Keep him on the ground," a bodyguard instructed while Santi secured the cuffs.

"We need to find a place to lock him up," Beckham instructed. "Santi, do you think you could get into the old jail?"

"You can't lock me up!" Theodore screamed. "I am the Paramount Chief of Carnot! How dare you treat me like this?" He flailed on the ground, trying to break free.

Ignoring his pleas, Santi replied to Beckham. "I can try my best to get into the jail. And in the meantime, I can do you one better. My guard shack was built with a bomb shelter underneath. We can keep him locked down there for the time being."

"Perfect," Beckham approved. "I'm leaving this situation up to you."

"Aren't any of you going to help me? How dare you turn on your leader like this?!" Theodore continued to yell. "No one has the power to arrest me! I can kill you all!"

Sensing no one was listening to Theodore, Beckham bent down to the ground, about a foot away from his face and taunted, "I hope it was all worth it."

Margaret and Summer tried to tie and hold clothing to Martin's chest, but each piece was quickly becoming soaked with blood.

"Stay with me, buddy," Vienna tapped Copeland's cheeks as his eyes began to fade. She heard faint sounds of ambulances growing louder by the second. "Copeland, I'm sorry," she cried. "I was a fool to push you away."

Copeland's head swayed back and forth, as he appeared to fade in and out of consciousness. "It's okay, Vienna... I'm still here. I love you."

Vienna didn't know if it was the loss of blood or his true feelings talking, but she didn't have time to reply either way. The ambulances pulled up and two paramedics came racing to Copeland and pushed her out of the way.

"We're losing him." Summer was holding Martin's head. "We're losing him!" She was hysterical as she felt his head turn to dead weight. She watched his chest and no longer saw any movement of his lungs.

Two other paramedics rushed to Martin and moved them out of the way. Margaret held Summer closely to her chest as they both cried.

A young paramedic held Martin's wrist, checking his pulse. "I'm not getting anything," she announced.

"He's lost a lot of blood," her partner replied. "We need to get him to the hospital for surgery."

Margaret didn't like the sounds of "surgery" for Martin, considering the doctors of Carnot essentially never had to perform it. Though they'd kept the up the practice of medicine since Carnot was formed, they hadn't needed to use it very often. People would very occasionally receive Ivy Letters informing them they'd die from surgery complications, like blood clots, which didn't make her feel confident about their ability to perform a successful surgery. But Martin wasn't supposed to die this month, so she prayed they'd be able to heal him.

The paramedics brought out a stretcher and placed Martin on it. They quickly wheeled him to the back of the ambulance and Margaret and Summer followed closely.

"We can only take one of you," the woman announced.

"You go," Summer immediately offered, and Margaret did not argue.

"Thank you," she replied as she hopped in the back.

"It's been two and a half minutes without a pulse," the paramedic announced to her partner.

Margaret held Martin's hand tightly. "Please, come back. Please, please come back," she cried. She squeezed his left hand tightly in hers and held it up to her face. "Please," she continued to beg.

Suddenly, Martin let out a huge gasp and opened his eyes. He coughed violently.

"He's back after three minutes," the paramedic said. "Stay with me, Martin," she tapped his face. "We need you to stay with us for a few more minutes."

Martin managed to stay conscious for the rest of the ride to the hospital. They unloaded him and wheeled him back as quickly as possible, leaving Margaret nervously pacing in the waiting room. After less than a minute, she was joined by Vienna as they took Copeland back.

"How's Martin?" Vienna asked.

"Not good." Margaret was honest with her. "He was lifeless for three minutes but came back. I am hoping they can remove the bullet and stop the bleeding but let's just say, I don't have a lot of confidence in our Carnot medical team." Margaret tried her best to make light of the situation, in fear she might otherwise collapse if she really felt her emotions.

"Me either," Vienna sighed.

"How's Copeland?"

"He's doing alright. His bleeding had slowed significantly by the time we reached the hospital."

"That's great."

"Where's Beckham?" Vienna asked.

"I don't know," Margaret replied, she was slightly ashamed she hadn't noticed he was missing. "I'm guessing he's still at Carnot with Summer."

"Hopefully, he's holding down the fort," Vienna said. "I really hope things didn't explode."

"Me too," Margaret sighed.

Chapter Fifty-Four

After Theodore was dragged away, and Copeland and Martin were taken to the hospital, the crowd was muttering. The street in front of Carnot stayed swarmed with people, all at a loss for what to do.

Summer and Beckham stood motionless, watching the sea of people.

"At least no one is fighting," Summer commented.

"That's true," Beckham agreed. "But what do we do now?"

"I don't know," Summer admitted. "I think you should take control. Tell people what to do."

"Me?" Beckham questioned. "I don't know what to do. Who am I to instruct them?"

"Beckham, you've wanted to work in the government your entire life. Here is an opportunity, on a silver platter, for you to take your first step," Summer said. "Lead them. They need you."

Beckham took a deep breath. Summer was right. This was his moment and he needed to take advantage of it, but that definitely sounded a lot easier said than done. He cleared his throat loudly. "Excuse me!" he called. "Can I have your attention please? Excuse me," he called again, when no one reacted.

The crowd began to quiet down and people were tapping and shushing each other, pointing to pay attention to Beckham. After a few moments, even Beckham was surprised at how quiet it had become.

"I know the events we all witnessed just a little while ago are extremely hard to take in, but the fact of the matter is even in the 'safe,'" he used air quotes, "society we have all grown up in, we have all witnessed many tragedies like this before. We have all lost loved ones to this system and been forced to live and believe in this charade. We've been raised to believe everyone around us is good and acting on our behalf, when in reality, this is not and has never been the case. The original intentions of today were to show you all that everyone has the option to make choices. Despite the way we were raised, we have the opportunity to choose good or bad and the obvious hope is that everyone still continues to choose good. I am not sure if we accomplished our mission this afternoon, but I plead with you all, think for yourselves. We don't have to live in this fake bubble anymore. We can live with freedom. We can live with the benefits of perpetual life but with the ability to choose our own paths and think independently and uniquely. I believe by allowing us all this opportunity, we will be able to propel Carnot to be a more successful nation than we ever thought possible."

The crowd seemed unnervingly quiet and Beckham worried his words were falling on deaf ears.

"So, with all this, I ask, who's with me?"

Beckham's stomach dropped as it seemed the crowd

was unresponsive. He felt like he could hear a pin drop when suddenly, an eruption of cheers filled the streets. It was as if a veil of darkness had been lifted and all of the residents were set free. A group of men raced to Beckham and lifted him up above the crowd.

"Carnot is free! Carnot is free!" the men started to chant, and soon enough, the entire city was chanting along with them.

Chapter Fifty-Five

Copeland awoke the next morning in a hospital bed with Vienna in a chair next to him.

"Good morning," he greeted.

"Good morning." She smiled. "How are you feeling?"

"Better now. How's Martin?" Copeland's face was suddenly struck with concern.

"He's doing well," she assured him. "His heart stopped beating for three minutes yesterday but he came back. It was quite the miracle actually. He's a few doors down but recovering well. They say he should be out in a week or two."

"Wow." Copeland sighed in relief. "That's incredible. And my father?"

"He's locked away," Vienna answered. "And probably will be for life."

"And Carnot?" Copeland asked. "How did everything shake out?"

Vienna grabbed the newspaper that had been sitting in her lap and handed it to Copeland.

On the cover a large, color photo of Beckham being raised up by a celebrating crowd was featured with the headline. "A Free Nation of Freer People." He continued to read, "Yesterday, will forever go down as the most influential day in Carnot history. Thanks to the sacrifices and risks of six loyal citizens, Copeland Howth, Archie Beckett, Beckham, Vienna and Margaret Tunston, and Summer Nile, Carnot can rest easy with the veil of perfection lifted."

"I guess that means it went pretty well." Copeland smiled up at Vienna. He didn't care to read the rest right now. He was still completely exhausted.

"Yes, it did."

Copeland reached out his hand for Vienna's and she held it tightly. Her mind raced as she wondered what to say next. *Does he remember what he said yesterday? Does he remember what I said?*

"You were a fool." He grinned. "An ignorant fool." He answered as if he'd been reading Vienna's mind.

"I'm so sorry." She kissed his hand.

"It's quite alright. We're here now and I'm never letting go."

"Me either." Vienna squeezed his hand tight and leaned down. "I'm never letting go," she whispered before kissing him.

Chapter Fifty-Six

A few days later, Copeland was released from the hospital and everyone gathered in Martin's room. Margaret had hardly left his room over the past couple of days while the kids had been coming and going.

"I can't believe after everything that happened that the six of us are all here today." Margaret was beyond thankful.

"Me either," Vienna agreed.

"I think we all owe Beckham quite the thanks for keeping things going in my absence," Copeland complimented.

"Agreed!" Summer clapped and the others followed suit.

"I can't believe everything actually ended up working out." Martin admitted, "I don't know if you guys knew this or not, but I really had no idea what I was doing."

"Ohh, I think we had a pretty good idea," Margaret laughed, and the others joined in.

"It all worked out in the end." Vienna smiled and squeezed Copeland's hand tight.

"I know it's not the most important topic for

discussion, but I have been thinking about Copeland's birthday party," Margaret started.

"What about it?" Copeland questioned; it had been the last thing on his mind.

"I was thinking it could still be good to have," she replied. "It could serve as a new beginning for Carnot. A fresh start for everyone."

"I agree." Copeland suddenly seemed more interested. "It can serve as the coronation of our new leader as well."

"What?" the room collectively questioned.

"I'm stepping down," Copeland declared.

"What are you talking about?" Martin asked.

"You can't step down," Vienna argued.

"I can," Copeland said. "To serve with pride and honor, means making the best decision I can for my nation and appointing myself to rule is not the best decision. Which is why, with great pleasure, I announce to you the new ruler of Carnot, King Beckham Tunston." He gestured toward Beckham who was standing across the room. "I think King sounds better anyway," he casually added.

Beckham's heart skipped a beat. He couldn't believe Copeland's words. "Are you sure?" he asked.

"Positive," Copeland replied. "I couldn't be more sure about a decision. Carnot has its work cut out for it as we move forward with a new system, and I can't think of anyone better to lead the charge. You will do big things as our leader and I'd be honored to serve you."

"Thank you," was all Beckham could say.

"Congratulations!" Summer hugged him and pulled him in for a passionate kiss.

"I guess you didn't *exactly* know what you were going to do when you grew up." Vienna winked from across the room.

"I guess you're right," Beckham laughed.

The weeks went by at an unbelievably quick pace as Margaret had been put in charge of planning the party (which was now *actually* deemed the party of the century). They all agreed to hold the party on the original date to ring in the new year.

It was five o'clock on December 31st and Margaret was pleased with how smoothly the set-up had gone. The party was set to start in an hour, but she had nothing left to do.

The kids were already getting ready on the second floor, even though they wouldn't be officially entering the party until 7:00 P.M. Since everything was ready, Margaret decided to take a break and check on them. She walked up the grand stairs and checked on the girls first.

"Wow, you two look magnificent," she said as she walked in the room.

"Does anyone not look magnificent in one of my designs?" Zelda rhetorically asked as she fluffed out the bottom of Vienna's dress. Her team was buzzing around the room, adding the finishing touches to their hair and makeup.

Summer donned a red evening gown that flared out at her hips and fell seamlessly down the rest of her body. Her long, brown hair was perfectly curled and half of it was pulled back into a braid. Vienna wore the ombre blue, glittering gown that Copeland had originally picked for the party. Her hair was pulled back into an intricate updo, which highlighted the large, gorgeous, diamond drop necklace and matching earrings she was wearing.

"Thanks, Mom," Vienna replied. "How's everything looking down there?"

"We're good to go."

"Great! We were about to go see the boys. Want to come?"

"I was planning to head there next," Margaret answered.

"Me too," Zelda added. "Give us two more minutes to finish up and we'll all head that way."

When they were ready, they walked down the hall, with Zelda's team towing all sorts of bags and supplies.

"Your dates look much better than you," Margaret teased when she walked in the room.

"Hey, now," Copeland defended them. "We still have two hours and our team of professionals has just arrived." He gestured toward the now-filled room. "You just wait and see."

Margaret laughed. Seeing the four of them together made her illuminate with pride.

"Where's Archie?" she asked.

"He should be back any—"

"Right here," Martin answered as he walked in the room. He was released from the hospital only two days earlier and he looked as good as new.

"Good!" Margaret beamed. "Before the events of the night begin and we're celebrating and being pulled in every direction," she stopped. Zelda was instructing her team members loudly and pointing them around. "Hey, Zelda, could you just wait one minute, please. I want to make an announcement."

"My apologies, Mrs. Tunston," Zelda replied. "We will wait to get started. Let's give them some privacy," Zelda instructed, and led her team back out to wait in the hall.

"Thank you." Margaret continued when the room was quiet, "I just want to take a second to thank you all for everything. Thank you for loving me and accepting me even after all of my mistakes. Thank you for throwing Theodore in jail for the rest of his life and keeping him far away from me." She looked at Summer. "Thank you for loving my son and taking such wonderful care of him." Her gaze shifted to Copeland. "Thank you for trusting Beckham with this nation and for helping him each step of the way. And thank you for loving my daughter the way I always dreamed she'd be loved. Vienna, thank you for forgiving me when you had every right to hold on to your anger for the rest of your life. Thank you for working so hard to do right in the world. And Archie, thank you for leading us and never giving up on your grandfather's plans. It's thanks to you we are all standing here today." She looked to Beckham. "And last but certainly not least, thank you for being such a wonderful leader. I never dreamed you'd rule this nation, but I should have because I have so much faith in you and I know you will do a phenomenal job. I am beyond lucky to call you my son. Thank you, thank you, thank you to all of you. I love you all more than you will ever know."

Chapter Fifty-Seven

Vienna and Copeland stood opposite Summer and Beckham at the top of the steps. They'd been instructed to wait until their names were announced to make any movements.

"I now introduce you to Mr. Copeland Beau Howth and his date Ms. Vienna Marie Tunston," she heard a voice announce over the loudspeaker. She wrapped her arm around Copeland's, and they made their way onto the steps. The crowd clapped feverishly and a smile beamed across Vienna's face. She'd never felt appreciation like this before. Halfway down the steps, there was a wide platform where they'd been told to stop to wait for Beckham and Summer. Vienna was thankful when she'd made it to the platform without tripping. They took a step off to the side and waved to the crowd. Cameras were flashing and people were screaming but all Vienna could focus on was being arm in arm with the love of her life.

"It is now my pleasure to introduce to you, Ms. Summer Joy Nile and for the first time, Sir Beckham Penn Tunston, King of Carnot," the voice announced.

The room exploded with cheers and applause as

Summer and Beckham made their way down the steps. They stopped when they reached the platform and joined Copeland and Vienna.

The four of them stood waving to the hundreds of people below.

"I can't believe we actually did it," Beckham said through a smile. The moment seemed too surreal.

"We did it," Vienna agreed. She still couldn't quite believe it herself. "We restored Carnot."

Acknowledgments

As an author, to dream of publishing a book is often that... only a dream. Thank you to Shellville Press for taking a chance on me and making my dream a reality. To Katie, thank you for your incredible editing skills and the countless hours you spent working to make this book the best it could be. And to Shelly, thank you for working tirelessly on cover designs, editing, marketing and so much more, to make my vision for *Ivy Letters* come to life.

To my mother-in-law, Julie, who started a conversation that turned into an idea I couldn't get out of my head and onto paper fast enough, thank you. To you and Paul, thank you for your support and for so graciously accepting me into your family.

To Mamaw, who reads more books than anyone on the planet, thank you for instilling the importance of a love for reading to me from an early age. And to my grandparents, thank you for your contribution to my education, which has allowed me to learn and grow in immeasurable ways.

Thank you to my friends who are really family, Bruce and Debbie. I can always count on your support and encouragement. I hope you "have a moment" while reading this.

To Molly, my seester, thank you for your love and always being by my side. I am incredibly lucky to have you in my life, not only as my sister, but also as one of my very best friends.

To my parents, who have always been my biggest supporters, I can't thank you enough. To my mom, who is always the first person to read my early drafts and encourages me to keep going (because at least someone in the world wants to know how it ends), thank you. One of the biggest compliments I receive is that I'm your mini-me. From your work ethic to your positivity to your eagerness for dancing whenever the mood strikes, I'm blessed to be like you and to have you as my role model. And to my dad, who sacrificed his career to stay home with us, thank you for inspiring me daily to never stop thinking creatively and for helping this book come to life in more ways than I can list. You have taught me the value of pursuing what I love and this is a tangible example of one of those dreams coming to life.

And lastly, even as an author, I cannot find words meaningful enough to express my thanks to my amazing husband, Josh. From your constant encouragement to your help with plot lines to your ability to suggest character names at any given moment and everything in between, this book would not have been possible without you. Thank you for being my better half and best friend. I love you most.